The River God Orpantha

Sequel to *The Death of Valdez*

Michael Seirton

First published in Great Britain in 2023 by STA BOOKS

ISBN 978-0-9933957-8-9

Cover Art – Abbe Fardon

A CIP catalogue record for this title is available from the British Library.
This novel is entirely a work of fiction. Names, characters, businesses, organisations, places and events are either the product of the author's imagination or used fictitiously and any resemblance to actual persons, living or dead, is purely coincidental.

ARTHUR WILLIAM CHAMBERS

My Uncle, A True Gentleman of This Country
A kind and Amazing Insightful Uncle, who nurtured
a creative spirit through a dark and troubled
childhood, preparing me for what creative
opportunities that lay ahead, through taking me to
auctions, giving an insight into the beauty of
collectable items, the quality of period furniture and
textiles, key information that would later serve to
establish a very important career in theatre, films and
writing.

Having passed away when I was seventeen, I can
only pray that his beautiful spirit has been with me
throughout every stage of this amazing life.

Acknowledgements

With special thanks

Primarily to my agent, Fiona Spencer Thomas, for her continuing support and for getting the second novel of this unpredictable series published.

With grateful thanks to Abbe Fardon for yet more amazing cover art.

Many thanks to my editor, Ian Howe, for his careful editing and understanding of these important characters, abandoned in an unthinkable situation.

Thanks also to Joss Marsh for her earlier editorial notes.

The River God Orpantha

Chapter One
Aftermath

The sharp clank of metal on tin was filtering through Geoffrey's unconscious state, along with the sickly odour of chloroform and the grating of a saw. He was distantly aware of the agonising pain in his hands and the reek of scorched flesh.

When he finally awoke his mouth was locked open by some torturous metal apparatus and in his paralysed state he could do nothing to remove it. He could just make out a shadowy figure moving through the haze of light, which was all that remained of his sight. He was also uncomfortably aware that he was completely naked except for the dressing on his face and the mass of bandages around his torso and hands.

"Praise God, you are awake," Marguerite's voice said, close to his head.

In the background he could hear a bubbling sound strangely reminiscent of the science lab at his old school.

"Sip this liquid, Geoffrey. It will help your recovery."

He tried to respond but it was impossible to do anything except breathe. He was propped up on a makeshift cot in his father's laboratory, with no idea how she could have got him there on her own. Through his blurred vision he focused on her apron, splashed with blood, presumably his own. He desperately wanted to ask after Rosamund but in his weakened state, could barely make a sound as another wave of nausea began, followed thankfully by a welcome blanket of darkness which carried him far away from the nightmarish reality.

As the hours passed, Geoffrey was aware of being moved, as though cradled lovingly in the comfort of his mother's arms. Yet he knew that was impossible and wondered if he was on his way to join her. Once out in the cool night air, mingled with a light rain, the desire for this to be his final journey faded. There was no sense of fear from the touch of naked flesh pressed gently against his own and he even felt unexpectedly comforted by the faint aroma of male sweat before he was laid gently onto a rush bed in a cooling draught of air.

"I cannot thank you enough," Marguerite said in the darkness, her tearful voice more loving than Geoffrey could ever remember.

During the night Geoffrey was awakened by Marguerite's voice from the next room, no words but a series of moans and for a moment he panicked, wondering if the marauders had returned. Hearing nothing more, he began to think he'd been dreaming until, in the final moments before sleep he heard the low sound of a male voice and the creak of a door as it closed.

Waking fitfully during the night, Geoffrey felt his inert body being moved into a more comfortable position and someone placing dampened cloths around his throat and brow. He could only conclude through the odour of his sweat as he leant across him that this was the same man as before.

Geoffrey awoke from a long and troubled sleep on a woven rush bed, set up on the bungalow's veranda. Though similar to what the local natives used it was intricately crafted and the weave, while firm, was less rigid than usual, helping ease the stiffness of his body. The restrictive metal implement had been removed from his mouth and his breathing felt easier.

"Just breathe through your mouth, Geoffrey. I have done the best I can to reset your nose but the plaster will not be removed for a while." Marguerite was bending over him so that he could see her face. In her hand was an invalid cup, the spout of which she tipped forward gently into his mouth, allowing the liquid to trickle slowly into his throat.

The process was repeated throughout the following days but how many days it was impossible for him to judge. Even so, he knew that he had to swallow the vile concoction and eat the crushed-up food she gave him, some of it bland, some positively disgusting. On other occasions it was a male figure that appeared through his distorted vision and he knew that there would be less compassion in the feeding process.

What Geoffrey found confusing was that this was evidently not the same man who had carried him onto the veranda and sat with him throughout the night. There was nothing gentle in the way this man's hands impatiently forced his mouth open to be spoon-fed whenever Marguerite wasn't there and being washed down by him was becoming a daily nightmare. On the third occasion Geoffrey noticed, as he had begun to suspect, that the man was spending longer in washing his genitals than was strictly necessary.

"Get your hands off my cock, you filthy bastard!" Geoffrey hissed through clenched teeth at the blurred form, his outrage enough to find his voice for the first time since the incident.

"Missy say you need I wash," said the figure. "You no want I make clean?"

"Touch me like that again and I swear you will pay dearly," Geoffrey said, though aware how pathetic his threat must seem.

"What you do me, Inglese pig, if you no move?" the dark shape sneered, looming ever closer.

"Not me but I know someone who will, you twisted South American bastard," Geoffrey retaliated, praying that somehow Archie would know they were in trouble and come to find them.

"Then why him no here?" the man jeered, gripping Geoffrey's wounded thigh with tremendous pressure as if expecting him to cry out.

"He is coming, you can be sure of that," Geoffrey said through gritted teeth, determined he would make his torturer pay dearly. For now he made do with spitting directly into the man's face, inches away from his own.

The shadowy figure scurried away, leaving Geoffrey's body uncovered and his mind in torment. How long he remained in that desolate state was impossible to determine but it only ended when his sister rushed to his side.

"Maggie, is that you?"

"Praise God you can speak again, Geoffrey," Marguerite said, placing a towel over him. "I feared it would be impossible after that dreadful beating."

"Who is that animal you sent here to wash me?"

"I will have a word with him later. His name is Drangoo, a novice monk from the Mission at Guava. Father Fitzgerald sent him to help with our situation. I am so sorry that he left you like this."

"I do not want that monster to ever lay hands on me again."

"You need to be washed, Geoffrey and I cannot do that with everything else. Rosamund needs my constant attention. She cannot be left alone for any length of time."

"Then who is with her now?" he asked, dreading it would be the brutal monk.

"The Otter is the only person Rosamund will allow anywhere near her. She screams for Mother constantly when the demons possess her. If only she was alive, Mother would know how to calm her," Marguerite's voice quavered but there was something more important he needed to ask.

"Did that monk give Mother a Christian burial?"

"He and Lorenzo did it together. It was a simple ceremony but moving. She was laid to rest in the burial ground with Father and the children."

"Lorenzo was here?"

"Only for the shortest time but when he returns he will take over from Drangoo. Until then you must allow him to help you."

"If Lorenzo was here, then why did he leave?" Geoffrey wheezed, exhausted from the effort of speaking.

"To get here is difficult overland. He had to bring Drangoo on foot and then stayed overnight before setting off to collect bark from a holy tree at the Temple of Light. It is a long way from here but he assured me its will help to restore your sight and speed up your recovery."

"Did he take the dog with him?" Geoffrey asked. He wished the hound was close by as not only was he barely able to see and unable to move but he was convinced it would prevent any more unwelcome attention from the monk.

"That creature has gone too. It follows him everywhere."

"... and what about that renegade priest?"

"Father Fitzgerald is due here in around a month on his missionary circuit. Lorenzo and Drangoo will then accompany him when he moves on."

"How long do these circuits take?"

"It depends on the seasonal rainfall but could take between eight and ten months."

"So I take it we have no option but be imprisoned here until they decide to return and take us back to civilisation? Surely a priest could offer a little more Christian charity?"

On the following day, when Drangoo began cramming food into Geoffrey's mouth, he bit down so hard on the probing fingers that the monk's howls caused Marguerite to appear on the veranda.

"What have you done, Geoffrey?"

"All I did was bite into what I thought was a piece of meat," Geoffrey lied, comforted that the monk would be more wary in future.

"I do not believe that for a second, Geoffrey. Your sight has begun to improve a little, has it not?"

"Slightly perhaps, it is no worse anyway," he said, as she began applying cream to the weeping sores on his body."

"I was worried the improvement from yesterday was only temporary but there are no extra patches of infection on your skin. One can only hope the virus has either been halted, or praise God, is on the retreat. If so, it must mean that distilling the roots is working."

"You mean that awful drink is distilled from those roots the Otter eats?"

"I thought you knew?"

"So does this mean you have an antidote?"

"I think the proof is that you and Rosamund are still alive. She was infected too, though to a lesser extent."

"Will I be able to move my limbs again if this works?"

"I honestly cannot say. The virus does appear to have been prevented from advancing and the fact that you can speak proves that the creeping paralysis has eased on your vocal chords but beyond that how far you will recover is a mystery."

"You mean I could be like this for the rest of my life?" Geoffrey asked, horrified.

"I cannot answer that, Geoffrey. I only wish that I could. Apart from distilling those roots I know nothing else to aid your recovery. We must rely on Lorenzo's knowledge of native cures. He seemed confident the bark of this rare tree would help." She sounded sure but her expression belied her tone.

"How can you put faith in what that red-haired freak tells you? How could you remotely imagine that some piece of tree bark, however holy, will ever get me back on my feet again?"

"Lorenzo's mother was well versed in all manner of natural cures and remedies."

"Then why not send her over instead?"

"Because the poor woman is no longer alive. She was executed as a witch and in the very temple Lorenzo has returned to."

"Is it safe?" Surely it cannot be the only place where this tree grows?"

"Apparently it is the only one of its kind. Lorenzo has assured me the bark from this tree will begin the healing process." He noticed her radiant expression when mentioning his name.

"And what happens to this trainee monk when your miracle worker arrives? Can we get rid of him at least?"

"I understand and how embarrassing this must be, Geoffrey, having someone wash you down and feed you but please remember, Drangoo is only trying to help. Although I must admit he does seem rather old to be a novice, unless he took to the cloth later in life, which might account for any lack of experience."

"This monk knows exactly what he is doing," Geoffrey said bitterly. Unable to control anything in his life, barely able to see, eat or even turn his head without help, he felt like a sacrificial object, subjected to the will of others, or some caged animal. Trapped within his own body by the paralysis, not knowing if he would ever move, feed himself or play music again; for Geoffrey this was a living Hell.

After watching him drift off into a troubled sleep, Marguerite pinned the sketch of Archie above Geoffrey's cot where he would see that reassuring face when he woke.

It was still two days until Lorenzo's expected arrival and although there was a slight improvement in Geoffrey's vision and his breathing was a little easier his limbs had remained as inflexible as rock. The daily body-washes under Drangoo's rough, insensitive hands was no less distressing and, had his home-made spear or Archie's knife been readily accessible he would gladly have plunged either into the side of the insidious monk. As it was, the only way he could stop the inappropriate fondling was to shout to his sister.

"You must stop calling for me, Geoffrey. I cannot keep dashing here all the time. It would be inappropriate for me to wash you myself, I do not have the time and Drangoo is more than capable."

"I not make wrong, Missy," Drangoo complained.

"I would rather smell like a dog than have this bloody moron ever touch me again," Geoffrey snapped.

"Well you will have to get used to it, Geoffrey. The last thing you need is another infection so you will have to put up with the embarrassment a while longer. You must be kept clean after using the lavatory. You cannot do that on your own and neither should you expect me to. It is better for a man to do it, so just be grateful we have Drangoo here to help you." Marguerite turned and left, huffing with exasperation.

Geoffrey resigned himself to the unwanted attentions of the monk, dreading nightfall when the novice would assist him to the commode and then clean him afterward. At least finding Archie's image close by offered some minor comfort.

During that night he woke up to hear Rosamund screaming his name. He called for Marguerite but she didn't come and in his panic and in his desperation to get to his sister he rocked to and fro in the cot until he crashed to the floor, where he lay in a heap until dawn when Marguerite found him.

"Geoffrey, wake up, wake up!" she cried.

"Leave me… you must help Rose. She was screaming for me in the night," he gasped, barely able to focus on her face.

"I heard nothing and my cabin is much closer to hers. You must have been dreaming, Geoffrey dear, reliving past events," she said, easing him up so that he could breathe more easily. "Anyone who has suffered in the way you have, is bound to be traumatised."

"This was different. Rose did not call for me to help back then. She took matters into her own hands," Geoffrey said. "Just tell me this… have you seen her this morning?"

"No I have not. I came over here first."

"Then go to her now, Maggs, please."

"Not until I have got you back in the cot."

"That will be impossible on your own."

"I will get Drangoo to help. Then I will go to Rosamund. I promise." She scurried away but returned alone.

"Where is he?"

"I cannot find him, although I suppose he could be praying at this hour."

"Then for Pete's sake leave me here and check on Rose; that pervert might be over there."

"Very well but you are misguided in your opinion of him. He is a devout Christian," Marguerite said, before leaving.

It was some time before a clearly troubled Marguerite returned with the monk trailing at her heels.

"I cannot understand why I did not hear her calling out in the night, if both you and Drangoo did," she said, as they helped Geoffrey back onto the cot.

"He was there last night?" Geoffrey asked, blinking furiously to clear his vision and trying to turn his head to look at the novice. There was a series of long gashes along his right cheek. "So how can he explain these?"

"Drangoo has already explained that he was trying to stop Rosamund from doing herself harm," Marguerite said.

"Then why would she be calling to me to help her, if she was intent on hurting herself? That does not make sense."

"I can assure you, Geoffrey, that is what occurred last night. Why would a man of God lie?" She lowered her voice so that Drangoo wouldn't hear.

"Why indeed? Did he say what was she supposedly harming herself with?"

"Rosamund had a pair of scissors from Mother's sewing basket."

"After what those hunters forced her to do, Rose must hate the sight of any man. If those scissors were in her hand when that monk went into her cabin, I can guarantee the bastard would not be alive now. I know how Rose thinks, better than anyone. She would have stabbed him and not just clawed his face," Geoffrey raged.

"You are mistaken, Geoffrey. It is not only men she fears but anyone at all, including me. The only way I can get her to drink the antidote is have the Otter take it in."

"Then why was the door open if the Otter was not there?"

"Lady Rosa, she think me Otter," Drangoo said, speaking for the first time.

"Liar… Rose would never mistake a man's voice for a child's. I want to see her now and get to the bottom of this," Geoffrey said angrily.

"That is impossible, Geoffrey and even if you did she would not know who you are. That is how she is with me, blanking out everything and everyone from her memory."

"Except that Rose was calling for me by name and if I ask she will tell me exactly what happened." Geoffrey wished he had retrieved Archie's knife from under the steps. If what he suspected were true, he would gladly use it on the monk.

It was late afternoon when Geoffrey's heightened hearing caught the sound of a dog barking in the distance. No one else in the compound suspected anyone was approaching until, as silent as night, Lorenzo appeared on the veranda and was leaning over the cot before even Geoffrey became aware of his presence.

16

"You came back," was all Geoffrey could say.

"Who this?" Lorenzo asked, as if about to touch the drawing of Archie.

"Do not touch that... not ever!" Geoffrey snapped, desperate to escape the intense gaze of those fathomless eyes but unable to turn away in his paralysed state.

Gently, as if he could read his thoughts, Lorenzo slid an arm beneath Geoffrey's upper body and leant across him, angling him into a more comfortable position. From the musk of sweat, he now knew exactly who it was had helped his sister carry him from the laboratory on that fateful night and whose hands had most likely made the beautifully woven cot he was sleeping on.

"Close eyes. Lorenzo him go bring mix, ease pain," Lorenzo said, before disappearing from Geoffrey's line of vision. Only then did he feel the wolfhound's cold nose pressed against the flesh of his arm and the dog's warm, damp breath on his skin, a contact more comforting than a thousand words could have expressed. Hearing sandal-clad footsteps approaching, he realised this wasn't Lorenzo returning but the monk.

"How you get on side?" Drangoo said, wrenching Geoffrey onto his back, unaware of the dog's presence until he heard the rumble of a warning growl.

"Get your bloody hands off me, you twisted bastard, or my dog will kill you!" Choking from the rough treatment, Geoffrey expected another jolt of pain in retaliation. Instead he heard Drangoo squeal like a trapped animal as he was sent reeling into the veranda railings and fell to his knees.

"What you do him, Drangoo?" Lorenzo hissed, having returned as silently as he had left.

"I no hurt man, Lollen, I here make better," the monk whined fearfully.

"No touch Massa… comprende?" Lorenzo threatened, easing Geoffrey back into position. Producing a jar of red paste, he began to gently massage it into his neck, elbows and knees. The process lasted for over an hour, at the end of which the joints, although still locked in position, felt warm and less painful.

"Thank you," Geoffrey said as Lorenzo leant over him and, like an animal, sniffed at the bandaging around his head.

"This need change," Lorenzo said to Marguerite as she arrived, flustered but glowing, with the Otter at her side.

"I was unsure what to do, so I left them alone," she said, resting her own hand close to his on the starch-like dressing. Geoffrey was aware of a light webbing of skin linking the fingers on Lorenzo's hand.

"Sod the bandage, Maggs, just get rid of this awful thing on my nose," he complained.

"I need to be sure that your nose has set properly before I remove the plaster of Paris. If it comes off too soon your beautiful nose will stay crooked."

"What the hell does that matter now? The shape of my nose is the least of my worries. What I need is to breathe more normally in this infernal climate."

"Maybe tomorrow when there is more daylight," she agreed reluctantly, only then removing her hand from his head and away from Lorenzo's.

"This I help with, Señorita," Lorenzo said, examining the plaster.

"Tomorrow morning it is then," she smiled. "Will you be joining me later, Lorenzo?"

"I need be here…" Lorenzo began but Geoffrey was having none of it.

"I will be perfectly all right on my own. I do not need any company," he said but Lorenzo still did not follow his sister inside.

"La noche… much dangerous time. I stay."

"Just leave the dog with me and I will be fine," Geoffrey said.

"You need I stay," Lorenzo said, settling down on the floor as easily as if it were a comfortable bed.

Geoffrey awoke with a start to find himself being lifted from the cot and seated on the commode. Lorenzo's skin was damp with river water.

"I do not want you doing this," Geoffrey hissed, not wanting to wake his sister.

"You want Lorenzo fetch Drangoo?"

"Very well but please… go away until I have finished." Geoffrey dreaded the inevitable moment when he would need to be wiped down, washed and put back into the cot. Yet to his surprise the experience was much less embarrassing and painful than he had feared, as Lorenzo was so gentle and considerate.

Later, however, with his sister now in attendance, there was no way to ease the suffering as the crushed tree bark was massaged painstakingly into his aching joints. After another dose of the liquid Marguerite had distilled from the roots, Lorenzo started to replace the bandaging and apply a fresh, stinking poultice.

"I refuse to have you bandage that cowpat back on my head, Lorenzo. I have had enough torture for today."

"This much good, you need me do this," Lorenzo said.

"Not yet. First I must go to the burial site and pay my respects to Mother."

"What you are asking is impossible," Marguerite said sternly.

"Not at all. All I need is to be strapped onto the travois I made for the hound and get that idiot Drangoo to drag me up there." Geoffrey was determined to achieve something, if only to prove he could do it.

"I could not ask that of him, Geoffrey and hauling you up there might harm you."

"No Drangoo… Lorenzo him take Señor Jeffy," said the young man.

"That bloody monk can do it. He is useless at everything else," Geoffrey insisted.

"Drangoo make you more pain," Lorenzo said but although Geoffrey knew he was right he was determined to get his own way.

"What the hell does that matter? I am in pain anyway!"

"Travois not so good; I make harness," Lorenzo smiled.

"What… so you can drag me up there?"

"You much stiff, Señor Jeffy… it better me carry," Lorenzo said adamantly.

In less than half an hour, Lorenzo had returned with an armful of reeds and a quantity of vines. Seated cross-legged against the wall he began to weave a simple but practical harness. Every now and then he would break his concentration to take a measurement of Geoffrey's body before returning to the project in hand, working methodically but with remarkable speed.

During this period the Otter squatted beside him, wide-eyed at his skill and chattering to him in some strange dialect.

Seeing them so relaxed in each other's company, Geoffrey began wondering what their relationship might be.

"Is the Otter your son, Lorenzo?" he asked, which caused Lorenzo to smile broadly.

"Nada… him no. Otter mi hermano… my brother," Lorenzo explained, never for a moment breaking concentration from his weaving. "I not have son, not yet."

It was midday by the time the harness was complete and in the intense heat the climb to the burial site would have been torturous for anyone, so Geoffrey reluctantly agreed to wait until sunrise the following day before they set off.

"A wise decision, Geoffrey," Marguerite said happily. "In the meantime, Lorenzo has suggested he removes the bandages."

"Where is he now?" Geoffrey asked.

"Down at the river making a fresh poultice. He said that your head wound will take a long time to heal. The gashes were frightfully deep."

"Gashes or not, I refuse to have any more of that evil-smelling horseshit strapped onto my head. Haven't I got enough problems?"

"It might not be as awful as you think," she reasoned.

"You would not be saying that if it was strapped to your head!" Geoffrey snapped.

He didn't even hear Lorenzo approaching before he felt him begin to unwrap the first of the bandages. Once again Lorenzo took care not to inflict any unnecessary pain, bathing the dried area where the bandage was stuck together until the leaves underneath could be lifted off in one solid piece.

"This much good," Lorenzo smiled, offering up the bundle for Geoffrey to see a mass of dried blood mixed with a layer of green and yellow slime. "Bark from holy tree make head much good; no smell like what horse shit, like you say." He laughed easily.

"That is a relief then," Geoffrey said more amiably.

Lorenzo next removed the bandages on his arms and gradually rubbed in a mixture of the red bark before he applied damp leaves over the healing wounds, binding them with a thin vine. He cleansed the other wounds on Geoffrey's torso, back and legs with river water before attaching poultices, packed in yellow and orange leaves and bandaging them in place.

"How did you learn about this bark?" Geoffrey asked.

"Mio madre, she much holy; this no teach, she give in here when I born." He placed a hand on each of his temples with a look of great sadness. "She priestess in Temple of Light... now many years dead."

"Then I am truly sorry. What do you remember about her?"

"She born and she die in Guava."

"Surely there must be more you remember?"

"Si... mio madre have same hair and skin like me. We River People."

Looking at Lorenzo's his pale, golden skin and European features, Geoffrey wondered who his father could have been.

"How old were you when she died?" he asked.

"She die few days after Lorenzo him born."

"That is terrible!" Geoffrey said, wishing he'd never asked.

"You no sad, Señor Jeffy. Padre, him take much care of Lorenzo," he said, putting the finishing touches to the dressing.

22

"Are you saying that Father Fitzgerald... the priest is your real father?"

"Si, esta es correcto," Lorenzo admitted with a smile but what shocked Geoffrey even more was his confirmation that both Drangoo and, as they had suspected, the Otter were also the priest's sons, all by different mothers.

"Can you get rid of these grotesque bandages on my hands, Lorenzo?" Geoffrey asked, needing to change the subject.

"This I no do. Señora, she say much damage and must leave more time for heal."

"Can you not at least take a look, Lorenzo? Everything you have done so far has made things so much less painful."

"It need more days. When time it come, I need mix many barks with sap from other trees. These Lorenzo no have and need find," he insisted and there was no use arguing.

Another issue presented itself when the time came for the harness to be fitted onto Geoffrey.

"You cannot carry me without any clothes on, it is not decent!" he protested. The only item Lorenzo wore was a belt with a hunting knife and a leather flap to protect his genitals.

"It too hot, so I no need."

"... but what about me. All I have on are bandages!" he said in a fit of rage, which made Lorenzo laugh.

"You carried on Lorenzo's back. If him no care, why you?"

"Bollocks, you bloody halfwit!" Geoffrey retorted, an outburst that immediately brought to mind a similar response he had made to Archie Westbrook. That seemed a lifetime ago now and he wondered what the Irishman would have made of this impossible situation.

"Why you make so much noise? Lorenzo only want help," he asked.

"Because… I am a gentleman, not a savage. You cannot strap me into that. Not like this, without any clothes," Geoffrey ranted. The imminent prospect of being strapped against Lorenzo's naked back was of increasing concern.

"Why you need, Señor Jeffy? They make too hot, this bad for you."

"I do not give a damn about the heat. I am not being exposed, paralysed or not!"

"Who see you? No me."

"For God's sake, that is not the point, you bloody idiot. I am not one of your blasted natives, I am not going anywhere without a pair of trousers and that is final."

"If you say, Señor Jeffy…" Lorenzo said, walking away.

"I still want to go, you blasted fool… You promised!" Geoffrey called after him. He was beginning to question his own prudishness but remained determined to get his own way.

When Lorenzo returned a short time later, he was holding up a pair of baggy underpants for Geoffrey.

"Where did you find those?"

"Them your Papa, they his," Lorenzo said, slipping them onto Geoffrey before he had time to change his mind. Attaching the harness, he then strapped it across his shoulders and fixed a lower strap around his waist, securing Geoffrey against him.

"The handcart would be a damned sight easier to get me there than this," Geoffrey said, remembering how he'd hauled the bodies of his father and the children up the steep incline to the burial site.

Even partially clothed, the friction between their naked bodies and the scent and touch of sweat during the seemingly endless climb was an unparalleled episode in Geoffrey's young life and an experience that would haunt his nightmares for years to come. As the nausea and stomach cramps grew on the final section of the jolting ascent all Geoffrey even began to hope he might be dead on arrival so that he could be buried alongside his mother, whom he had loved more than life itself.

As the wolfhound circled protectively around them, his only other comfort was that the potion Lorenzo had massaged into his aching joints before setting off had already eased the pain considerably. Even so, his limbs remained as rigid as before as Lorenzo sat him down on a rock and unhooked the harness. From this vantage point he could see only his father's burial place and had he been able he would gladly have pissed on his grave for being the catalyst that made his beloved mother travel so far, only to meet such a horrific end.

"What is that awful stench?" Geoffrey protested, unable to react as Lorenzo removed the baggy underwear.

"This I clean, Señor Jeffy," Lorenzo answered simply.

"May God in Heaven forgive me!" Geoffrey cried, now aware of another revolting smell rising from his chest. "Have I been sick too?"

"Si, I make good." Lorenzo unhooked a coconut shell from his belt, filled it with water from a nearby stream and began gently cleaning Geoffrey's face.

"You should not be doing this!"

"You need, Señor Jeffy. This heat much bad for you."

"You could have refused to bring me here," Geoffrey said, trying to conceal the embarrassment of having his underwear removed and washed.

"I do this for… tu madre. It much importante, you here."

"How can you be so kind, when all I have ever done is behave like an idiot?"

"The ancients know you great warrior," Lorenzo said, looking around at the magnificent trees surrounding the clearing. "They see happen, like Lorenzo," he continued, looking first towards the area where Geoffrey had stabbed the headhunter with the garden fork and then at where he and the dog had dealt with the boa constrictor. "You save Perro, this I see much clear."

"How on earth could you… how could anyone know what happened here?" Geoffrey protested.

"Lorenzo, him see many things," he answered simply, pressing his fingers against his temples. "Señor Jeffy kill hunter and then snake; this brave."

Once Lorenzo had rinsed out the clothing he sluiced handfuls of water over Geoffrey's shoulders and then, carrying him over to the stream, sat him in the water and washed him down until his entire body was spotless.

"Where is Mother buried?" Geoffrey asked hoarsely, needing to see but not wanting to.

"I put she here." A small mound lay in the shade afforded by a gnarled tree that looked as if it had been there since time began.

In that moment of utter despair, had he possessed the physical ability, Geoffrey could have willingly plunged Archie's knife deep into his own, useless heart.

"Can you move me over there?" he asked, using his eyes to indicate a rock at the cliff edge, overlooking the river. "I need to be alone."

Lorenzo lifted him gently and carried him there, close to where Geoffrey had pitched the dead hunter over the precipice.

Once Lorenzo was out of sight, Geoffrey began to put into action what he had planned. First he started the same rocking motion that had tumbled him out of the cot and on to the floor, his objective this time was to pitch himself over the edge of the cliff but, within moments, the wolfhound began howling and Lorenzo came sprinting back to grab hold of Geoffrey and haul him to safety.

There was no hint of condemnation of Geoffrey's reckless action, only an expression of the purest tenderness and understanding as Lorenzo carried him back and propped him up in the shade of the trees.

Lorenzo sat a few feet away, cross-legged beside Lady Claudia's grave as if in a trance. Placed on the mound was a wilting spray of flowers Marguerite had left, among them a single red bloom that had miraculously survived since the burial.

"Was there a ceremony, Lorenzo?" Geoffrey asked.

"This no happen. This we do, Señor Jeffy."

"If I had a violin and my bloody hands were not in plaster, I could have played for her!" Geoffrey wailed, tears streaming down his cheek unchecked. Gradually he became aware of Lorenzo chanting. To begin with the sound was barely discernible but increasing steadily. At times his voice seemed barely human, a wild, primeval sound that sent shivers along Geoffrey's arms. Every intonation and change of rhythm and tempo was like nothing he had ever heard, all the elements blending together so that it seemed more like a three-dimensional image than any ritual incantation. As the sound become more passionate, the leaves of the ancient tree above him began to rustle violently, as if caught up in a storm, yet every other plant and bush around the clearing remained deathly still.

As the chant ended the rustling of the leaves also ceased and at a tiny red butterfly emerged from the living flower on his mother's grave and fluttered in a circular motion around the mound. Seconds later another red butterfly, then another, emerged from the flower, until there were dozens of them clustering together into a fluttering red cloud.

Seemingly oblivious, Lorenzo crouched at the head of the grave, listening intently until he glanced over to Geoffrey. At precisely the moment his keen hearing detected the faintest sound of a violin, music that was indistinct at first but was soon recognisable as one of Geoffrey's own haunting pieces. As the volume increased he knew that he must be going crackers. Every nuance of the movement confirmed this was his own work, as if Lorenzo had miraculously achieved the impossible in granting him the wish to say goodbye to his beloved mother through his own emotional composition, plucked from the air.

Geoffrey leaned forward with his mouth agape, saliva running down his chin as he stared intently towards the mound where his mother lay, longing to be with her, far away from the living hell of his life. Just as he was about to overbalance, the wolfhound pushed its body against him, leaning him back against the rock as the colony of red butterflies, their wings all fluttering in perfect time with the music, began spiralling upwards until they were just above Lorenzo's head. Here the vibrant red wings of the colony fluttered into an isolated shaft of sunlight penetrating the canopy of leaves. The higher they went, the lighter the red of their wings became, until finally, there was no trace of colour at all. The pale, beating wings continued fluttering higher until they fused into the translucent winged form of some mythical spirit, launching effortlessly into the sky like a plume of pale smoke.

At the precise moment the music reached its climax in a note only achieved by Geoffrey once and barely perceptible to the ear, the spirit evaporated into the brilliant light.

With his impaired vision it was difficult to focus on Lorenzo, still and scarcely breathing and seemingly enveloped in the same shaft of light. The young man's exhaustion was clear, as though he had lost almost all his bodily substance. His naked torso was barely an outline, showing no muscular definition; it was a shape that defied any logic, as if Lorenzo was somehow evaporating before his eyes.

"Lorenzo!" Geoffrey cried, unable to move as his companion crumpled onto the ground like a deflated balloon, as if drained of every atom of energy. He searched frantically for any sign of life as the hound went and lay beside the still figure but once the shaft of light had faded it was possible once more to make out the flaming auburn hair and the damp glistening skin of the man and not just an empty carcass.

How long Geoffrey sat in that position, watching for the restoration of life and praying that Lorenzo would recover, he could not tell but after a time he became aware of a crack that was appearing in the soil over the infant Benedict's grave. After a few moments the crested red head of a tiny lizard peeked out, the bluish tinge of its scales becoming more pronounced as it wriggled free and emerged into the open. For a short time it lay motionless on the surface of the grave, its scales becoming more vibrant as the sun broke through once more. Caught in a ray of sunlight, the crest on its head gave the impression of being in flames.

The creature's tail twitched, its eyes scanning the other infants' graves until another lizard crawled out from the cracked earth above Abigail's plot and within moments three more lizards had emerged. All four lay perfectly still until the bluish tinge of their scales became as vibrant as the first lizard, to which they were identical in both shape and colour except for the dramatic flaming crest.

Once their colours matched, they scurried away, clustering together behind the red-crest who now moved rapidly away from the burial ground, passing only inches from Geoffrey's feet. Skirting the undergrowth they headed towards the stream that would carry them to the river. Geoffrey recognised their instinctive knowledge of how to reach home, a journey he feared he would never undertake. If ever he did find his way home, he knew he would never take the English countryside for granted with its scent of freshly mown grass or the sound of a skylark ascending above an ancient meadow. Instead, he was imprisoned within his own body, the humidity was becoming unbearable and he was parched and desperate for a drink. There was still no sign of movement from Lorenzo, who lay with the wolfhound as if dead beside Lady Claudia's grave.

"Lorenzo, please wake up… Someone is coming," Geoffrey cried in desperation. The urgency in his voice, along with a low growl, rumbling in the dog's throat, appeared to get through to Lorenzo, who stirred and made an effort to stand but sank back on to his knees as Marguerite stumbled into view, out of breath from the climb.

"Geoffrey what happened?" she exclaimed, quickly transferring her attentions to the exhausted Lorenzo.

"I am not sure."

"Why did you insist on making him do this?" she challenged, trying to help Lorenzo to his feet.

"Lorenzo him no need help," he said shakily, rising unsteadily and holding on to the tree trunk for support.

"What the hell am I supposed to have done?" Geoffrey retaliated, feeling his sister's glare.

"I would have thought that was obvious, exhausting the poor man by having him carry you up here in this damnable heat." Marguerite hovered near the naked man, as if expecting him to fall.

"You no speak him bad," he admonished her, before grasping the wolfhound's ruff and walking unsteadily towards the cliff edge. "It much hot, Lorenzo him need swim."

"Lorenzo, do be careful… you might fall over the edge!" she screamed.

"Me, I back soon." Lorenzo paused on the brink before diving over the edge and plunging into the river below.

Having peered down from that exact spot a short time earlier, Geoffrey knew it was a terrifying height for anyone to consider diving from and with a gathering of caiman basking close to the river's edge immediately beneath, he feared they would never see Lorenzo again. Yet after less than half an hour he reappeared, evidently fully refreshed and once again perfectly in control of the situation. With sunlight gleaming on his gold-auburn hair, he looked every inch the human counterpart of the red-crested lizard.

Chapter Two
Confusion

The journey downhill, although steep in places, should have taken much less time but because Lorenzo was carrying Geoffrey on his back, extra caution was needed because of the tree roots that had become exposed over the years from rain erosion. That afternoon the humidity was more intense than it had been in weeks and sweat was running down Geoffrey's face in rivulets by the time they reached the compound. However that was the least of his concerns after the jolting and close bodily contact.

Once they were back on the veranda and Geoffrey was waited to be unharnessed, he could only pray for a swift death before Lorenzo was able to detach the equipment and expose his erection. To make his situation even worse, Drangoo had appeared on the veranda and was making his way towards them.

"Cover me up, Lorenzo, before that rotter gets here, I beg of you. I did not want this to happen, I swear I did not," Geoffrey pleaded, red-faced.

"You man, Señor Jeffy. You not feel shame," Lorenzo said, placing the recently washed underwear quickly around his waist. "Why you want here, Drangoo?"

"Missy say you no well, Lollen, want me help with Señor esta noche, no you."

"Lorenzo make Señor Jeffy ready for sleep."

"Missy she much angry if you no come, Lollen, she want you eat with her. Want rest inside, no here."

"It better Lorenzo, him stay. Señor Jeffy no well, no me." He gently eased Geoffrey into a more comfortable position.

"It is better you get some rest yourself, Lorenzo, after whatever sorcery you called upon to create that beautiful service for my mother." Geoffrey felt infinitely more relaxed now his embarrassment was no longer an issue. "All I ask is that you leave the dog with me, then I will be safe." He knew the monk's fear of the animal would keep him away and allow him to rest uninterrupted.

"Perro and Lorenzo, them both stay."

"Why you no go Lollen if Padre no here? I no tell," Drangoo said slyly.

"What did he mean by that?" Geoffrey asked suspiciously.

"Drangoo, him only think with this," Lorenzo said with annoyance, briefly holding his own genitals to demonstrate.

"Then what you want me do?" Drangoo asked.

"Señor Jeffy, him need you go, I much working for make Señor well."

"Why use devil witchcraft like tu madre?" Drangoo jeered. "Why no pray to Christian God, like me, I do… and tu padre?"

"Mi madre, she River People. Esta noche, Lorenzo, him make Señor Jeffy swim."

"Are you completely bonkers…? How can you expect me to swim if I can't even move my legs?" Geoffrey said in panic.

"No fear what in river, Señor Jeffy. Night water… this good."

"You think I give a brass farthing about what you think? You are not putting me in that bloody river, you freak.

Night or day, it doesn't matter. We would both get eaten alive."

"It no problema para mi, Señor. We go this night."

"Like hell we do. I am not going in any water, whatever you think! I need to see Rose; that's much more important," Geoffrey snapped.

"No, Señor Jeffy, la bella señorita, she much remember evil, have much hate."

"Not against me… I am her brother. I saw what happened. That is why I must see her."

"Lady Rosa, she want see no one, she many times much loco. I know you want this happen, Señor Jeffy but that no help."

"I cannot accept that. That thing you did with your chanting, to evoke music and transform butterflies. Surely if you can do that you can do something to help Rose?"

"It no Lorenzo make this. I call forest spirits for help; them take tu madre into our temple. This I make for you. Give peace," Lorenzo said.

"… and I thank you but I cannot allow another day to pass without being with Rose. She is more important than anyone else on this earth and she needs my help. I would be with her now if I could move and that is why I need you to help her through this."

"Only man Señorita let close is Otter; it no you, Señor, it no Lorenzo."

"Then what can I do to help her, Lorenzo? I must do something."

"First heal body, Señor Jeffy. Make walk again. Help Señorita after."

"Very well, if that is my only option." If Lorenzo thought he could get some mobility back into his limbs, Geoffrey was determined to do whatever it would take.

"Estar noche, we go," Lorenzo promised before leaving, making barely a sound.

Towards evening Lorenzo returned, his skin gleaming from swimming. His dark auburn hair was wet and dripping water and he seemed radiantly happy, crouching down to clean his hunting knife in the earth.

"Have you killed something?" Geoffrey asked cautiously, recalling the witch doctor's gruesome medicinal preparations at the galleon.

"Lorenzo no kill, him take what forest give, for help Señor Jeffy in water," he said.

When darkness came Lorenzo carried him, like a papoose, along the riverbank to an inlet where his beautifully decorated canoe had been hauled onto the bank. Further along the bank was an area that Geoffrey had no idea existed. Here a waterfall cascaded down the rock face at the far end of a lagoon, tumbling in the moonlight like a cascade of glittering diamonds. This was a magical place and for the first time since the brutal attack Geoffrey felt relaxed and at peace.

It was clear from where Lorenzo placed him that he had been preparing this area for the nocturnal event. Straddled across two large boulders was a framework of saplings, stripped of bark that had been lashed together to form a bed. Beside this were four bundles of moss and lichen. There was also a large enamel jug that he recognised from the kitchen and three earthenware urns, one much larger than the rest.

"What the hell is that for, Lorenzo? Are you going to bake me?" Geoffrey said.

"No this night. This para mañana… tomorrow."
Lorenzo laughed easily, the lilt of his voice reassuring.

In this part of the lagoon the water was still and
incredibly clear, unlike closer to the river where the
undercurrent was fast and often turbulent. There was a full
moon that night, reflecting off the water so that Lorenzo's
body appear tinged with green as he began to mix a handful of
crushed herbs with some of powdered bark, sprinkling them
into a tin of river water. Using a stick he stirred the contents
into a soft paste, which he then heated over a small fire.

Once this was ready, he removed Geoffrey's underwear
and worked the warm paste into every joint on his body for
what felt like an hour. When that was done, Lorenzo removed
his belt and with it the hunting knife and pouch and leaving
these close to the edge of the bank, guarded by the wolfhound,
he carefully lifted Geoffrey into his arms and carried him into
the water.

Any fears Geoffrey may have had of being attacked by a
shoal of red-bellied piranha, water snakes or black caiman
were not what concerned him most. Rather it was the intimate
bodily contact with Lorenzo, making him question everything
he had been brought up to believe was sinful, since this strong
physical attraction he was feeling towards another man was
surely the very thing he had so despised in Noel Effingham.

On that first night Lorenzo waded into the water only
until it covered his waist, lowering Geoffrey onto the surface
while supporting his body.

"Why is the water so warm?" Geoffrey asked as the
pain in his limbs began to ease almost immediately and he
sensed that this was the first stage in unlocking the paralysis.

"This from mineral spring in temple below, it good for
make repair."

"Temple?" Geoffrey asked but there was no response as Lorenzo began to support him in the middle of his back with alternating hands, massaging each of the painful joints in turn before they eventually returned to the bank. Once there, Lorenzo worked in the remainder of the paste before he put Geoffrey back into the baggy underwear and, strapping him into the harness, carried him to the compound.

Although it was still impossible to move his limbs there was undoubtedly less pain and Geoffrey slept more soundly that night. After a week of intense nightly sessions at the lagoon, he began to notice a distinct tingling sensation of pins and needles throughout his body.

"What about the baking rack, Lorenzo? I thought you were going to cook something on that?" Geoffrey asked at the end of that first week.

"When you ready, then Lorenzo, him use. You no good bake Jeffy, much too bony for me eat," he laughed, working more of the green slime into each joint.

At the beginning of the second week, Lorenzo caked Geoffrey all over with a revolting black mud until he resembled a large chocolate cake. Once this was done, he placed him on the stretcher of narrow boughs close to the water's edge. He then set fire to pieces of lichen and moss and inserted the smouldering clumps underneath the open rack, immediately beneath Geoffrey, who lay face up on top. Not so long before, Geoffrey would have screamed for his elder sister to rescue him but, after a week of gentle manipulation under Lorenzo's competent hands, he felt no fear at all.

Throughout this lengthy procedure, Lorenzo vocalised strange, unintelligible sounds from deep in his throat and as he wafted the smoke evenly over Geoffrey's body the animalistic sounds morphed into primeval chants. Similar to what he had heard at the burial ground, they had a vibrating rhythm, which echoed back from the ancient trees surrounding the clearing.

This time there were no butterflies but a flurry of large flakes, yellow and vivid green, lifted from the coating that covered his naked body. With his head fixed in one position, Geoffrey gazed up into a myriad of stars. For a moment, gliding across them, he was sure he could make out the same winged creature that he and Marguerite had seen briefly from the boat but the vision was broken as Lorenzo lifted him bodily from the stretcher and carried him into the warm water, where he peeled off the baked covering and Geoffrey discovered his shoulders and neck were noticeably more flexible than before.

Midway through the second week, after Lorenzo had dosed him up with an evil-tasting liquid, Geoffrey found that he could move his head properly. By the end of that week, after Lorenzo had doubled the length of time he spent on manipulating them, every joint in his body had a tingling sensation, as if he was being jabbed with red-hot pins. It was rather an unpleasant sensation but Geoffrey was prepared to put up with it for the rest of his life if it meant that Lorenzo had miraculously forced the paralysis into retreat.

When they returned to the compound in the early hours, much later than on previous nights, they were confronted by an impatient Marguerite seated on the veranda steps with the Otter at her side.

"Where have you been all this time?" she asked in a way that made Geoffrey fear the worst. "You have been gone most of the night."

"Why? Has something happened to Rose?"

"No, not at all," she said.

"It me keep Señor Jeffy long time. No him," Lorenzo said in his back-to-front way.

"There is no need to apologise, Lorenzo," she responded in a sickly-sweet tone that she used with her pet spaniel at home.

"Lorenzo was explaining, not apologising, for Pete's sake. Why are you behaving like some neglected fishwife when you know perfectly well he is helping me?"

"I worry what might be lurking out there in the dark. You have been gone a very long time."

"It was not through choice, I can assure you. Lorenzo has been brilliant about this and never complained once, working on my joints in the water when God knows he ought to be back here asleep."

"You were in the water? That is even worse!" she said, horrified. "I will come with you next time."

"You can't. It wouldn't be proper. Lorenzo needs to work on my entire body, so I have to be naked and, quite frankly, I am not having you or anyone else looking on," Geoffrey snapped back.

"What he say much right, Señora, Señor Jeffy him safe in water with me. If you alone on bank, you no safe in dark."

"Oh very well… have it your own way," she said moodily "but promise me, Geoffrey, you will not stay out there too long in future."

"I cannot promise anything. It will take as long as it needs."

"Why must this work happen only at night?"

"Ancients no can help in sunlight. Starlight this much good," Lorenzo said, which seemed to satisfy her.

"What about my hands?" Geoffrey asked. "When are you going to remove this plaster? It soaks up the water and weighs a ton. Surely they must have healed by now?" He was desperate to scratch an itch on his nose when, to his amazement, Lorenzo not only scratched it for him but in exactly the right place, as if he had read his mind. When that thought flashed through his mind, Geoffrey could have sworn Lorenzo smiled but it was impossible to be certain.

"I could do it tomorrow but I would need Lorenzo to help," she said reluctantly.

"Why does it need two of you? They are only bandages."

"If you want them removed, Geoffrey, then I insist Lorenzo must be there." She turned on her heel and disappeared into the bungalow, closely followed by the Otter.

Despite all Geoffrey had suffered since they had docked in Pernambuco, nothing could have prepared him for the moment when his sister finally removed the plastered bandages. It was all he could do to stop himself from screaming with horror, desperate to convince himself that he was dreaming and the butchered hands belonged to someone else but the grotesque shapes were real enough.

"What have you done to my hands, you twisted old bitch?" Geoffrey screamed.

"I had no choice, Geoffrey. It had to be done. There was nothing on earth anyone could have done to reattach your fingers. They had to be removed to prevent infection."

"You did this atrocity to prevent me getting a bloody infection! You mutilated my hands for that? Jesus Christ. Why not just leave me? I was dying anyway." Geoffrey twisted back and forth on the cot in a wild fury until Lorenzo leant over to calm him.

"Señora, she save life, Jeffy."

"My life…! What good is that to me now? Do you think I want to live with these butchered claws instead of hands?"

"I could not leave you like that, Geoffrey. I had to do something… the missing fingers were only attached by skin."

"Where are my fingers? What have you done with them? What have you done with them, you evil bitch?" Geoffrey screamed, struggling to examine his grotesquely misshapen hands. On the left hand, the third and fourth fingers were missing. On the right, the second, third and fifth had been removed. "Answer me… What did you do? Feed them to the bloody piranha?"

"I buried them, with Mother. I swear I did not know what else to do," Marguerite said fearfully as Geoffrey lurched forward in his fury.

"I swear I would kill you for this if I could reach you. How could you have taken my music away from me, the only thing I was ever any good at? Instead you have turned me into a bloody freak! I hate you… I will never forgive you for what you have done to me, NEVER!" Geoffrey screamed at her terrified figure as she backed away.

"Señora no bad, Señor Jeffy, she try help," Lorenzo reassured him. Closing his eyes, he moved to place his hands on either side of Geoffrey's head. "You make music again."

"That is something I can never do. I couldn't even lift an instrument now, let alone play with these stumps she has left me with, you bloody moron."

"This Lorenzo help make."

"Go to hell… both of you!" Geoffrey yelled, clamping his eyes tight shut.

"Will Geoffrey survive, Lorenzo? I cannot bear to think this is all my doing," Marguerite asked, almost to herself. She turned away abruptly as Drangoo appeared, stumbling along the veranda. His robes were torn and his face was streaming with blood, not so much from the fresh gouges on his face as from the clump of hair that had been torn from his scalp.

"Drangoo, what on earth happened?" Marguerite cried, stepping forward to support the monk as he fell to his knees.

"Lady Rosa, she loco… crazy woman!" Drangoo whimpered.

"Rosamund did this to you?" Marguerite asked, to no response. "Lorenzo, you must do something. You know I cannot get near her. The Otter must not be involved in this; he might get injured."

"Si, I go," Lorenzo said, making to leave.

"Not without me," Geoffrey hissed. "You cannot leave me here with them."

"It no safe you go. Bella Rosa, she need me help, no you, Jeffy."

"Safe… you think I give a damn about that any more? Rose is my sister. Whatever is wrong, she will listen to me. If she has gone round the bend then I can understand why. I was there. I saw every horrific thing those men did to her."

"You no strong yet," Lorenzo said, trying to restrain him.

"There is nothing wrong with my voice and if you do not take me, I will crawl if I have to!" Geoffrey said, already beginning to rock himself out of the cot.

"You no need, Jeffy. I take," Lorenzo said, lifting him bodily.

"When we get there, you must leave me alone to talk with her."

"If this you want, I do," Lorenzo said, carrying him down the steps.

42

"Geoffrey no…. Rosamund might kill you," Marguerite called after them.

"Better that than Lorenzo. At least he is some use in the world, unlike this bloody cripple you have turned me into!" Geoffrey yelled over Lorenzo's shoulder.

Before they had come close to the cabin they were confronted by the Otter, fleeing towards them, his eyes wide with fear. On their arrival they discovered one of the windows had been smashed and the door, although broken off its hinges, had been barricaded shut from inside.

"Set me down on the veranda, Lorenzo and then leave," Geoffrey ordered.

"If you here, Jeffy, I stay."

"And I say you do not. Rose will listen to me but only if no one else is here."

"I not go," Lorenzo said, setting him down on a broken crate.

"You must. Rose cannot see you almost naked like this. Even dressed you would present a threat to her."

"Then Lorenzo, he get clothes," he said.

"For God's sake piss off… I need to do this on my own and I do not need any bloody chaperone. Just button up my shirt before you go; I do not want any flesh exposed."

"If Lorenzo no here, it no safe for you."

"I know what I am doing. Just make sure that she can see me through the window," Geoffrey said in desperation, with half a hope his sister might even be crazy enough to put an end to his own life.

Once Lorenzo was out of sight Geoffrey began calling his sister's name but there was no response, only a slight movement beyond the shattered window.

"I know you are there, Rose. Please come out and talk. I cannot move, otherwise I would batter down that barricade and come inside. It is me, Jeffy… I need to see you," he shouted.

After what seemed like an eternity he heard the sound of furniture being moved away from the barricade and eventually the door creaked open.

"Jeffy?" Rosamund's voice called from the shadows.

"Yes, Rose, it is me. I cannot move, so you need to come out where I can see you."

"I have been waiting here all day for Mama to come and take me home, Jeffy. I hate this place. Where is she?"

"Mother cannot be here today because, because she is… ill. That is why I am here instead."

"Then you must take me home, Jeffy."

"I cannot do that, Rose, not today."

"Then why are you here?" Rosamund demanded, stepping closer to the opening but keeping her face deep in the shadows, so that only the lower part of her torn and filthy gown could be seen. Dangling from her fingers was a pair of scissors, dripping with blood.

"I… I thought I could ask Maggs to find you a clean dress," Geoffrey lied.

"Why, do you not find this appropriate?" she asked.

"Please hand me those scissors before you hurt yourself," Geoffrey pleaded, forcing his agonising joints to reach out and hoping not to scare her off with the sight of his mutilated hands.

"Why should I? Get your own, I need them."

"What would you need them for?"

44

"I need them in case I have missed anything. If I am going home, I need to look my best," she said, at last stepping forward into the light.

"Oh my God… What have you done?" Geoffrey gasped. Her scalp was raw and bleeding where she had hacked off almost all of her beautiful hair, leaving only tufts that had been impossible to reach. There were dark rings around her hollow eye sockets that gave her the appearance of a manic doll.

"Is that monster with you?" she asked nervously. He noticed the bruising around her throat and a savage red hand mark across her pale cheek. There were fresh cuts to both knees.

"I am sorry, Rose. I could not get here on my own. I asked Lorenzo to carry me over," Geoffrey said, wishing he could reach out and comfort her. "The monk told us you were barricaded in. That is why I am here."

"If that filthy animal comes near me again, I swear to you, Jeffy, I will plunge these scissors into that black heart and send him back into Hell without it!" She began screaming, wild and demented, stabbing the scissors repeatedly into the doorframe until, broken and exhausted, she sank to her knees, sobbing.

"Lorenzo… where are you? We must help her!" Geoffrey cried.

"No, Señor Jeffy. We need leave, give time for devil in head to escape," Lorenzo whispered from the shadows.

"We have to do something for her," Geoffrey pleaded, only able to watch as Rosamund struggled to her feet, the scissors still clenched like a dagger in her small hand.

"Come with me, Rose, where you will be safe. You should not be in that cabin alone," Geoffrey called but she grasped the neck of her torn gown, pulling it up tightly against her throat and retreated into the gloom where she stood for a moment.

"I am not a whore, Jeffy… I am not… I am not!" she shouted, her agonising cries reverberating throughout the overhanging trees as she wrenched the partially hinged door back into position.

"Rose… Rose, do not do this. Come back outside!" Geoffrey cried, barely aware of Lorenzo kneeling at his side.

"It much soon, Señor Jeffy, you no can help."

" I have to do something. I cannot leave Rose like that. She needs me," Geoffrey hissed. Only after several minutes did he eventually realise that she wouldn't return.

"La Bella Rosa need much time for heal," Lorenzo said, massaging the back of Geoffrey's neck. "What you need, Señor Jeffy?"

"What you cannot possibly give me, Lorenzo. No one can, not even you."

"If you tell, I much try?"

"That pervert Drangoo must be punished for this and I will find a way. I swear!"

"Nada, Señor, Lorenzo, him do this," he said reassuringly.

"I also want revenge on those bastards who raped her. They must suffer after what they have done. What I need more than anything else on God's earth is to hunt down and kill every last one of them but how can I, like this?"

"Lorenzo, him make Jeffy whole again."

"Look at me… how could anyone resurrect this useless body? Rose could have got away if only she had tried and she would have survived but she stayed, thinking she could protect Mother and this broken body of mine. Look what has happened to her... that. I could not help her when she needed me most."

"You try help Bella Rosa, I know."

"For what good it did!" Geoffrey said bitterly, remembering every vivid detail. "Had I been strong like you, I would have hunted those bastards down to the very ends of the earth." Tears were forming, though he tried his utmost not to cry.

"If this you need, Jeffy, Lorenzo, he show hombres die."

"That is impossible... How can you?"

"Lorenzo make see, him know how." He calmly picked Geoffrey up and carried him back to the veranda where Marguerite was waiting.

"Where be Drangoo?" Lorenzo asked.

"I have no idea. He took off soon after you left," Marguerite said.

"Him no say where go?" Lorenzo persisted.

"To ask forgiveness, he said but not where."

"Lorenzo, him know where Drangoo pray. He go find."

"Be gentle, Lorenzo. I did the best I could to stitch back the scalp but he is in a lot of pain," Marguerite called after him as he left. She turned to her brother, white-faced. "Please forgive me, Geoffrey, for having to do this to your beautiful hands."

"How can you expect my forgiveness? Just stay out of my sight and help Rose. You have no idea what's been going on under your nose."

"What do you mean, Geoffrey?"

"Ask Lorenzo after he finds that lunatic monk and drags him back here."

When Lorenzo returned there was fresh blood on his knuckles and a satisfied look on his face and Geoffrey chose not to enquire while Lorenzo offered up no explanation. The following morning Drangoo was ushered onto the veranda with Marguerite at his side. His mouth was badly cut and swollen, his sallow cheeks bruised and cut in several places and there was a bandage around his torn scalp. It was also apparent Marguerite had been unable to repair his broken nose, which was oozing blood.

"How could you do this, Lorenzo? Drangoo is your brother," Marguerite said accusingly. "You are the last person I would have expected to be so brutal and with no provocation at all? Drangoo was praying!"

"Drangoo, him no touch la bella Rosa more. I make promise he no live if him do," Lorenzo said.

"You should be thanking Lorenzo, not berating him," Geoffrey said.

"You actually condone what Lorenzo has done, Geoffrey! How could you?"

"Quite easily, as it is no more than I would have done myself, or worse, if I were still whole. Why not go and see Rose for yourself before you make any more assumptions?"

"Rosamund will only allow the Otter anywhere near her."

"Then save your unwanted cynicism until you have seen her," Geoffrey said bitterly.

It was a great relief when night came and Lorenzo harnessed him up and carried him back to the isolated lagoon, which not only offered some hope of being able to use his limbs again but also allowed them to get away from his sister and the monk.

48

Lorenzo laid out a rectangle of stones and then another smaller circle at the far end of the space. In this he piled a mixture of red moss and a bluish tree bark before he trailed lengths of riverweed over the mound.

"This for help Jeffy, understand much," Lorenzo said, turning to leave.

"Understand what?" Geoffrey shouted after the departing figure, already merging into the dense undergrowth without even a shaking leaf to show his passing.

This time there was no massaging of Geoffrey's joints when Lorenzo returned, carrying a small woven bag slung across his broad shoulders. Cradled in his arms was a bundle of wood unlike any Geoffrey had seen before. The bark had a translucent and silvery blue sheen.

Once he had piled the wood into a cone over the moss in the centre of the small circle, Lorenzo squatted in the oblong section, facing the pile, his arms folded across his chest and his eyes closed. As he began a strange guttural chant, to Geoffrey's astonishment, the cone of wood almost immediately caught fire. This was not a warm orange and yellow blaze but was made up of blue and green flames, like Geoffrey had seen as a child when he had thrown salt on the fire at home but, unlike then, this colour didn't fade. Instead, the turquoise flames increased as if in response to Lorenzo's mysterious chant.

Once the fire was blazing, the wordless chant began to change into a spoken dialect, fiercely dark and intimidating and, at the moment this recitation ended, a mass of sparks erupted from the cone and the flames died away. For a short time afterwards, Lorenzo stayed cross-legged within the stones, his head bowed, his bronzed hair hanging loose, masking every feature.

"Lorenzo?" Geoffrey called anxiously, uncertain if this was to be a re-enactment of the incident at the burial ground.

"Lorenzo, he good, time for make Jeffy see," he responded, folding his arms over his chest just as before and uttering strange, echoing sounds from deep in his throat. When this altered once more into the unrecognisable dialect, the cone again burst into flames. This time, however, Lorenzo took longer to recover.

"You must stop this, Lorenzo, before it makes you seriously ill," Geoffrey cried. His companion merely smiled as he began removing items from the woven bag.

"For Lorenzo this done… it now you," he said. In his hand was a dark, gooey paste that he applied liberally to the sockets around Geoffrey's eyes.

"What are you doing?" Geoffrey said with alarm as Lorenzo put some of the paste onto two purple leaves, firmly spitting on each one in turn.

"Close eyes, Jeffy, you see." Lorenzo placed the leaves carefully over Geoffrey's eyes, binding them around his head with a thin vine. Once this was done, he carried him over to a shelf of rock overhanging the river, seating him so that his knees were at the very edge, his legs hanging free.

Holding him steady, Lorenzo climbed onto the rock and sat close behind, easing Geoffrey back into his body so that the young man's arms were over Lorenzo's bent knees, with his head positioned on his lower chest, with barely a fraction of an inch between them. Unable to see but having the reassuring pressure of another naked body against him, Geoffrey found this disturbingly comforting,

"What are you going to do?" he asked.

"You want see, Jeffy? I show," Lorenzo said, pressing his fingertips lightly on either side of Geoffrey's temples.

Within seconds, Geoffrey felt a tingling sensation where Lorenzo had placed his fingers and a sizzling sound penetrated his skull, as if a thousand wasps had been released inside his head. The leaves covering his eyes became intensely hot.

"What is happening to my eyes, Lorenzo?" Geoffrey said in panic, as searing, orange flashes shattered the darkness of his vision before fading to leave a light green mist.

"I make see what happen," Lorenzo reassured him, speaking close to Geoffrey's ear. "You listen me speak, you watch, much learn."

Although Geoffrey had no idea what was happening, his trust in Lorenzo was unshakeable, so he said nothing, not even when another dramatic sequence of colour flashed across his vision. He tried to relax, listening intently to Lorenzo's hypnotic voice until the flashes ended and he could make out a rain-sodden shape sprawled in the churned-up, blood-soaked mud. To his astonishment, he recognised the shape as himself, with Rosamund hunched up on the bottom step against the handrail.

"This what happen, Jeffy."

It was as if he were somehow watching a re-enactment of that terrible day from a high perspective. Geoffrey heard the two pistol shots from inside his mother's cabin, then Scarface staggered screaming from the doorway, clutching the section of his face that had been shot away before dropping into the mud. Following immediately behind was the albino, clutching a bundle of objects wrapped hastily in his mother's embroidered shawl. Trampling over his dying companion, the albino did not run towards the steamer but cut away into the trees and within seconds, the fleeing figure was deep in the forest.

After that, a silvery mist descended then cleared to reveal the staging by the river where Marguerite was standing with the revolver in her hand, exactly as he remembered but now he was close enough to see every gory detail as she carried out the calculated execution.

As each shot was fired, Lorenzo somehow relayed to him every word Marguerite uttered as she emptied the revolver into the writhing body of Valdez, right down to the moment when his sister lifted the hem of her skirt to press her foot into the bloody mass, deliberately pushing the wretch into the river.

"This for you give peace," Lorenzo said, placing his right hand on Geoffrey's forehead and his left over his heart.

"It was horrible but what she did was justified but what became of the others?"

"You see," Lorenzo said, easing Geoffrey into a seated position. He took a small amount of red powder from the pouch and applied this around Geoffrey's eye sockets, before he smeared more of the dark paste onto the leaves and spat on them as before.

Once the blindfold was back in position, Lorenzo seated himself behind Geoffrey on the rock and eased him into the same position against his chest. He reconnected his fingertips on Geoffrey's temples and the sizzling and tingling intensified until Geoffrey was convinced this time his head would explode. Finally it resolved into a swirling bluish green mist through which leaves were taking shape and a narrow tributary was flowing below.

"What is this place?" Geoffrey asked.

"This make for justice," Lorenzo whispered into his ear, as clearer images began to appear before Geoffrey's eyes. He saw a giant snake, which somehow he immediately understood was a legendary creature that had been worshipped among the River People for generations, a gigantic anaconda that had grown to double its natural size. It was a giant that had long outlived its allotted time and, with the advancement of its great age, had become increasingly slow in the hunt for prey. As a result it was ravenously hungry.

Geoffrey saw the serpent clearly, waiting as still as death, concealed among the thick overhanging boughs that spread above the river, lying in wait for anything edible that might come within reach. Only the creature's eyes shifted warily as it sensed the approaching boat and aboard it the two men, not the most tender food source but palatable enough.

As the one-armed ruffian steered the rusting boat warily towards Geoffrey's vantage point it was clear that he had sensed danger, not only lurking in the murky waters of the narrowing channel but among the dense foliage flanking either side. Yet he paid no attention to the dark canopy of leaves and boughs above him. It was also evident that Geoffrey's attempt to infect him with the deadly virus had worked, his eyes already showing the characteristic covering of grey film and leaving him unable to focus in the reduced light from the overhanging trees.

As the steamer chugged slowly beneath them, it was clear too that the aggravating infection between his fingers was making it increasingly difficult for his one hand to grip the wheel and steer the vessel away from the banks. He cursed with frustration as the engine abruptly cut out and the boat drifted into a mass of floating vegetation.

Covered by a filthy mosquito net to keep away the swarming insects, his mutilated companion lay groaning in the rusted prow. He was barely alive and, to alleviate friction on the mass of eruptions covering his skin, he was stripped naked with the incongruous exception of his hobnailed boots, the instruments of torture that had crushed Geoffrey's fingers.

Firing up the engine once more, the one-armed man was about to crank the boat into reverse when he looked up. From his confused reaction it was clear he thought a bough had broken free from the tree above them and snagged on its way down and he made to heave it over the side as it crashed onto the deck. Only then did the realisation hit home as he stared at the enormous head of the serpent, its hypnotic, calculating eyes focused on him, as the boat drifted even closer. The sound of his fearful cries and the jolt of crashing gears roused the cyclops, who sat up in alarm as the boat juddered slowly through the floating vegetation, bringing him ever closer to the snake.

Clanking noisily, the propeller snagged against a thick root system projecting from the bank, bringing the boat to a standstill as the engine spluttered and then cut out once more. Petrified, the helmsman could only watch as the serpent coiled itself around his companion, hauling the writhing body up into the tree above them like a small child. The terrified screams of his comrade prompted him into frenzied action, tearing at the clumps of weed that were clinging to the propeller.

Barely a few feet above him, pinioned among the tightening coils of the reptile, the other man's ribcage audibly shattered as the snake found a more comfortable position above the river. There was no hope of escape as the giant anaconda prepared to squeeze out the remainder of his agonised breath.

The one-eyed man's screams were as high-pitched as a girl's as with a chilling hiss the broad, flat head of the serpent dislocated its lower jaw. Immediately beneath this tableau, the one-armed hunter watched petrified as the snake thrust his comrade head first into its gaping mouth, swallowing the naked man whole. He began slashing wildly at the remaining weed as one of his companion's boots crashed onto the deck against him, clanging off the metal handrail before it splashed into the water.

Finally free of the tangled weed he managed to restart the engine, all the time screaming to the Almighty for forgiveness as the boat veered crazily in reverse from bank to bank and into the dark, fetid waters of a swamp where blackened, jagged stumps reared up out of the water like prehistoric monsters.

It was abundantly clear to the watching Geoffrey that the situation was becoming more hopeless the deeper the boat penetrated the swamp. There was barely enough fuel left to stoke up the boiler and nowhere to moor the boat and gather more wood. Crazed with fear, the surviving hunter steered further into the gloom until finally, the spluttering engine cut out and the threatening silence became overpowering. The dank air was as still as death, until a rumble of thunder heralded the searing flash of crackling lightning, momentarily illuminating his hellish incarceration.

In desperation, he managed to pole the boat forward a short distance but, to keep the boat moving, he needed every ounce of strength as he fought against the dangling trails of vine from the overhanging trees, brushing against his face like imaginary snakes.

When the next thunderclap came immediately overhead, he dropped the pole, clamping both hands over his ears and screaming with terror as another searing flash speared into the darkness. He groped about in the water to retrieve the pole until, with a splintering crash the decrepit craft came to a juddering halt, speared through its rotting hull by the remains of a petrified tree. Now the rain came sheeting down and with it a surge of stinking water rushing into the boat.

Despite the teeming rain, Geoffrey could make out a pair of eyes glistening amid the fallen logs surrounding the sinking craft but after another bolt of lightning flashed across the scene, the eyes were gone and the boat shifted in the water as Rodrigo tried to cram whatever he could get hold of to block the hole and stem the flow.

The first sign of the new threat was a blurred flurry of squawking egrets as they took flight. Startled, the man unsheathed his hunting knife, backing away from the damaged prow before screaming wildly as he spun around and stared into the gaping jaws of a caiman. Its rancid breath blasted into his face before the jaws clamped hold of his right arm, piercing the flesh to the bone as it yanked him bodily out of the boat.

In the thrashing water a larger and more ferocious caiman now grappled for ownership of the prey and within moments had secured possession, leaving the first reptile to retreat with the dismembered remains of his one good arm. The insanity of his dying screams echoed above the surface long after the man was dragged bodily beneath the water, his withered left arm flailing uselessly, his legs kicking wildly and his final breath gurgling from his lungs.

Geoffrey could barely speak when Lorenzo removed the covering from his eyes and cleansed them with fresh water. Even though he had every justification to welcome the savage deaths of the two hunters it was hard to come to terms with what he had witnessed.

"Could I be left alone for a while?" Geoffrey asked, growing nauseous as he tried to focus back onto the real world around him.

"Si... Lorenzo he go swim." Within seconds he had plunged into the lagoon as Geoffrey began retching until his entire body ached.

Though he glanced up several times there was no sign of Lorenzo. He continued to stare across the vast expanse of still water for what seemed an eternity until Lorenzo's head suddenly appeared and he swam strongly to the bank.

"Lorenzo sorry him go, if Jeffy much ill," he said with obvious concern.

"I am perfectly fine," Geoffrey lied, unable to stop replaying the terrifying images that were etched into his brain.

"Why you no tell Lorenzo?"

"Was what I saw real?" Geoffrey blurted out. "It was horrible!"

"Si, this why I show. You no want them die?"

"Of course I did but ... but not to be a part of it."

"Why this trouble Jeffy, make sick?" Lorenzo asked, collecting some fresh water to clean Geoffrey's body.

"I suppose because it was such a shock seeing it all happen," Geoffrey said, remembering the calculated execution of Valdez by his normally mild-mannered sister.

"La Señora, how you think now of what Lady, she do?" Lorenzo asked, as if he had interpreted those thoughts.

"Truthfully? I am amazed at her determination to make that filthy bastard pay for what he did to Rose and to me." Geoffrey stared down at his butchered hands. "I saw very little of what happened and could never have imagined that my sister would done that. Marguerite is a devout Christian and it goes against everything she believes."

"Then Jeffy understand why she do this?" Lorenzo asked, reaching over to massage the mutilated stumps of his fingers.

"In time I suppose I may but not yet. I only wish I could see everything else as clearly as I could see what happened when my eyes were bandaged." Geoffrey blinked furiously.

"Soon Lorenzo make see," he said reassuringly, wetting his fingertips in his mouth before stroking them lightly over Geoffrey's closed eyelids.

"Any improvement would be a blessing," Geoffrey began. He paused as his sharp hearing picked up the sound of someone who was clearly trying not to be heard but whose approach had also been noticed by the wolfhound, which had begun to growl.

"Who is that out there?" Geoffrey shouted irritably.

"This Drangoo, Señor; loco Perro, it no let through."

"What the hell do you want?" Geoffrey asked.

"It Missy, she want you come back."

"Well tell her that I cannot, not yet."

"What you do there with Lollen?" Drangoo taunted from beyond the bushes.

"What we are doing here is none of your damned business, so piss off back to the compound and tell that control freak who sent you that I will come back when I am ready and not before!"

"What you say, Señor, Drangoo him no understand what this… piss off it mean?" he called back, before shrieking with panic at a series of ferocious growls from the dog. Moments later he could be heard crashing away through the undergrowth.

"It time we go. I can no more do," Lorenzo said, strapping Geoffrey into the harness. "We need make Jeffy walk soon, not carried like bambino."

Chapter Three
Dark Visions

During the following three nights, Lorenzo massaged and manipulated each of Geoffrey's joints relentlessly until he was convinced his limbs were about to fall off. However, at the end of each session the tingling sensation had increased throughout his entire body and his previously rigid limbs were noticeably more flexible.

Once each session was over they spent an hour in deeper water, Lorenzo supporting him bodily and encouraging Geoffrey to perform the motions of swimming, which, with the aid of the mineral waters, assisted with the increasing mobility.

On the fourth night of the third week, Lorenzo applied a slimy paste around his eye sockets and it felt as if he was administering a series of sizzling jolts through his fingertips right to the back of Geoffrey's neck. He then carried him out into the deep water.

"What are you doing?" Geoffrey shouted in panic as the lower part of his body was allowed to sink, leaving only his head facing Lorenzo's above the surface. Despite Geoffrey's confidence and trust in him, he feared for a moment that Lorenzo's intention was to either kill or let him drown.

"Lorenzo help make see," he replied, cupping Geoffrey's head in his hands.

"What am I supposed to do?" Geoffrey panicked, unable to tread water and fearing he would sink like a lead weight if Lorenzo let go.

"You no speak and eyes keep open, it much importante. Lorenzo no let drown," Lorenzo said, as if reading his thoughts.

After inhaling deeply, Lorenzo planted his mouth onto Geoffrey's, forcing air deep into his lungs until Geoffrey feared he was about to explode. His alarm grew as Lorenzo now dragged him beneath the surface, until he became aware of a phosphorous light that illuminated a cavernous space below them. Swimming underwater as easily as any aquatic creature, his rich auburn hair glowing like waving seaweed, Lorenzo seated Geoffrey on a flat rock opposite him.

By now Geoffrey no longer felt any sense of panic, even though he had been underwater for longer than at any time in his entire life. The oxygen pressed into his lungs gave him time to evaluate his surroundings. The enormous space was a submerged temple, with a central avenue of carved stone columns that had once supported a massive roof.

It was strange that there was no sign of any black caiman, water snakes or shoals of red-bellied piranha, yet a group of dolphins were swimming gracefully among the columns. He watched in amazement as Lorenzo began swimming with them and performing exuberant, underwater acrobatics, as if this was an everyday occurrence.

The section of rock where Geoffrey was seated was pierced by a series of holes and through these pumped jets of hot, mineral-rich water in which shoals of small fish appeared to be performing balletic movements in the upsurge.

Geoffrey watched as Lorenzo now swam right around the column nearest to him, as much at ease underwater as he was on dry land. With a finger he indicated that Geoffrey should focus on a corroded piece of stone and as his blurred eyesight began to improve he realised it wasn't a crumbling rock at all but had been intricately carved into the shape of a dragon.

It was only as Geoffrey's clouded eyesight cleared that he saw three of the dreaded caiman and a shoal of red-bellies a little further off, yet not one of them was venturing close to the temple. It was as though an invisible screen surrounded the ancient building.

Geoffrey did not resist when Lorenzo put his arm around his chest and they wove slowly together in and out of the columns, swimming so close that he could make out the intricate detail on each of the ancient carvings. All too soon, however, the air left his lungs and he became light-headed. With Lorenzo still supporting him they returned to the surface, where the iridescent shape of a huge fish leapt out of the dark water, feasting on the hovering mosquitoes before plunging back as Lorenzo swam to the bank with Geoffrey clinging to his shoulders.

"What was that place, Lorenzo?" Geoffrey asked, recovering his breath as they lay together beneath a myriad of stars.

"The temple name… Orpantha."

"Orpantha?"

"Orpantha, him river god."

"Why do you smile?"

"Orpantha, this Lorenzo, him tribal name from mi madre. Lorenzo, my Papa, he give." Lorenzo laughed.

"Lorenzo is an easier name to remember for sure." Yet the tribal name resonated and they had stayed underwater for an extraordinary amount of time when anyone else would surely have drowned.

"Now eyes clear. You see many things in temple, yes?"

"Oh my God!" exclaimed Geoffrey, realising for the first time the clarity of the stars above them. "I can see again."

"If Jeffy happy, then Lorenzo, him too." He smiled as he began carefully removing the paste from around Geoffrey's eye sockets.

"You made this possible," Geoffrey said, staring up into the night sky. This was a truly magical place and one that Geoffrey knew he would remember for the rest of his life. At Geoffrey's request, they returned to the submerged temple twice more that week, each time spending longer underwater than before. On the second visit, after momentarily resurfacing Lorenzo forced more air into his lungs, enabling him to return beneath the water and ride on the back of a giant turtle through the temple, gliding over a sacrificial altar and medieval tombs, propelled between the avenues of elaborately carved stone screens, all cloaked in that eerie phosphorous light.

Every time they returned to the bank another batch of slime was freshly mixed and manipulated into every joint of Geoffrey's body and each session lasted longer than the one before. Although Lorenzo said very little and gave no indication there was anything wrong, there was a definite alteration in his mood. He had become even more focused on the areas of manipulation but even when Geoffrey cried out at the intensity the treatment didn't stop and extended into the early hours.

"Thank the Lord that is over!" Geoffrey finally exclaimed.

"I no mean hurt Jeffy." Lorenzo's voice was weary and leaving him within the circle of stones he plunged into the water, sinking immediately beneath the surface.

With no sign of Lorenzo returning, Geoffrey drifted into an erotic, dreamlike state and on awakening he had no idea if it had been real or imagined but rather than sprawled across him fast asleep, Lorenzo was crouched close beside him, staring intently.

"You no want move?" Lorenzo asked.

"You know I do… if only I could," Geoffrey grumbled morosely.

"Then it time!" Lorenzo grabbed hold of Geoffrey and lifted him bodily to his feet.

"Why are you not harnessing me?" Geoffrey panicked.

"This I do soon, first you make come to Lorenzo." He moved away, still standing close enough to catch him if he fell but far enough away to allow Geoffrey to make a step forward. After some initial tumbles he managed to stagger a few hesitant steps before Lorenzo supported him, helped him back down and strapped on the harness.

"This is a miracle!" Geoffrey exclaimed in awe.

"It you, Jeffy; good spirit in here make walk," Lorenzo said, pressing his clenched fist against his heart.

When they got back to the compound that morning, Marguerite was already pacing the veranda.

"You have been gone all night!" she said accusingly, once Lorenzo had left them. "What were you doing all this time?"

"You know exactly what!" Geoffrey resented her tone but was unable to look her directly in the eyes, still questioning the vivid reality of the dream.

"Whatever you were doing, you should have returned hours ago."

"I do not answer to you. You are not my mother," Geoffrey retorted.

"Not me, perhaps but that obnoxious priest will need some explanation of where you and Lorenzo have been. He arrived in the night and accused me of being a whore, demanding to know if Lorenzo was in my bed!"

"Where is he now?"

"I have absolutely no idea. He rode off on his mule at daybreak with Drangoo racing after him. I have not seen either of them since."

It was an hour later when the priest returned, seated easily on the back of a mule that was much larger than the one Geoffrey remembered from his last visit. His worn black robes were roughly repaired and bizarrely he was riding bareback.

The priest reined in the mule within a few feet of the veranda and dismounted with an agility that was unexpected in a man of his advancing years. Seen in the harsh light of day, his features were deeply lined from endless exposure to the sun and beneath the thinning grey hair, several areas of his scalp were severely blistered. His muscular legs, briefly exposed beneath the dark robes as he dismounted, were scarred and badly lacerated with recent cuts. His mud-encrusted feet, in worn sandals, were oozing blood.

Seeing him so close up, Geoffrey noticed that his face was severely scarred, particularly across the forehead where a savage gash from an animal's claw had separated his right eyebrow into three parts. There was a deep gouge that had missed taking out his left eye by only a fraction, slashing down across his cheek and cutting into the upper part of his lip.

Reluctantly, Geoffrey had to admit that this was the face of an intelligent man, one that had once even been handsome.

An ageing misfit, obsessed with the severity of his calling, alienated by the priesthood from any form of cultured society.

"I understood you were paralysed!" Fitzgerald announced.

"As you can see, I am not!" Geoffrey defiantly gripped the handrail, determined not to fall over. "The reason is all due to Lorenzo's skill."

"Then he has done well. Where is Lorenzo?" He looked up at the ominous cloud formation. "We must set off before the storm breaks."

"He cannot leave here. We need him."

"What you need is of small consequence, Englishman," the priest growled. "Lorenzo is not one of your servants. He is an instrument of God and we have a mission to spread the Lord's message. As a gesture of goodwill I could maybe spare Drangoo but that is all."

"I could not imagine anyone… less helpful." Geoffrey wished the priest would leave so that he could sit down without being scrutinised.

"Very well… I will allow you one hour to reconsider. However, I strongly suggest that you think this over carefully before you continue with these childish objections."

"There is nothing childish about not wanting that bloody pervert roaming about here," Geoffrey retorted angrily.

"I reject your warped opinion of Drangoo. He is a dedicated Christian. It is time you faced up to the fact that you will need someone here to help out for the next few days, at lest until he can arrange transportation for you and your sisters to the Mission of Guava."

"Why the hell would we want to go there?"

"One good reason would be for the safety of Lady Rosamund until she has recovered enough to travel." The priest stared at Geoffrey's claw-like hand, bleached white by the effort to hold onto the rail. "Now you have made the point that you can stand, Geoffrey, it is about time that you sat down, before you fall over and break a leg, or something worse."

"'Geoffrey'? Who the hell do you think you are talking to?"

"Obviously to someone who expects to get their own way but, as I am sure you are well aware, this is a far cry from the shores of England. Here nobility counts for nothing, only the art of survival."

"You imagine I am not aware of that?"

"Since you question leaving Drangoo behind, then I do wonder. Quite frankly, I doubt if you are able to walk at all without having something or someone to hang on to. Whatever you have in mind that will not be my Lorenzo."

"I do not give a brass fart what you think, Fitzgerald and you will kindly address me as Lord Geoffrey!"

"I will allow your two sisters the courtesy of addressing them in the manner of their given titles but not a self-opinionated little prick." The priest moved closer and forcibly removed Geoffrey's mutilated hand from the rail, supporting his body as he carefully eased him onto the cane lounger.

"You did not need to do that. I could have managed," Geoffrey protested.

"Never mistake Christian charity for anything other than that. I have no respect for people like you, Geoffrey, the weak and privileged," he said, stepping back.

"Nor I you, you... pompous ass," Geoffrey spluttered, convinced he was going to pass out from the excruciating pain in every joint.

"I do pity these injuries in one so young but maybe this is God's way of making a man of you yet, now that you have put aside that fiddle."

"For a man of God, you do talk a load of bollocks!"

"It is not a sign of weakness to admit you need help, Geoffrey. If not for yourself, then at least consider my offer for the sake of your sisters."

"If it was anyone else but Drangoo I probably would," Geoffrey croaked.

"Then consider this. Once Drangoo knows his rightful place, his presence here could be of some use to the ladies, who will be in need of assistance."

"Perhaps but how can I control him if I am immobile like this?"

"Drangoo fears Lorenzo and that hound more than the wrath of God himself. That might be a start."

"How will that help if they are hundreds of miles away?"

"If you accept my offer, which any man in his right mind would, I will arrange for the animal to stay here with you but be aware, you have one hour to decide and not a moment longer. Once we leave this compound, do not expect to see any of us return for nigh on a year. There are distant tribes in great need of the Christian message and it is my intention to fulfill that mission."

It was less than an hour later when the priest again confronted Geoffrey but this time, he was accompanied by Lorenzo and the monk, who was cautiously holding the temperamental mule's bridle.

"Well, Geoffrey, it is time. Have you come to a decision?"

"If Lorenzo will allow me to keep the hound, then I would be very grateful for the assistance here, however temporary." Geoffrey's agreement sounded firmer than he was feeling, realising he couldn't be with Lorenzo again for almost a year.

"Lorenzo, him make this; keep Jeffy safe when swim."

The armlet Lorenzo attached around Geoffrey's bicep had been intricately woven from strands of his red/gold hair and fashioned into a webbed design that closely resembled the broad mesh collar worn by the hound.

"Why would anyone want to swim in such treacherous waters?" Geoffrey asked, examining the intricate workmanship. "Other than you, I suppose."

"You need swim much each day, Jeffy. Make for strong body which much need." Lorenzo ran a finger along the mesh. "In water, caiman, them much fear sign of Orpantha, they no harm."

"And what about those awful piranha and water snakes?"

"Si... them too, they much fear token of Orpantha, keep Jeffy safe. Perro, him have same." He smiled and crouched down beside the animal, muttering unintelligible words into its ear before he vaulted over the veranda rail, spear in hand, disappearing into the dense undergrowth and leaving no sign of his passing.

"I bid you good day, milady.... and you also... Geoffrey." Fitzgerald crammed a battered clerical hat onto his head, mounted the saddleless mule with the agility of a young man and cantered off at a furious pace, the shapes of priest and mule obscured in a cloud of dried earth.

By late afternoon, although clearly resentful Drangoo had made himself useful by helping Marguerite get the fire under the kitchen stove alight and stocking up with wood. Geoffrey did what he could to continue the improvement in his ability to walk, hobbling and limping around the compound perimeter until he stumbled exhausted back up the bungalow steps.

"Where did you acquire that lovely armlet, Geoffrey? Why have I never seen this before?" Marguerite asked, running her fingertips lightly over the intricate mesh.

"It was a gift… from Lorenzo."

"Then perhaps you can explain why he would leave something like this for you and nothing for me?"

"I have no idea but since you ask, perhaps it is a symbol of bonding. If you look closely, you will see this is a matching pair to the one that he made for the hound. We fought as a team before and we will again but only after I have built up my strength."

Geoffrey was increasingly irritated that it seemed Marguerite could barely bring herself to look at the armlet without an expression of resentment.

"If you like it so much, why not draw the damned thing in your journal and see if that will get it out of your system," he snapped.

"If you had any feeling at all, you would have given it to me," Marguerite said peevishly.

"Even if I wanted to I could not. It is impossible to get the damned thing off!"

"Excuses…!"

"If you think that, then try taking that one off your wrist, the one Churuma gave you. It's woven from the same fibres as this one and when you cannot, then tell me I am being difficult!"

"I never said that."

"It was implied and that is enough. It is on my arm, not yours and that is where it will stay. It links me and the hound together and that is more important."

"That dog will need a name if you are going to keep it," Marguerite announced as she began sketching Geoffrey's armlet into the journal.

"He already has one... Lorenzo named him Perro."

"That is just the Spanish word for dog. It needs something else. You cannot just call it 'dog'."

"Why not; that is what he is."

"Why not name it Frankenstein instead? With all of those scars it might have been assembled from spare parts," she said acidly.

"That is cruel and you know it!" Geoffrey retorted.

"It was meant only in fun, Geoffrey. However, you should come up with a name if it is going to be staying here until they return."

"Very well, then I shall," said Geoffrey. He pondered an appropriate name for an Irish wolfhound before inspiration struck. "I will call him Bog Boy, if that makes you feel any better."

"Why choose such an odd name as that?"

"Why indeed?" Geoffrey smiled, offering no explanation, rather happy with the secret connection to Archie Westbrook, who he was convinced would have been outraged if he had known. "If I decide to enter him at Cruft's when we get back, then I will explain; otherwise I could always shorten it to Bog if that makes you any happier." His laughter was aimed not at his sister but at the drawing of Archie pinned above his cot.

Chapter Four
Survival

Although Geoffrey had initially rejected the offer of Drangoo's help, he soon realised it was essential to have an able-bodied man helping out but when Marguerite insisted the monk continue with the daily massage of Geoffrey's joints, he would have none of it.

"If you let that creep anywhere near me, I swear I will set the dog on him and do not think that is an idle threat. That pervert can find a more practical use for his hands, because they are coming nowhere near me," Geoffrey snapped, as he worked on the exercises Lorenzo had shown him.

"Very well but understand this: I cannot be expected to take over. There are other more important matters to be attended to." She broke off before rushing to the railing, where to his surprise she vomited over the edge.

"What is wrong with you, Maggs?"

"I have been feeling unwell for the past few days. It will soon pass."

"Are you showing any signs of the infection?" Geoffrey asked fearfully.

"There is no rash, only mosquito bites. It could be something I ate."

"Even so, you should take some of that anti-viral potion you are distilling in the lab, it cannot do any harm."

"I have already tried but it only makes me feel worse. Rosamund is suffering with the same thing too but not as severe."

"Well that is a blessing. She has enough to deal with," Geoffrey struggled to his feet, helped up by the wolfhound, which seemed to know instinctively where he needed support.

"Rosamund has been asking for you," Marguerite said, putting a hand up to her mouth and running into the building.

A week after Lorenzo's departure, Geoffrey was able to walk the length of the veranda without stumbling. By the end of the second week he had managed to navigate two circuits of the compound before he was totally exhausted but he continued to improve every day by pushing himself to the limit each time. By the end of the third week, he was able to achieve his ultimate goal and reach the lagoon. After that he swam for an hour each morning, returning again before dusk to swim for a further hour. Within a month there was a tremendous improvement in his flexibility and, as the months progressed, his wasted body grew stronger until he began to acquire the muscular physique of a swimmer. The woven mesh seemed to have expanded with his muscular development, although Geoffrey was never able to remove it, not that he would have tried, as the glow from the armlet somehow repelled any threatening predators, which kept their distance.

A fortnight after Lorenzo had left them, it seemed that Marguerite's mystery illness was no longer affecting her, unlike Rosamund, who was suffering badly from severe stomach cramps that brought on terrifying convulsions.

"Rose will injure herself if she continues like this," Geoffrey exclaimed, dodging as she hurled a piece of pottery through the window as they approached.

"There is nothing we can do, Geoffrey; even the Otter is afraid to get too close. He leaves her food at the door, which she will not collect until he has gone."

"Then let me try." Geoffrey reached to take the tray of food from her hand.

"No, Geoffrey, her moods are so unstable there is no telling what she might do if you get too close."

"I have to try. Without any contact from us, Rose could go completely mad and be lost to us forever. If I take Bog Boy in with me, that might help. You know how she loves dogs."

"I know you care about this dog, Geoffrey but it is more of a savage than any I have ever seen."

"Then it seems he and I make the perfect team," Geoffrey said grimly, steadying the tray with what remained of his fingers. "At least with Bog at my side I will never feel like a freak in a sideshow!" As he saw the tears well up in her eyes, he immediately regretted his words. "I am sorry… I should not have said that."

Two weeks of Lorenzo's intense rehabilitation programme of manipulation, oils and paste, with complete rest between the sessions to allow time for the treatment to penetrate deep into the rigid joints, had left Geoffrey no time to visit his sister until now. Although he had been prepared for some alteration during that time, the nightmarish creature confronting him through the window was barely recognisable. Rosamund had patches of rouge smeared on both cheeks, taken from the stack of cosmetics for his father's harem and a vivid gash red of lipstick concealed every part of her soft and expressive mouth. Dark shadows emphasised the sunken hollows of her expressive eyes. Beneath each of these, clown-like, she had drawn the stark outline of a teardrop with Indian ink, colouring them in with the scarlet lipstick.

Into the pieces of hair that had grown back Rosamund had knotted gaudy ribbons, tying more of them around one of her bruised wrists and since only her head, face and hand were visible through the gap, Geoffrey dreaded finding out what clothing – if any – she would be wearing in this manic state.

"Who are you?" Rosamund demanded, backing away from the window.

"It is me, Rose. Jeffy… Please let me inside."

"Liar! Jeffy would never leave me alone in a place like this!"

"I had no choice; otherwise I would have been here sooner. You know I would never leave you alone; it was because I was injured." Geoffrey offered up his claw-like hands for her to see.

"Was Mother injured too? Is that why she is not here for my party?"

"She is resting. Mother would come, if it were possible. Just allow me inside and I will wait with you until she arrives."

"Is there anyone else with you? This is a private function."

"I have brought Bog Boy along because you like him. There is no one else, Rose, I promise," he lied, praying she would not see Marguerite close by.

"Do I know this friend of yours?"

"You met him before the accident, so you may not remember," Geoffrey said, leading the hound to where his sister could see him.

"Oh you mean a dog… how delightful… do bring him inside," Rose said, moving the barricade from the door.

Safely inside, Geoffrey did not know what to say. His sister was barely dressed in a gaudy skirt that had once belonged to one of his father's mistresses and wearing nothing at all on her top half. Her small breasts were badly scarred and seemed unnaturally swollen, with flies continually buzzing around the enlarged nipples.

"Will Mother approve of this new look?" Rosamund asked, twirling around to fan out the material of the skirt.

"Who could not?" Geoffrey said, looking desperately around for something to cover his sister's tortured body.

"I knew you would like it," she said, losing her balance from giddiness so that she crashed onto the unmade bed among the piles of harem clothing.

"You might consider adding this, Rose," Geoffrey gently suggested, holding up a beautifully embroidered shawl. "These birds are truly magnificent. I swear I have never seen the like of them before, even out here."

"If you really think Mother will love it, then I will." She allowed him to drape it around her shoulders.

"Might I suggest knotting it to cover your chest? The flies here are quite beastly and can give a nasty bite." Geoffrey relaxed a little as she allowed him to knot it loosely.

"How perfect this is," she said but the troubling gaiety was gone in a second, as if someone had switched off a light, replaced with a look of suspicion as she picked up a pair of scissors from the bedside table. "Are you sure no one else came?"

"There is no one… only me and the Bog, I promise."

"Are you sure? That devilish monk was staring at me through the window earlier." Rosamund looked cautiously out through the broken gap.

"He will not be troubling you again, Rose." Geoffrey reassured her, ready to deal with Drangoo severely if he caught him snooping.

"I know that, Jeffy but I am well prepared to drive him away if he gets inside here." Rosamund stabbed the scissors viciously into the table. "He is not invited to the party. Mother would loathe him."

On his return to the bungalow Geoffrey went in search of Marguerite, finding her in the laboratory distilling more of the Otter's bulbous roots.

"What have you done with Mother's clothes?" Geoffrey asked.

"I have done nothing. Everything has been washed and folded away in the camphor-wood chest," Marguerite said.

"If you show me where the clothes are, I would like to go through them."

"Not until you explain why."

"I ask only because Rose needs something decent to wear."

"There is no point; they would never fit her. Mother's clothes are too large. Bring me some of Rosamund's back with you and I will wash them through. She has some lovely clothes of her own."

"Not any more; most of what she had has been slashed into pieces."

"Then what is she wearing?" Marguerite protested.

"What little she has on today belonged to one of Father's mistresses and that has to change. There must be something in that chest that will fit."

Geoffrey could see the reluctance in his sister's face.

"But they will get damaged, Geoffrey. What if she shreds those too?"

"So what if she does? They are no use to Mother now and there is no other reason to keep them. Sentiment is no use in a situation like this."

"Not even if I would like to wear some of them myself?" Marguerite retorted.

"You…? Mother was a fraction of your size. They would split at the seams if you tried them on."

"I have lost weight since we have been stranded here… if you could be bothered to notice."

"To begin with perhaps but not enough to make any difference; in fact I would rather say you were putting it back on again. What the hell is wrong with you anyway, behaving like this? Rose is the one who got raped and needs some decent clothes, not you."

"I do apologise; of course Rosamund must have whatever she needs. We will go through everything together." He could see that Marguerite was verging on tears and already regretted what he'd just said.

"Very well… and by the way, you have lost some weight and you do look better for it. I am only worried that Rose will never regain her sanity again, not if she dresses up like a circus clown."

After his initial breakthrough with Rosamund, Geoffrey became a frequent visitor to his sister's cabin, making sure that she ate properly, washed and took the mysterious tonic that Lorenzo had prepared for her before leaving.

At the end of two more weeks, Geoffrey found he was not only beginning to enjoy his intensive swimming regime but that he could walk properly and was even able to jog slowly alongside the hound for a short distance. The progress encouraged him to begin a more rigorous exercise routine to rebuild the strength in his hands, enabling him to grip and accurately throw a spear should the need arise. Each day he would find a quiet place where, despite his missing fingers, he began to perfect his technique until eventually his accuracy was deadly.

Twice during this period Geoffrey and the hound had narrow escapes, first when they were able to repel an attack from a ferocious jaguar and then a few days later when they were ambushed by a black caiman. Working together, they began to develop a combined skill in the art of a survival. It was an instinctive collaboration that gradually transformed them into a ruthlessly efficient killing machine.

Although Geoffrey was aware the rainy season would be coming soon, he had no idea when it would begin or how long it would last. If the rains were particularly heavy the lower section of the compound, where all but one of the cabins were located, could be flooded, which would at the very least increase the danger from the many caiman he saw daily, sunning themselves on the riverbank. What was also increasingly clear was that they could not survive for much longer without access to more provisions.

For a while he considered killing animals for their meat but because nothing would stay fresh for longer than three days in that climate, Geoffrey gave up on the idea. Although his father's store of canned food had served them well, the stocks wouldn't last forever.

Since the confrontation over their mother's clothes, Geoffrey had paid more attention to Marguerite's altered appearance and while it was clear that she had lost a lot of weight over the past few months, he suspected she had recently put some of it back on again. The effect was not unpleasant as the alteration now made her appear more womanly, rather than the bloated sausage she had once resembled. Her features were also altering, transforming her looks so that she now began to resemble her mother before the illness. This was in marked contrast to Rosamund, whose once beautiful face was now bloated and taut and whose slim legs, like her entire body, had swollen out of shape until she was barely recognisable.

"You must come with me today when I visit Rose. I am really worried about her. She just waddles around all the time, holding on to her side."

"How is that possible? The Otter never takes Rosamund more food than we have ourselves."

"I am well aware of that. That is why I need you to go over there and see for yourself."

"There is nothing I can do, Geoffrey. I have tried so many times to get inside that cabin but Rosamund will not allow me anywhere near her."

"Then you must try again, Maggs. Rose may not survive much longer, not if she continues to swell up like this. There must be something you can do to help."

"Very well, I will try but do not expect miracles. I am no doctor."

"Maybe not but you do have some medical knowledge and I suggest that you wear some of Mother's clothing when you go inside."

"Why would you ask me to do that?"

"Rose is not reasoning properly. She believes that Mother is still alive. If you wear your hair in a similar way and her shawl with the dragon embroidery, Rose might mistake you for her."

"That is a preposterous idea. Rosamund would never mistake me for Mother… whatever I wore."

"Well at least give it a try, unless you have a better idea." In the harsh reality of daylight it did seemed improbable this idea would work but there was no other way of getting his elder sister into the cabin.

"You cannot really expect me to wear Mother's shawl in this heat!" she protested.

"You must… and get rid of that old straw hat. It is impossible to see anything of your face under the brim."

"Lowering the veil keeps the mosquitoes from eating me alive."

"Strewth, Maggs, stop making excuses. I am not asking you to remove the damned thing forever. You can put it back on once you are outside."

"We will never get away with this dressing-up farce, Geoffrey, however much you want it to work. I look nothing like Mother."

"Then maybe you can come up with a better idea."

"You know that I cannot, otherwise I would have been to see her long before now."

"It might help if you wear Mother's sapphire earrings handy. That would definitely help convince her. Mother loved those earrings more than anything else."

"Earrings and a shawl would not convince anyone I am her," Marguerite protested.

"All we need is for her to mistake you for Mother long enough to get you through the door," he pleaded.

"Very well, I will give it a try but you must go in first and remove any sharp objects."

And so it was agreed. Yet Geoffrey was not remotely prepared for the transformation in his sister when she reappeared. Admittedly her shape was considerably fuller than his mother's had ever been but that was successfully hidden by the shawl, draped about her shoulders in exactly the way Lady Claudia would have worn it. More unnerving was seeing Marguerite's dark hair coiled loosely behind her neck, exactly the way his mother preferred, thus showing the dangling sapphire earrings to great effect, glittering brilliantly with the slightest movement of her head. It was also shocking to realise how very closely his sister's features actually did resemble their late mother's.

Although the idea of confusing Rosamund was born from desperation, it could not have worked out better to getting Marguerite inside the cabin. Even though Rosamund was fully clothed, it was clear that her pitiful appearance was having a bad effect on his elder sister, though she masked her distress well.

"Why are you not examining her?" Geoffrey whispered urgently.

"There is no need. I know exactly what is causing this swelling."

"She is not going to die, is she?"

"No she is not. We can speak of this when we are alone." and that was all the information Geoffrey was given until they had returned to the main cabin and were seated quietly on the veranda.

"What is wrong with her, Maggs? Has she contracted some awful bloating disease?"

"There is no need for concern, Geoffrey. There is nothing wrong with her physically."

"That awful swelling, that cannot be normal?"

"This does occur in some women, when they are with child," Marguerite admitted reluctantly.

"What the devil are you saying?" Geoffrey cried with horror. "Surely there must be a way to prevent this from happening? If not, it will push Rose over the edge. There must be something in Father's laboratory you could give to… to abort this… this awful thing. She would never recover from that."

"There is nothing we can do, Geoffrey; her time is too far advanced. We must allow nature to run its natural course. When this is over, the infant can always be adopted."

"And that is it! You are not even going to try?"

"What you are asking is impossible. It would require an operation to remove the child and I could never attempt that."

"You can operate, I know you can. It did not stop you from lopping off my fingers," he protested.

"No it did not but what I did was to help you, not to endanger your life, rather to save it. There was no option other than to amputate them. This is different and you must accept that Rose will have her confinement in around five months."

"Lorenzo would know of a way to help her."

"I am sure that he would but he is not here, as you so often remind me... and we are."

"Then what should we do?"

"Nothing… and when the time comes, then you must help Rosamund in every way you can to deliver this child safely. She has always relied on you more than anyone else."

"Me! I am not getting involved in anything like that… how could you even suggest such a thing? Even if I could, I would be useless with these bloody claws you have left me with. This is down to you, Maggs… you are a woman, you know about these things."

"I might not be available," she said, somewhat reluctantly.

"Why the hell not? What else could you be occupied with that would take priority over this awful event that you are trying to hand over to me? Sketching more useless plants for that bloody journal of yours?"

"Of course not… What do take me for? I would be there if it was at all possible but I cannot guarantee anything, not for sure."

"What are you babbling on about? What could be more important than helping Rose deliver this, this monster, not unless you are ill… are you?"

"No, I am not, not in the way you imagine." Her cheeks reddened.

"Meaning what exactly?" Geoffrey persisted, now concerned that she might have contracted the virus. "Whatever it is, I need to know."

"Very well, if you insist. I have been wondering how to broach this for some time but the opportunity has never arisen until now. Even so, I am at a loss for words."

"If you are not ill, what could be more important than helping her?"

"None, except that I am also expecting. My own confinement should be a lot more straightforward."

"What confinement? Why are you talking in riddles?" Geoffrey wondered if he was losing his hearing now that his sight had recovered.

"I am also with child."

Geoffrey was momentarily lost for words. Staring at her, he spluttered, "How can that be? If you are angling for sympathy, then forget it. You were miles away when they raped Rose and they were long gone when you returned. Why on earth would you lie about something like this?" He stared at his sister, convinced she was losing her mind.

"It is not something I would ever lie about, Geoffrey. My own confinement will happen soon after Rosamund's." She was evidently unwilling to say more.

Lost for words, Geoffrey hunted through his memory. Only now did he remember having been woken by her moans and a creaking bed beyond the veranda wall and hearing a male voice in her room at night.

"Then Drangoo must be the father. So that is why you are always defending him!"

"How could you think that? Drangoo did not arrive here until the following day. It was Lorenzo who comforted me that night."

"You are a LIAR! He would have said something if it was him," Geoffrey blurted out, in an instinctive effort to blank out the unlikely but undeniable truth.

"I am not a liar!" she called after him as he stormed off the veranda.

His mind racing, Geoffrey made his way up to the store cabin, where he could be alone and think the shocking revelation through properly. After a sleepless night he was in no mood for further conversation with his sister and stayed away until the following afternoon, when hunger eventually dictated his return. Even so, it was two more days before they brought up the subject.

"How could you do that with Lorenzo?" Geoffrey said angrily, trying to block out his own failings and unable to look her directly in the eye.

"You must believe me when I say it was not done intentionally. I was distraught after what had happened. The thought I would also lose you and Rosamund, after Mother, was too much to bear. When Lorenzo offered me comfort, I did not resist."

"Then why did he say nothing about this child of yours?"

"That is because he has no idea. You are the only person who knows."

"You are making this up."

"Why? Is it really so improbable that any man would be interested in me in that way?" she snapped, her tone verging on hysteria. "I am fully aware of my appearance and I know I am not as desirable as Rosamund but I am a woman nevertheless, a woman who has physical needs and Lorenzo was there when I needed him most."

"For an old spinster like you to do that with a younger man, it is obscene."

"I am twenty-seven. That does not make it impossible for me to have children," she said angrily.

"... but you are unmarried."

"What if I am? It does happen. My child will arrive soon enough and when it does, like Rosamund, I am going to need your help to deliver it safely."

"If you imagine I am getting involved you can think again. You got yourself into this bloody awful mess, so you can figure out another way to get out of it but whatever it is… do not include me," Geoffrey retorted.

"If there was any alternative, then I would, Geoffrey but, apart from you and the Otter, who else could I ask?"

"I am sure that monk Drangoo knows the anatomy of a woman's body well enough. Get him to assist you. At least he will have God on his side to lend a hand."

"Blasphemy is not going to help with this situation, Geoffrey."

"Well something needs to, because I cannot. Even if I could, there is nothing I could do with these bloody useless claws."

"Just having you do what you can would be enough."

"I am your brother, for Pete's sake. You cannot expect me to handle things, not down there… not in your private parts. You must ask that deviant monk. Not me. I refuse to be any part of this."

"Even if I agreed, that would be impossible now. Father Fitzgerald ordered Drangoo to leave here as soon as you had recovered and rejoin him on their missionary circuit."

"Then you must ensure that he sends Lorenzo back here immediately. This is a problem of his making, not mine. Let him clear up his own mess."

"I have no intention of informing Lorenzo about this child. I will get through this, with or without your help."

"What if you both start having these children at the same time? Have you thought about that? Lorenzo must be informed, so that he and the monk can be here, not me."

"Lorenzo will never be told about my condition and Drangoo knows nothing of this. He left early this morning."

"You allowed him to leave without telling me?"

"There was no point since you disliked him so intensely. You should be delighted by the news," Marguerite said decisively, bringing an end to the conversation.

Chapter Five
Initiation

With Drangoo gone, there was more for Geoffrey to deal with in the passing months than he could ever have anticipated. In her current condition and especially in the increasing heat and humidity, there was little change from when Marguerite had been so grossly overweight and could only waddle along at a snail's pace. Fortunately her cooking skills had improved and since the outbreak of the virus she had become obsessive about spotlessly clean linen and dishes and maintaining a tidy kitchen, such as it was. All this was essential to infection-free living but beyond that, everything else was down to him.

"I must show you how to distil those roots, Geoffrey," Marguerite said unexpectedly.

"What on earth for? That vile concoction you came up with must have cleared every trace of the damned virus by now."

"I agree but if another outbreak ever occurs we must be prepared. It might look a little bit odd but it works." She led him to the back of their father's laboratory to examine an ingenious amalgamation of glass rods and rubber tubing, all hooked up to a copper kettle that had been secured in place on a metal trivet above three Bunsen burners.

"Strewth, Maggs, this contraption would make any crackpot scientist green with envy. How on earth did you come up with this crazy set-up?" Geoffrey laughed.

"Desperation, I suppose. There were a few failed attempts to begin with. Fortunately I found an article on a distillery in one of father's books. I based my own version on that and it works." She examined the few dried-up roots that remained. "We need to restock these, Geoffrey. It will only take me a day to collect them."

"You cannot go paddling a dugout in your condition," Geoffrey said with alarm.

"I am with child, Geoffrey, not an invalid."

"Maybe not but the way your backside has spread out this past week you would never fit into that dugout any more."

"How dare you… how could you be so insulting," she retorted, bright red in the face.

"I dare only because it is a fact and not because I mean to be rude! Anyone could see that you would never get in that canoe in a million years and that is the truth, like it or not. So, what's going to happen is this. I will get whatever you need to make more of the stuff," Geoffrey said.

As the months passed Geoffrey found that wherever he went he was followed, not only by the dog but also by the Otter. With the added responsibility he'd had to take on the boy was a great help, especially as he didn't gabble on about nothing, the way most children of his age did back in England. Geoffrey had no objection to him helping collect dry wood for the stove or gather fruit and anything else edible, to supplement the depleted selection of tinned food in the cave.

"We need more of that tinned food before the supplies get too low," Geoffrey said one afternoon to his sister.

"How long will it last?"

"Probably a few weeks but not much longer; the problem is that once the rainy season has started we cannot afford to run out of food. It might take an age before Rose is well enough to travel. In the meantime, we will be stuck here with two extra mouths to feed."

"The rains started months ago."

"I do not think it's just the rain that the old priest was concerned about," Geoffrey said.

"There has been no evidence of anything more than a bad thunderstorm in all the time we have been stranded here."

"Maybe not but Fitzgerald was concerned about getting away from here before the heavy rains began the last time."

"Well that never happened, did it?"

"Maybe not that time but if a seasoned missionary is that concerned it must mean something. In Grifka's book he states that the rainfall is sometimes unpredictable, so we should take precautions and stock up with provisions," Geoffrey said, watching Rosamund as she wandered aimlessly up and down the veranda of her cabin, clutching her enlarged belly, staring with unseeing eyes at the blanket of rain.

"Then I am at a loss about what we can do. I doubt the trading post would stock any imported tinned food."

"They do. There were definitely some crates of it that Father had not collected. Once I have the roots you need, I will go to the trading post and collect them."

"Do you really think they will still be there?" Marguerite asked.

"I cannot imagine anyone else around here would want to buy them, not when they can go out and kill whatever they want for free."

Geoffrey had planned to set off with the Otter to dig up the roots at daybreak but because Rosamund was in an unusually distressed state their departure was delayed until midday. Marguerite had found him a canvas bag to carry the bulbs. As a precaution, Geoffrey coiled a length of rope into a bandolier, which he hung from his shoulder and across his chest and strapped the bag on to this against his hip. As he and the Otter went down to the canoe, the hound was trailing close behind and, for the very first time in their relationship, the animal refused to go back when told.

"You cannot take that dog with you, Geoffrey. It is far too big. There is hardly enough room in the canoe for you and the Otter as it is," Marguerite called as the wolfhound leapt into the cramped space, leaving Geoffrey barely enough room to paddle.

"Well he seems determined to come with us, whether I like it or not."

"Then it seems you two are perfectly suited. Whatever happens, do try and get back before dark, Geoffrey. It will be treacherous out there in the swamp," she called after them.

The afternoon was cloudy, yet although there was no sun Geoffrey thought the animal's woven collar appeared to be giving off a reflective glow, as too did his own woven armlet.

As they approached the dank, gloomy area of swamp, he thought he couldn't help but admire his sister's earlier determination to collect the roots, at a time when she could not have been certain her plan to distil them into a liquid cure would even work. Yet she had overcome her fear of water and whatever horrors might be swimming below the surface.

They paddled the dugout further into the rapidly darkening everglade, where creepy trails of moss dangled down from a few surviving trees, sinister and repellent, brushing across his face when they passed beneath them. In that light, each touch made him shudder even more, for fear it might be a snake.

It was clear that parts of the area were already flooded from the constant rainfall and had the Otter not been instinctively aware of which direction was safest the canoe would have soon run aground on the partially submerged land, or been speared by one of the petrified trees that loomed up fearfully from the water.

Having been convinced they were lost, Geoffrey breathed a sigh of relief when the Otter pointed out a section of firm ground, projecting no more than two feet above the water level and as nightfall was imminent this seemed to be the safest place where they could set up camp.

Once they had tied up the canoe, Geoffrey and the dog followed by the Otter to a rocky area, where they rigged up a canvas awning as shelter between the sagging boughs of a tree. As an afterthought, he hung the remaining section of canvas at the back, which he then anchored down with rocks against any crosswind.

The campfire had almost gone out when Geoffrey woke with a start, grabbing the spear instinctively when he saw the hound staring beyond the fire, a low, warning growl rumbling in its throat. He hurled the weapon with deadly accuracy, embedding it between the glinting eyes of a black caiman, barely a few feet away from the sleeping Otter. Even as he grabbed hold of the boy and dragged him away from the reptile's thrashing tail, the dog's focus had transferred to the back panel of the shelter, the hackles on the back of its neck rising.

Within moments the savage claws of a jaguar shredded the canvas, its snarling head pivoting around as the ferocious wolfhound moved to the right of the predator while Geoffrey instinctively went to the left, Archie's hunting knife grasped in his claw-like hand. In a single coordinated movement they moved in on the creature, the hound leaping on its back where it sank its teeth into the animal's neck, the weight dragging the jaguar to the ground where Geoffrey, avoiding the slashing claws, thrust the blade deep into its throat.

At daybreak, an examination of the dog revealed two small gashes on its hindquarters and a slash over one eye. Geoffrey treated the wounds as best he could from the makeshift first-aid kit Marguerite had insisted he bring with him. There was also a nasty gash on his own chest that would need stitches when he returned. As a temporary measure he applied a pad soaked in an antiseptic cream from the kit and bound this onto his chest with a torn strip from the shredded awning.

To Geoffrey's surprise the Otter seemed barely troubled by the sight of the two carcasses as they prepared to leave the campsite and was clearly more concerned by the increased level of water rising up around them.

"We need come back soon, Massa Jeffy," the Otter said, grabbing Geoffrey by the hand after securing the dugout to a higher section of the bank.

He followed the boy out onto an area of lush vegetation. Here, banks of unidentifiable orchids bloomed in profusion along the sides of a small and elongated lake, fed by a sparkling waterfall a short distance away. The surprise of finding such an unexpected oasis in this intimidating area of swampland momentarily distracted Geoffrey from his natural wariness.

"No, Massa!" the Otter yelled, pulling Geoffrey's hand away as he was about to inspect an extraordinary orchid-like boom, huge and staggeringly beautiful. As he watched an unsuspecting lizard dashed across the surface to escape the intruders, where it was instantly clamped over by the spring-loaded petals of the spiked flower.

"What the hell was that?" Geoffrey shrieked, his shout prompting all of the remaining blooms to snap shut.

From then on Geoffrey took care to follow in the Otter's footsteps and touch nothing, however temptingly exotic, until they reached their final destination at the edge of the lake. Here clumps of bulrush-type plants grew in great quantities, leaving only small gaps between them for any access to the water.

"No, Massa Jeffy!" the Otter said urgently, leading Geoffrey away from the first of these gaps, where he could now make out two blue poison dart frogs, creatures he remembered vividly from a coloured illustration in one of his father's books.

Avoiding the second break among the reeds as a precaution, in case any of the frogs were gathered there too, the Otter led Geoffrey to a much wider opening where thick, tulip-like leaves were clumped together. Sprouting from these were slender flower stems, each one producing clusters of dark violet blooms. Without hesitation the Otter got to his knees and began digging the roots out with a hunting knife, indicating that Geoffrey should do likewise.

Because the plants were growing in water, Geoffrey wrongly assumed they would be easy to remove but instead, every plant they dug out required a desperate struggle and in his efforts, the Otter fell into the water headfirst. Geoffrey grabbed hold of his arm and yanked the boy out. When this happened a second time and the boy didn't reappear, Geoffrey leapt into the water, becoming submerged in seconds.

A few feet below him, the Otter had sunk up to his knees in the mud and was struggling to get free. Treading water and fearful to stand on the mud in case he also sank, Geoffrey could barely see anything to hold on to through the murk, even with the radiating light from the glowing armlet, until the hound plunged into the water beside him, generating more light from its woven collar. Only then was Geoffrey able to catch hold of a thick tree root and grab the Otter's waving arm but even then, the suction was so great the boy was impossible to move.

Almost out of breath, Geoffrey removed the bandolier from across his shoulder, looped it over the dog's neck and, by crooking his elbow into the loose end, caught hold of the boy's seemingly lifeless arm, praying the animal would know what to do.

Instinctively, the hound began paddling furiously, churning up the muddy water like a steamer and, within seconds had released the boy from the deadly suction. Holding on like grim death, Geoffrey and the Otter were dragged to a sloping section of the bank where he immediately began pumping out water from the boy's lungs until he was breathing normally.

While waiting for the Otter to recover, Geoffrey hauled up more of the purple tubers and packed them into the bag. The boy was in no fit state to walk, so he made a primitive harness with lengths of twisted vine, thinking back to one Lorenzo had made for him and strapped the boy to his back. When he became too exhausted to continue, fearing they wouldn't get clear of the swamp before dusk, he straddled the boy on the hound's back, supporting him in position with the harness. After that they made good progress to the moored canoe, sloshing over an area of boggy ground that he didn't remember from earlier.

When they reached the canoe in the rapidly fading light, it was clear that the water level had risen considerably higher up the bank in just a few hours and what had been a good two feet between the dugout and the water had been reduced to just a few inches. Watched by a group of caiman he loaded the Otter and dog into the canoe before casting off and jumping aboard, praying they would clear the swamp before dark.

Although the Otter was unable to paddle, he had at least recovered well enough to guide Geoffrey through the gloomy everglades. By the time they had reached the main tributary it was already dark and Geoffrey decided to make camp on a rocky outcrop that seemed high enough from the river to be safe, immediately lighting a fire to keep any predators away and planning to stay awake, re-stoking the fire and armed with his spear and hunting knife. He was jolted awake at dawn by a downpour of warm rain. The embers of the fire had already washed away and he found the Otter kneeling beside him with a piece of peeled fruit.

In less than half an hour both Geoffrey and the Otter were paddling furiously against the fast-moving current until the boy manoeuvred the canoe into a slower tributary, where they could progress more easily until at last they reached a rotting section of staging at the rear of the compound.

"Thank heaven you are safe, Geoffrey," Marguerite said, stitching up the gash in his chest as neatly as she could.

"Heaven had nothing to do with it. It was Lorenzo's band on my wrist."

"How could that protect you?"

"Well it did, whatever you think and I'm sure the collar around Bog's neck saved him too."

"There is nothing magical in these bands, Geoffrey, however lovely they are. That wolfhound you dote on has a killer instinct. That is why you both survived."

"You saw how badly injured he was when I first brought him back here. Any other animal would have been dead before it even staggered through the bushes and yet it saved my life and helped me get free of that boa constrictor. Trust me when I say these woven bands have supernatural powers."

"If so, then why did it not prevent Churuma from being killed? He wore one too."

"We both know he was not wearing it that day, because he had given it to you," Geoffrey said, yet she remained unconvinced.

"These are boyish imaginings, Geoffrey. You have an overactive imagination, most likely brought on by those adventure books you were always riveted to at home."

"I cannot believe you still think I have boyish imaginings after what we have been through!" Geoffrey retorted.

"What I am trying to say is that the reality of life is different from what you might have read in those fantasy novels by the likes of Jules Verne."

"This was no fantasy, whatever you think. What I am telling you is fact and not some bloody piece of fiction! You will realise it one day."

"If you say so," she said moodily, bandaging up his chest. "However, what I need right now are more tins of baked beans and bully beef from father's store, otherwise we cannot eat this evening." She picked up the bag of bulbous roots.

"Then I shall get on to it," Geoffrey said.

"While you are gone, I will get these liquidised. I want you to begin taking a week's course of this medication, starting tomorrow."

"Do I have to? It has been three months since we contracted that damned virus and bear in mind I will not be able to get back to collect any more until after this downpour has ended. God alone knows when that will be."

"I cannot face the thoughts of another five months of this. The rains must surely ease off soon," she said, contemplating the churned-up mud of the compound. "There is an account of the effects of the rainy seasons in one of Father's books." She slid the volume across the table but he ignored it.

"Then I hope you are right. Where these roots came from yesterday is probably three feet underwater by now."

"Would it still be possible to reach the trading post for more supplies, do you think?"

"It seems I must try… just as long as you realise I might be gone for about a week, or perhaps even longer if I have to stay to negotiate with that female gorilla who owns the dump."

"Will you be taking the Otter?" she asked tentatively.

"No, he must stay here to help out with Rose. I will be fine on my own."

"Presumably that animal will go with you?"

"Bog must remain here too, to protect you and Rose."

"There is absolutely no need, Geoffrey. I have a gun and you know I can use it should the need arise. That creature should be with you at all times, not here. On top of that, it would be impossible to make a deal with that dreadful woman without some protection. Having the dog by your side would be enough to scare anyone and it might give you the advantage you need in the negotiations."

Having the hound travelling with him gave Geoffrey all the confidence he needed to set off downriver two days later. As his mother had once done when he went off hiking in the

Dales, Marguerite had filled the canvas bag with fruit and some of her flatbread, which looked and tasted like soggy cardboard but was at least edible. Along with this was some of the distilled anti-virus liquid in a Thermos flask of his father's and a jar of Marguerite's home-made antiseptic cream – just in case!

Chapter Six
A Dangerous Mission

The journey took four long days of paddling, with only a few short overnight breaks on the bank. For protection from the sun when the rain eased, Geoffrey wore his father's wide-brimmed panama hat. By the end of the second day the palms of his hands were sore and blistered and he bandaged them with pieces of cloth Marguerite had put in the bag in case the need arose.

Towards the end of the third day, having taken a diversion along a tributary to avoid being rammed by two fallen trees that were heading directly towards him, Geoffrey manoeuvred the canoe along a short section of fast-moving rapids, where his hat was blown off and swept away down the river. By nightfall the blisters on both hands had burst, leaving his palms raw and bleeding. Once he had applied the antiseptic ointment and rinsed out the bandages, he had no option but to tear up his father's only surviving shirt into strips and rebind his hands. With the state of them, this was a more difficult operation than he had anticipated and one that was only accomplished by tying the loose ends with the other hand and his teeth.

Geoffrey cursed his own stupidity for not having thought things through logically before tearing up the shirt, leaving his naked torso exposed to the blazing sun when he could have used Marguerite's canvas bag instead. The swarms of mosquitoes clouding the riverbanks presented another threat to his newly exposed flesh.

Without wasting any more time, Geoffrey slashed along the side-seams of the bag with Archie's knife. Once it was opened out on the ground, he cut two armholes. Finally, he placed a remnant of the canvas over his hair, binding it in place with the handles which he knotted together, leaving a flap over the back of his neck to keep off the sun.

The light was already fading as the trading post came into sight, so Geoffrey and the hound bedded down on an open section of ground away from the river, where he warily kept the spear close by in case their canoe had been spotted by anyone in the elevated building.

After an uninterrupted night, Geoffrey smeared more of the antiseptic gel onto the open wounds of his palms and bound his hands again, this time not against friction from the paddle but to allow more flexibility for handling the spear if the need arose. What he hadn't considered was how the bandages only emphasised the mutilation of his hands.

It was soon apparent their arrival had not been noticed as the owner appeared, turbanless, wandering out of the cabin. Her frizzy and badly dyed bright ginger hair waved in the wind like a coil of angry snakes as she lit up a large Havana cigar. Inhaling the smoke eagerly at first, she began to choke as she caught sight of Geoffrey, the wolfhound at his side, making his way towards the place where he had last seen his father's crates. Deliberately ignoring her bellowing and unintelligible enquiries he barely glanced in her direction, scouring the lean-to in search of the twelve crates of imported canned goods.

Geoffrey turned quickly as the owner approached, her oversized turban back in place and glittering with baubles. She was surrounded by six of her muscular security force. One of these men, he noticed, was considerably younger and much lighter skinned than the others and wore a broad gold armlet on one of his bulging biceps. He had an impressive golden rod through his nostrils, which seemed to signify him as someone of importance. Alongside him was an intimidating brute, Herculean in size and shape, armed with a bow and a quiver of arrows.

Another burly native, positioned close to a stack of caiman hides, was armed with a bloodstained machete, while two more brandished traditional spears. The sixth member of the group was obscured by the burly man at the front, so Geoffrey had no idea what weapon he was carrying but still felt ready to take on every one of the natives if the need arose. For a few moments after their arrival it was as if there was a standoff among the men, seemingly uncertain about how to proceed and waiting for instruction from their female leader.

Only then did Geoffrey become aware of what a fearful sight he must have presented to the group that morning, his straw-like hair protruding from beneath the makeshift headgear, the warrior-like scars on his chest and arms and the spear clasped in his bandaged, claw-like hands. With the equally scarred wolfhound at his side, this was a combination that presented a terrifying spectacle and appeared to have rendered everyone speechless. The exception was the turbaned Gorgon, who now began challenging his reason for being there with a cross-section of languages, until at last she tried his own.

"You... wild man... What you want here?" the owner called, straightening the turban imperiously, on which was fastened a treasured Queen Anne cameo that had once belonged to his mother, crudely stitched with coarse button thread among other pieces of glittering jewellery. It was clear she had no idea who he was.

"I came for these," Geoffrey said, indicating the boxes.

Nervously the woman began fingering the emerald necklace that was tightening in the restrictive folds of her bullish neck as she spoke, another exquisite item of jewellery that was instantly recognisable as having belonged to Lady Claudia. Its nine square-cut emeralds were all flawless with the exception of the one in the centre. This had been damaged in his grandmother's day when the missing section on the lower right corner of the stone had to be repaired with a filling of gold. With its stylish imperfection Rosamund had loved it more than any other item of her mother's jewellery and had been allowed to wear it on the first evening when Lorenzo and the priest had arrived at the compound. With growing anger Geoffrey realised that both pieces had last been seen in his mother's bedroom, which meant that none of them had been used in exchange for the revolver. So how had this woman got her hands on them?

"How you know speak Inglese?" the grotesque woman asked suspiciously, with a theatrical jerk of the head causing the pantomime-like pendant drops of vibrantly coloured glass beads crudely strung together shook as they dangled from her large earlobes.

In the silence, waiting for his answer, she glanced furtively towards the burly native positioned nearest to the stack of caiman hides who was inching away revealing the man concealed behind him. Geoffrey instantly recognised the albino and immediately, the connecting pieces began slotting into place.

"Why you no say speak Inglese?" she asked, as if wanting more information but the sly look in those bullfrog eyes made it clear she was trying to keep him distracted, especially as both the albino and his muscular companion were no longer visible.

The hound's collar was glowing and Geoffrey could feel the warmth from his own armlet, a sign that he now recognised as alerting him that danger was imminent. Even so, he kept up the pretence with a shrug of the shoulders but listened intently for the slightest movement from beyond the stack of hides, constantly aware of every movement the albino and his companion made, circling around behind him, masked by the bales of cured caiman hides.

"So... why you want crates?" she demanded, continuing to act out the charade of trading long enough for her thugs to take him unawares.

"They have my father's name on them, if you need a reason," Geoffrey responded, playing along with her deadly game but fully aware of the imminent threat as he heard the low, warning rumble from the hound's throat, its eyes fixed on the bale closest to where they were standing.

"They much cost, what you want pay?" she said, unconsciously stepping backwards in preparation for what would come next.

"Nothing; all twelve crates have already been paid for by my father, Oliver Saint Hubes."

"You no get, if no pay!" she said, her eyes narrowing into slits.

"I will pay you nothing for what is rightfully mine," Geoffrey retorted, increasingly aware of the bodyguards closing in behind him.

"I only let take, if you bring Misqualla Lally Olibo's blue ice, then you have!" She tugged at her earlobes expectantly.

Geoffrey remembered how this hulk of a woman had stared so enviously at his mother's sapphire earrings but kept up the charade of negotiation.

"Allow me to be perfectly clear, madam. I bring you nothing here in trade for what is rightfully mine but perhaps you can explain how you are wearing my mother's necklace?" Geoffrey said icily.

"This no Lally Olibo's, this Misqualla's," she said indignantly, fingering the gems, her shifty eyes glancing towards an opening between the stacks of hides close to where Geoffrey was standing.

"Then you are a liar and a fool, madam, if you expect me to believe that and I have a good idea how you really acquired them, because my mother certainly did not offer that item to you in trade."

At that moment the burly native suddenly appeared through the gap wielding a machete. Partially concealed behind him was the albino, loading a blowpipe. Just as Geoffrey was about to hurl the knife in the hope of wounding at least one of them the hound hurtled past him in a blur, leaping at the burly native as the man hurled his weapon, which flew past Geoffrey's ear and became embedded in one of the crates.

At the moment of contact the dog sank its fearsome teeth into the native's calf, tearing off the tendons to the accompaniment of ear-shattering screams. He lurched backwards into the albino and sent him crashing into the stack of caiman hides, where he clutched at his throat, choking and gasping for air. Geoffrey realised he had swallowed the poison dart in the collision.

Taking advantage of the confusion, Geoffrey yanked the machete free from the crate, ready to face Misqualla's bodyguards and fully prepared to take them all on. What he hadn't expected was to see every one of them simply lay down their weapons, leaving their leader unprotected.

106

"Massa, no hurt Misqualla... what want, him take," she pleaded.

"Firstly, I want that necklace back."

"You no take, please Massa... this Misqualla's."

"Take it off now or I will cut the bloody thing off you myself!" Geoffrey demanded, wielding Archie's hunting knife in the claw of his right hand. The precious emeralds were quickly unclasped and handed over.

"Misqualla now go?" the woman asked, edging away.

"You can remain where you are; we are not done yet. Firstly, I want the loan of a large dugout, big enough to transport every one of these crates here. I also want a strong and trustworthy paddle-man to go with it."

"Si, you take Misqualla best boat, Massa Inglesi." She indicated a modest-sized dugout at the mooring.

"Do not forget the paddle-man."

"Si, Massa... you take Zanier, him much strong." She pointed to a muscular native with dyed ginger hair.

"I do not want that one," Geoffrey stated firmly.

"Why no take Zanier? Him much good," she urged.

"I would never trust him!" Geoffrey snapped, aware of the shifty glance she gave the muscle-bound Zanier, presumably the leader of her bodyguards. "I want someone else," he said, reaching over and yanking the turban off her head.

"Please, Massa, you no take," she wailed but Geoffrey was having none of it.

"Some of this jewellery was stolen from my mother. Be thankful I do not slit your evil throat for arranging the theft of these!"

"Misqualla no understand, Massa… what mean?" she complained, waving her arms theatrically, the multiple layers of bracelets jangling up and down her muscular forearms.

"You ordered those bastards to raid the compound and for what… a few pieces of jewellery and for that, inflicting rape and mutilation?" Geoffrey screamed, now barely able to contain his rage.

"Massa, him no kill Misqualla!" She squealed like a pig and he began to wonder why so many men had allowed this woman to become their leader.

"Just be thankful you are a woman, otherwise you would be lying dead with that vile albino bastard."

"Misqualla much thank Massa Inglese," she sobbed.

"Spare me your tears, you miserable toad. I guarantee by the time I have done with you, you will wish I had slit your throat!"

Less than an hour later, with the crates loaded into the dugout, Geoffrey made his selection of paddle-man for the trip, much to Misqualla's outrage and horror.

"No take Misqualla, Zanier, him no Señora!" she cried to the accompanying jangle of her countless bracelets as she gesticulated frantically with alarm.

"I would advise you to save your breath for paddling, you old hag," Geoffrey said with some satisfaction. With the breadth of her shoulders and her enormous hands Misqualla was the ideal choice for a paddle-man. On top of that, she would also be in the canoe with him and not left behind where she might hatch some other scheme to regain his mother's jewellery.

After a further hour's delay, a bodyguard brought down a bag of clothes and food for the trip, an extra tarpaulin for privacy and a box of cosmetics which Geoffrey made a note to sort through when they made camp, for any concealed weapons.

As an afterthought, Geoffrey had the Otter's dugout attached at the rear for towing. He also asked for two extra paddles but after a long wait he was given only one. What was beginning to concern him was that there was no sign of the muscle-bound Zanier, nor was there any further suggestion of him taking over as paddle-man. It seemed Misqualla had resigned herself to making the journey, though Geoffrey was not convinced.

They had been paddling down the tributary for less than an hour when he felt the warmth of the glowing bracelet. An outcrop of native huts could be seen in a sheltered clearing up ahead, structures that had been purpose-built on stilts to protect them against rising floodwaters. Close by, a few native women were washing clothes at the riverbank.

When the canoe drew level with the women Misqualla leapt to her feet, waving her paddle frantically and repeatedly calling out Zanier's name.

"Sit down before you tip the canoe over," Geoffrey shouted as her screams became louder and more frantic, the violent colours of her baggy dress flapping about her like a nightmarish wounded butterfly, the spectacle sending the women on the bank bolting for cover, leaving scattered items of clothing drifting out into the river.

His vision now fully restored, Geoffrey scoured each of the buildings until he caught a glimpse of Zanier's unmistakable ginger hair, where he lay in readiness to aim his bow and arrow. Out on the water in an open boat he knew was a sitting target and had no idea how to avoid the inevitable attack. Barely able to think amid the deafening screams, Geoffrey swung his paddle hard at Misqualla, catching her with a hefty blow to the side of the head, knocking her off balance so that she fell like a sack of potatoes into the bottom of the canoe.

Uncertain if he had killed her, Geoffrey quickly leant forward to see if she was still breathing, at the exact moment when the flight-feather of an arrow brushed against the makeshift flap that covered his neck and the projectile thudded into the far side of the canoe where he had been seated moments earlier.

Instinctively he rolled across to the near side of the canoe, pulling the hound with him. Their only hope of survival would be to stay out of sight, knowing that eventually the river's current would carry the dugout clear of the would-be assassin's range but Misqualla had dropped her paddle overboard when she fell, so Geoffrey could not afford to wait for long before peering over the edge of the craft to see if it was reachable. As he raised his head, in the space of a heartbeat a second arrow thwacked into the exterior of the dugout, quivering barely an inch below the top.

Two more arrows followed in rapid succession, skimming over the edge of the canoe and embedding themselves alongside the first. Zanier would not be giving up easily on the rescue attempt.

Finally the dugout drifted out of range and soon Misqualla had recovered well enough to paddle but it was impossible to stop her from bleating about the pain in her head until Geoffrey gave her two aspirin from the medical kit stashed at his end of the canoe.

"Your head is only hurting because you tried to get me shot!"

"Why you say this, Massa? Misqualla no try," she protested.

"Not you, that muscle-bound freak trailing us with a bow and arrow," Geoffrey said, yanking out the arrows from the side of the canoe, an action that served only to make Misqualla more agitated.

"Massa, them bad, no keep in canoe."

"Not bad for me, since they missed," Geoffrey said, examining the well-crafted projectiles.

"Why you want keep?" she asked, shying away as if he was holding deadly snakes and not shafts of wood.

"I might need them." He had no idea what for, other than that Misqualla's fear suggested the arrows might prove a good way of keeping her under control.

"Massa… no hold tip, it much poison," she said with evident relief as Geoffrey carefully wrapped them together in a piece of torn canvas.

Geoffrey insisted on paddling much further than he had intended before nightfall, fully aware that Zanier wouldn't be giving up easily and uncertain whether her henchman would be tracking them by canoe or over land on foot.

Having taken the precaution of confiscating Misqualla's shoes once her shelter had been erected on the other side of a clearing, Geoffrey slept under his own tarpaulin with the two remaining paddles at his side and Archie's hunting knife clasped in his right hand and the hound's body generating a reassuring warmth as it rested in the crook of his knees, watchful for any intruders and focused on the movements of the unpredictable Misqualla.

The following morning, after an emotional outburst from Misqualla, he allowed her to perform her ablutions out of sight but soon grew concerned that it was taking much longer than Marguerite or Rose might have needed. He was also beginning to wonder if forcing her to act as a second paddle-man was actually worth the effort. On the other hand, when the time came for his sisters to give birth it would be useful having another woman to assist with the deliveries.

Misqualla was proving herself to be surprisingly adept with the paddle and the dugout was not an easy craft to manage while towing the smaller canoe behind, especially when negotiating fast flowing cross-currents.

By travelling with the current whenever they could they made good progress down the river, even in a heavy downpour that lasted the whole of the third day. Geoffrey was all too aware of the rising water level against the banks. On the fourth night the rain was torrential but Misqualla still insisted on completing her toilet out of sight, protected by an oilskin poncho. When they ate, however, there was nothing ladylike in her habits; her portions were almost double Geoffrey's own and gone in less than half the time and he wondered whether their supplies would last until they reached the compound.

Having slept heavily that night, Geoffrey awoke the following morning with a splitting headache and severe stomach cramps, convinced that his captive had mixed poison into his food.

"Where have you been? You cannot have been washing all this time," Geoffrey said. There was a large amount of caked mud on her feet and what he could see of her ankles beneath her tent-like sarong.

"Misqualla need wash, Massa," she smiled, exposing clumps of lipstick on her yellow and blackened teeth that matched the bright patches of rouge on her cheeks.

As they were paddling away from the bank, Geoffrey noticed a fluttering strip of red ribbon caught in a bush close to the water's edge. In such a remote region, it was unlikely that anyone had set foot there in years and he suddenly realised that he had noticed something similar dangling from another bush after a previous toilet break. This was clearly a trail for Zanier, who was no doubt tailing them by canoe. Geoffrey decided against saying anything; she would be less trouble if she thought he had no idea about her plan. From then on he made sure to get rid of any ribbons that she'd left and as she deliberately didn't glance back when they paddled away, no doubt to avoid attracting his attention to her markers, his plan worked perfectly. However, Geoffrey knew he could only delay his pursuer for a few days before he eventually tracked them down to the compound. He hoped that would give him enough time to get his sisters out of harm's way and to recoup his strength in readiness for the inevitable confrontation.

On the fifth night there was only a light drizzle and, shattered from lack of sleep and the added exertion of paddling through treacherous rapids, Geoffrey abandoned the idea of setting up a makeshift camp with tarpaulins on an area of clear ground, deciding instead to utilise a group of abandoned native huts. Most of them were falling apart but, because of Misqualla's insistence on privacy, Geoffrey allowed her to take cover in the only building with a roof still intact, while he and the hound sheltered in a collapsed hut that he was able to prop up with poles.

"I much hunger," Misqualla said wearily.

"Good, then you can cook us both something," Geoffrey said. He continued working on the shelter, watching her warily as a fish was filleted, aware that she was taking care to block his view as she chopped it up with some diced mango. Even though he was starving he had no intention of eating any of it.

"Why you no eat, Massa?" Misqualla asked.

"You have it; you normally eat twice as much as me anyway," Geoffrey said, scraping all of his food onto her empty plate without asking.

"I no hungry," she lied, pushing it aside.

"You need to keep up your strength," Geoffrey urged but she wouldn't take another bite.

"You give Perro, Massa. Him need eat," Misqualla said slyly but cowered away when Geoffrey leant towards her, brandishing Archie's knife.

"Do you take me for an idiot, you old witch and think I would feed him poison? If I did not need you to help paddle this cargo back to base, I would force-feed this plate full of food down your own wretched throat!"

On the sixth day, even though Geoffrey had no real sense of homecoming in a place where they had seemingly been imprisoned for a lifetime, it gave him a little comfort when they paddled around a familiar bend in the river and were back at the compound.

Once the dugout was docked and the crates of food had been unloaded, Geoffrey deliberately removed both paddles and got Misqualla to take off her shoes.

"No Massa… Misqualla need," she called after his departing figure but Geoffrey was having none of it.

"Wait there until I come back. If I see you at the compound before then, I will set the hound on you!" Geoffrey threatened but waited until she was seated on the crates before he made his way to the buildings.

It was clear from the moment he saw her that Marguerite was unwell and in no mood to exchange information. A collection of exotic plants, set in an assortment of wicker containers, had been strewn across the veranda. Opened out on the table was a recent watercolour depicting one of these plants in her journal, an image so perfectly captured that it could have been the living plant itself.

"Where have you been, Geoffrey? I have been going out of my mind with worry," she asked, her knuckles bleached white from gripping on to the rail.

"What sort of idiotic question is that? Where do you think I have been, apart from collecting crates of tinned food? It was hardly an excursion along the Dove," Geoffrey retorted.

"I am aware of that, Geoffrey. It is just that you have been gone for almost two weeks."

"Two weeks to hell and back," he said bitterly but the look on her face made him wish he had been more tolerant. "So… why the outburst?"

"You would not understand. How could you? You are not a woman!" She leant forward and began retching over the handrail.

"Why don't you go and lie down, Maggs," Geoffrey urged, uncertain of what he should do to help.

"Just go away and leave me alone."

"I am not going anywhere until you explain. Is there anything I can get you?"

"Not for me but since you ask, Rosamund needs help. It has been a nightmare getting her to eat anything at all since you left. I can barely get anywhere near her. She is behaving like a caged animal."

"What do you think started this?"

"I cannot be sure, except that her stomach is so dreadfully misshapen. It is much too enlarged at this stage."

"She is bound to get fat after six months," Geoffrey reassured her, trying not to show how deeply concerned he was.

"So am I but it does not show as much."

"Yes… but you have always been overweight, so that does not really count," he said thoughtlessly, which put her into a rage.

"Oh very well, have it your own way!" she snapped. "I just cannot go on like this on my own. It is so unfair. I need Lorenzo here to help me through this!"

"There is no need to take on so and I did bring another woman back with me to relieve some of the burden." Geoffrey was about to name Misqualla but thought better of it, at least until his sister was feeling better.

"What a blessing you had the foresight to do that, Geoffrey."

"I must confess that it was under considerable protest."

"I am confident she will settle in once we get to know each other but only when I have had time to rest."

After Geoffrey had collected Misqualla from the quay he housed her in the smallest cabin, which was a single room and basically furnished with a narrow cot, a low table and a chair.

"Why no in there for sleep?" she asked, pointing to his mother's cabin.

"Because this is all you're getting and you're lucky to have this. Be thankful you have somewhere to sleep with a roof over your head and stop complaining!"

"Why Massa, him make Misqualla do this?" she griped as he once more made her remove her large, moccasin-like shoes.

"You will not be wearing these while you are here!" Geoffrey said, nailing them to the veranda post where she could not reach them.

"Massa…. Misqualla much need!" she protested loudly.

"Complain all you like. They're staying put. Without them you will not be tempted to run away."

"It no safe Massa; el frog azul, it have much poison."

"Protest all you like, there are no poisonous frogs here, blue or otherwise. They are out in the marshland."

"Misqualla much need shoe, Massa," she pleaded again. "Pit viper and man-eat spider, them aqui, here in forest."

"Then I suggest you watch where you tread. You will sleep and eat here alone and stay away from my sisters' cabins unless you are asked to go there. If you do otherwise, I will set the hound on you!"

Even though Geoffrey was anxious to greet Rosamund and assess her condition, it took every ounce of determination to enter the cabin as the missiles she hurled crashed into the wall behind him. Her grotesquely painted features looked even more deranged than he'd remembered, making him truly fear for her sanity. Yet once he was confronting her face to face and speaking normally, the ferocious attack ended as quickly as it had begun.

"There is nothing to fear from me, Rose… it is me, Jeffy, your brother," he said gently, barely able to look at the bloated figure that was scarcely recognisable as his beautiful younger sister.

"Then perhaps you can explain why it is that although I have continually asked Mother to make you come and take me away from this prison, you never have," Rosamund said, tears gathering in her eyes.

"I could not be here, because I had to collect the food Father left at the trading post. Otherwise I would have come sooner," he reassured her.

"Have you brought that dog?"

"He is waiting outside," Geoffrey said, relieved that she still remembered the hound and that he was allowed inside.

"You never did tell me his name," Rosamund said, sitting awkwardly on the floor to hug the animal.

"I have decided to name him Bog Boy. That is, unless you can think of anything else," Geoffrey said with a smile.

"Why on earth did you call him that?" she asked.

"It is just a nickname, after an old acquaintance of ours."

"What acquaintance would that be?"

"I doubt if you would remember him after such a long time, Rose, a lot has happened here since then."

"You mean, apart from me getting so horribly fat? I swear I am trying not to eat so much Jeffy but I keep on getting fatter regardless. I fear some days that quite soon I will simply explode and disappear forever." Rosamund stumbled to one side as she went to the window and peered cautiously out. "If you tell me the name, I might remember?"

"If you insist, it was the Irishman, Archie Westbrook."

"I sometimes dream that Archie rescued me from a building that was falling down all around us. I do wish he was here at this moment and he could rescue me from this prison." Her eyes glazed over as she stared blankly into the rainforest.

Geoffrey had expected Marguerite to have recovered enough to be up and about the following day but she only came into the kitchen for a short time, ashen-faced, barely speaking as she pumped fresh water into a tumbler before returning to bed and asking not to be disturbed on any account. He had come over with an armful of stained bedding and clothes from Rosamund's cabin, fully expecting to her to wash them through, so as an alternative Geoffrey immediately put Misqualla to work, washing everything thoroughly, making sure that each item was properly clean before she hung them out to dry on a line he'd rigged up along the main veranda.

On the following day, Geoffrey handed back Misqualla's shoes and forced her to help transport the crates of food to his father's makeshift storage unit in the cave, breaking off only to prepare a meal for himself and his sisters. One that Marguerite declined, still feeling sickly and Rosamund hurled at his head, missing him by only a fraction.

Needless to say, Misqualla was banned from the kitchen after her attempt to poison him on the journey and he supplied her with a tin of baked beans and another of bully beef and let her make do with that.

By the time the boxes were unpacked it was almost dark, so he nailed her shoes back on to the post after he had battened the cabin door to keep her inside until after his swim. Afterwards he went some distance away from the compound, not wanting the Otter or Marguerite anywhere near as he unwrapped the poisoned arrows and tried to work out how best to incorporate at least one of the heads into a practical throwing spear.

Concentrating hard to avoid touching the poisoned tip, Geoffrey had not been aware that his armlet was beginning to glow. He looked up only when the warning growl rumbled in the hound's throat, the hackles erect on the back of its neck. His keen hearing picked up the sound of crashing furniture and Rose screaming like a wild beast. Without pausing to think, he was running alongside the wolfhound, aware only then that he had left Archie's knife where he had been working and had no other weapon than one of the arrows, gripped in his claw-like hand. Even so, there was murder in his heart, for if Misqualla had dared to harm his sister the woman would be dead before she hit the floor.

What he had least expected to find was the sweating, half-naked Zanier, grappling with his raging sister before knocking her to the ground as Geoffrey crashed through the door. The shock of his sudden appearance caught Zanier momentarily off guard and, as he hesitated, Rose slashed through his Achilles tendon with a shard of broken mirror, bringing the hulking brute crashing to his knees, where Geoffrey thrust the poisoned arrow deep into his throat.

"Rose… Rose, can you hear me?" Geoffrey cried, scrambling over to the girl on all fours as she lurched back against the wall, her eyes wild and staring, her legs thrashing erratically, tearing at her clothes.

"JEFFY!" she screamed. "Help get this evil out of my body! I cannot see to cut it out myself. You must do it."

"I cannot cut you open, Rose. You will die if I do so," Geoffrey said, attempting to stay calm while kicking the jagged glass out of her reach.

"You must do this! Help me to die, Jeffy and take this monster with me," she gasped, writhing from another spasm of pain before she thankfully passed out.

It was clear from the amount of blood pooling on the floor that his sister was about to miscarry and Geoffrey had no idea what to do. Instead he made her as comfortable as possible and dragged Zanier's body into the far corner of the room, covering him with a bedcover in case Rosamund awoke while he was gone. With Marguerite unable to assist, he ran as fast as he could to get the only other person who could possibly help in that dire situation.

When he arrived at the bungalow, the primitive shower was cranking out water. Remembering her protracted ablutions during the journey downriver, Geoffrey had no intention of waiting for her to finish and yanked the door open. Unprepared as he was for the sight of Misqualla's naked body and the prospect of being confronted by that cringing expanse of human flesh, nothing could have prepared him for being faced by an erect penis.

"Jesus Christ... You are a man!" Geoffrey gasped with horror.

"Massa... no kill Misqualla..." the man pleaded, cowering like a trapped animal in the corner of the wooden cubicle.

Given his sister's predicament, even this devastating revelation didn't stop Geoffrey from grabbing the quaking Misqualla by the arm and dragging him out into the open. "Get some clothes on, you great tub of lard and come with me, NOW!" Geoffrey screamed.

"What want Misqualla do, Massa?" he whined, hobbling along behind Geoffrey in his bare feet.

"I have no idea... Just keep up!" Geoffrey shouted, knowing he had to reach Rosamund as soon as possible and do something, anything to help her, even without a woman's assistance.

By the time they reached the cabin, they were being tailed by the Otter, who Geoffrey ordered to stay outside with the hound as he went inside the cabin, dragging the reluctant

Misqualla behind him. From the tortured screams inside it was evident the child was about to be delivered at any moment.

Unsure of what to do when the misshapen, bloodstained form emerged, Geoffrey could only stare blankly at the dark orange creature writhing on the ground. Moments later, it was followed by a second and then a third, all partially formed infants, each struggling weakly to prolong its short life. Taking up the shard of mirror, Geoffrey carefully cut through each of the umbilical cords the way he had seen his father do when his border collie had delivered her litter. By the time this was done, all three of the pitiful, malformed creatures were already dead and there was nothing he could have done to prevent it.

"You, Misqualla... get me some sheets, clothes or anything to help stop this bleeding and bring them here. Don't bloody well sit and there with your mouth gaping, get them over here now!" Geoffrey commanded, doing what he could to stem the bleeding with one of the harem dresses until Misqualla returned with the sheets.

"What Misqualla do now, Massa?" the man asked, backing away from the lifeless creatures on the floor, then squealing as he stumbled over the body of Zanier in the darkened corner, disturbing the bedcover and revealing his face; yet the reaction was not one of shock but more of relief.

"I do not give a damn what you do... just get rid of them," Geoffrey snapped.

"Tell Misqualla where go?"

"How the hell do I know, just do it before Rose wakes and sees them and make sure that you come back here directly to help me with him. If not, I swear I will hunt you down and kill you on the spot!"

As Geoffrey waited for him to return Rosamund began to wake, groaning and thrashing about as she had when the birthing began. As there was still no sign of Misqualla it was becoming apparent that he would not be coming back at all.

Uncertain what to do next, Geoffrey went to the window and called for the Otter, who immediately appeared with the hound.

"What want, Massa Jeffy?" the boy asked, his eyes like saucers.

"Go and wake Missy and bring her back. Do not come back without her," he ordered. The boy almost collided with Marguerite as she appeared around the corner of the building.

"I heard screaming, Geoffrey; you should have woken me earlier," Marguerite said. To his relief she looked more like her normal self and with a hasty rearrangement of her hair and the dangling sapphire earrings it was oddly reassuring for him that she looked so much like their mother.

"The child was coming but that is now over," Geoffrey said.

"It has arrived... then where is it?" Marguerite asked, stepping over the body of Zanier to reach Rosamund.

"There was more than one of them... three altogether but I think there might even be another on the way."

"Why did you not call me sooner if Rosamund was in such distress?" Marguerite said, moving him out of the way to carry out a swift examination of her sister.

"You were ill. I did not think you could cope in the state you were in."

"Then why not get that woman to help? Where is she anyway? I might need her to help if Rosamund becomes violent."

"I am not sure. I asked her to take the creatures away to be disposed of and she never came back."

"Is Rosamund responsible for that?" she asked, looking over at Zanier's corpse.

"No, that was me. He was manhandling Rose when I got here."

"Who is he?"

"Zanier, one of Misqualla's bodyguards who must have tracked us here from the trading post."

"You brought that dreadful woman here to help. How could you?"

"There was no alternative. I needed a paddle-man."

"You actually arranged for a woman to paddle all this way? That was an inconceivable choice Geoffrey, even for you!"

"Maybe not, since you were not there and I was the one in a life-or-death situation. Admittedly I did make an error of choice but not in the way you think."

"What do you mean?"

"Although Misqualla might act and dress, like a woman, he is in truth a man and I can vouch for that having dragged him out of the shower to assist here."

Rosamund began tearing frantically at her clothing. "Is there another one coming, Maggs?"

"Thankfully not; this is all natural and comes out after the birth." Marguerite stood up awkwardly. "Can you get her onto the bed without my help, Geoffrey?"

"Yes, I can manage that." He carefully assisted Rosamund on to the cot. "Is there anything else you need from me?"

"I will need a bucket of fresh water and a block of carbolic soap from the kitchen and also some of that antiseptic cream I made up for you." She bent over her sister, the earrings shimmering blue.

"I am glad you are wearing Mother's sapphires."

"At your suggestion; Rosamund takes great comfort from seeing me wearing them."

"When you have what you need, I will get rid of this body." He dragged Zanier's corpse clear of the doorway and made his way hastily across the compound to collect what she needed. On the way he saw that both paddles had gone and with them Misqualla's shoes, which proved that Zanier had not been alone.

Once the items were delivered to his sister Geoffrey grabbed one of his spears and ran to the staging where the dugouts had been moored, determined that Misqualla and his accomplice would not escape. The larger dugout was no longer tied at its moorings and he presumed they had got clean away until a startled flock of egrets took to the air a short distance downriver and, realising they hadn't got far, he ran as fast as he could along an animal track that would lead him to a clear section of the bank.

Although he was too late to get ahead of the canoe he refused to give up the prospect of killing or at least injuring one of them. Misqualla and his companion with the gold armband were almost out of his throwing range but Geoffrey knew he had to try. Using every ounce of his strength and balance, he hurled the spear at its target, a shot that was fractionally too high to hit Misqualla but tore through the bulging muscles and tendons of the other man's shoulder, rendering his arm useless.

As the spear embedded itself in the hull of the dugout the bleeding native was back on his feet, rocking the boat precariously as he tried to stem the bleeding. The pitch of his agonised screams startled a flock of blue macaws into flight, screeching wildly as the dugout now rolled over, pitching both occupants into the river but close enough to the bank for them to evade the shoal of piranha that had scented the blood and three caiman that slid into the water from the opposite bank.

The last Geoffrey saw of them they were crashing away through the dense undergrowth. The dugout had righted itself and was drifting close to the bank, where he was able to reach it without wading too far and dragged it back to the clearing where he secured it to a tree. Luckily one of the paddles was still inside, as too was the spear, embedded in the wood. Removing both, he returned to the compound.

"Did you not you hear me calling, Geoffrey?" Marguerite asked when he entered the cabin a short time later.

"Sorry, I must have been too far away." Geoffrey was relieved to see that Rosamund was sleeping peacefully, with all of her clownish make-up gone and her body washed and covered with a sheet.

"I need you to collect some more of Mother's clothes, Geoffrey. There is nothing decent in here for Rosamund to wear." Marguerite bundled up another pile of harem clothing that had been cleared from the chest of drawers. "She will be terribly weak from the loss of blood and so one of us must be with her day and night until she has recovered."

"I will stay as long as it takes. Go and rest; you look all in. Leave Rose to me."

"What about Misqualla? Could she help?"

"Are you barmy?" Geoffrey protested. "That dressed-up gorilla got that brute over there to follow us and has just fled with another muscle-bound moron but at least I did get the canoe back."

"What about him?" she asked, staring at the dead Zanier.

"I must get on to that now, before Rose wakes." Geoffrey began to drag the corpse out by his feet. "The piranha and caiman can fight over him."

Chapter Seven
Son of Orpantha

Although Geoffrey could get Rosamund to drink, it took three days before she could keep any food down. By then it seemed the rainy season was finally over, leaving the ground saturated and the fast-flowing river high and close to bursting its banks. Not for the first time, Geoffrey wished Lorenzo could have been there to use some of his mystic gifts on her and help ease the suffering.

It took the best part of a month before his sister was able to move about properly, then another five weeks before she would speak to anyone, even Geoffrey, who was with her day and night. By now Marguerite was eight months into her pregnancy. Her legs were badly swollen and she had slowed down considerably on her workload.

Over the months Geoffrey and the hound had perfected a coordinated system to drive off nightly intruders. Twice they had repelled attacks from jaguars before Geoffrey was awoken at dawn by screams and, discovering he was alone, rushed outside to find an eighteen-foot green anaconda had cornered Rosamund on the veranda. A short and bloody skirmish resulted in two crushed sections of handrail and a nasty gash across Geoffrey's shoulders from the death throes of the now headless reptile, a shock that only added to his sister's unwillingness to speak.

The anaconda was so heavy that it was impossible for Geoffrey to drag its corpse more than a few feet before needing to stop but the soggy ground underfoot helped him slide the creature across the compound with a rope tied around its neck and it was as he hauled it along in a series of jerks that he uncovered the remains of his shattered violin.

It was clear that nothing short of a miracle could repair the instrument. Even so, he could not bring himself to discard it in respect for the artistry of the long-dead craftsman who had created it. Once he had dumped the body of the snake and covered it over with shrubbery, he took the shattered remains of the violin and placed them on a shelf in the store cabin.

By the time he got back down to the compound the sun was already high and intensely bright, the humidity increasing, as he sat down to eat with Marguerite.

"I had the strangest dream last night," she said.

"Hopefully not about snakes."

"No… it was about a stone circle."

"You dreamt about Stonehenge?"

"No, it was nothing like that. These rocks were laid out in a figure of eight."

"Now that is bizarre. Next you will be telling me they were set out near a lagoon," Geoffrey said, staring at her intently.

"Why, do you know this place?"

"Yes I do; I go there twice a day to swim. It is the place where Lorenzo cured my paralysis. I could show you… if you are up to it, although it is a decent walk."

"I am with child, Geoffrey, not an invalid!" she said, laughing for the first time in weeks.

On the following morning, leaving the Otter to stay with Rosamund while she was sleeping, Geoffrey took Marguerite to the lagoon.

"It is quite lovely here, so restful by the water," she said.

Geoffrey walked the hound to the lagoon's edge, peering into the water in the hope of being able to make out the submerged temple deep below. "How do you think Lorenzo and the priest will react when they hear news of this child?"

"I have no idea, nor do I care. I am more interested to learn how you feel about becoming an uncle."

"I have not given it much thought. I just hope it will not throw up all the time, like those belonging to Mrs whatever her name is at the village post office. She seems to have babies like clockwork every year, all smelling like the devil and screaming blue murder in that battered old pram."

"Babies are not all the same," she said defensively.

"So what do you remember about me as an infant?"

"Only that you screamed the house down whenever you needed to be fed."

"Well, now that you have raised the topic of food, we should think about getting back. Have you thought of names?" he asked, helping her stand.

"I would rather wait and see what it is first." She pressed her hands over her stomach. "Put your hands here Geoffrey; you can feel it kicking."

"I would rather not," Geoffrey said, though he wondered how on earth he would be able to help deliver the baby if he didn't have the nerve to put a hand on her stomach, let alone anywhere else.

Since there were no cradles in the harem and they had burned all the cots, he realised the newborn would need somewhere to sleep and decided he would try to make one, deciding not to mentioning this in case it didn't work out as planned. Nevertheless, it was difficult to avoid her questions.

"Where do you go to in the afternoons, Geoffrey? I can never find you after you have been attending to Rosamund," Marguerite asked as she added the final touches to a watercolour in her journal.

"What did you need me for?"

"Nothing, I was just curious."

"I have been trying out a few ideas."

"About what exactly?"

"Nothing much, just something to help pass the time. You have your journal to illustrate and I… well, I have other things, like exploring more of the area," he lied.

"Then I would be grateful if you would show me where the most unusual plants can be found. I have almost exhausted what I can paint in this compound."

"I will but only if you promise not to bring any more back here to pot up, otherwise there will not be enough room to sit down out here with all of these containers cluttering up the veranda. Why keep them anyway?" Geoffrey moved a basket away from his feet.

"I cannot bear to throw any away. In shape and colour they are extraordinary."

"Well quite frankly I think you are barmy. There are clusters of them growing everywhere."

"Not these I have potted. I have never seen their like before, not anywhere, even at Kew. I am convinced they are rare."

"But if they are in pots, why keep them up here on the veranda?" he said irritably.

"Because there is nowhere else that is not in full sunlight each day, Geoffrey. Most of these need shade."

"Then let me take them up to the store cabin when you have finished painting them. There is a shaded area in front of the veranda there that would be perfect."

In his father's workshop, Geoffrey's attempt at creating a practical crib began by utilising one of the small drawers from his mother's cabin that he fitted on to rockers, which took forever to shape from sections of another drawer. Once this was done, he glued together the damaged body of the violin, adapting it into a headboard. The broken neck was then positioned to project over the crib. From this he hung a canopy of mosquito netting to drape over the new arrival.

There were many times when Geoffrey almost abandoned the idea, since he struggled to manipulate the tools with any degree of accuracy. When the project was eventually complete it gave him a great sense of satisfaction to have been able to create anything at all and he decided then and there that he would utilise this new-found skill to construct a musical instrument that he could play. On a visit to the Academy of Music in London he had been shown a Stroh violin which, when played like a cello, produced a light and delicate sound akin to that of a viola. Though many traditionalists were sceptical of the design it was this he was determined to recreate, even though he was uncertain where he would obtain the materials.

On the night the crib was completed, Geoffrey felt an intense buzzing sensation in his head as he lay down to sleep. As he closed his eyes, a series of vivid and disturbing images began to appear. He could see himself clearly, standing waist high in the lagoon to lift a newborn infant out of the water before carrying it to the bank. The nightmarish scenario jolted him wide awake with a thumping headache and, realising it was already morning he staggered into the kitchen to find something to eat.

"Geoffrey dear, you look dreadful. You should let me take your temperature," Marguerite said, moving more awkwardly than ever.

"It is nothing, just a headache."

"Are you not sleeping well?"

"Not last night. I dreamt that you gave birth in the lagoon. How crackers is that?"

"That was your dream?" she asked, with a startled expression.

"I told you it was crazy."

"Not if I had the same dream," she said cautiously.

"You cannot be serious. Two people cannot have the same dream."

"I would never have thought so either and yet in mine, I asked you to carry my baby out of the water for me."

"Strewth... You actually saw that too?" Geoffrey almost choked on a piece of fruit.

"Is that what happened in your version?"

"It was exactly like that and I am sure it was a boy."

"You thought that too? I have been wondering about the delivery and have decided it might be sensible for me to be immersed in water for the birth."

"Are you barmy? You cannot do that, regardless of whatever you or I dreamt. The infant will drown."

"This has been done successfully before, Geoffrey. I read about it."

"For pity's sake, Maggs, no one in their right mind would risk giving birth in that way and you are the least irresponsible person I know."

"Well I can assure you this has been done before, in France in 1805 to be exact."

"Is that all you have to go on? This is verging on madness if you are actually considering such a crackpot idea!"

"There was mention of other babies being born in water successfully."

"How many were there?"

"I cannot tell you that. There was no more information about when or where in Father's books."

"What you are suggesting would be a terrible risk."

"At my age, giving birth in the normal manner would be perfectly acceptable if we were at home in Ashbourne but as we are not, I cannot afford to take any chances or risk infection."

"If this is about not taking chances, then you really are bonkers if you intend going ahead with this crazy scheme."

"If you read about the advantages to the mother giving birth in water, it all makes perfect sense."

"Not to me."

"Very well, then perhaps you can explain the reason why you and I both had exactly the same dream on the same night. I have made my choice, Geoffrey and whatever your opinion might be it is not going to change my mind."

Even if Geoffrey disagreed with her argument, it was her decision and he could not ignore the fact that Lorenzo was the father of this child and how perfectly at ease he had been in the water, nor his ability to remain submerged for an impossible length of time. So as his sister's decision appeared unshakeable, he concluded the lagoon above the temple would be the safest section of water for the child to be delivered.

After a day of rummaging through every drawer, cupboard and place of concealment, Geoffrey had managed to come up with all of the components he needed to begin work on the instrument. Although his father's wind-up gramophone had been smashed up during the raid, the horn speaker and pickup head both remained intact.

In addition to what he could remember of the actual Stroh violin in London, he had fortunately discovered an illustrated advertisement in a magazine of his father's for an ideal instrument that he could hold between his legs like a cello.

For the body he used a corner support from a damaged wardrobe in his mother's cabin, which it took him the best part of a week to chisel and carve before he could fit the four string adjusters. After making vile-smelling glue from ground and boiled fish bones he carefully spaced and stuck down a fingerboard from the teeth from a black and white comb. He still had the strings he had purchased from the street market and, luckily, he was able to dig out the violin bridge, undamaged, from the mud. The most intricate part of all was to fit the pickup head on to the strings, then attach this and the gramophone horn to the post, fixing them in place with a length of copper wire. Finally, he tested his creation with an undamaged bow that had been packed away in his shipping trunk.

Although the instrument he had created was far from elegant and even though Geoffrey played clumsily to begin with, the sound it produced had an eerily beautiful tone. However, any pleasure was soon changed into fury at his own inability to play anything of worth because of his missing fingers and he angrily threw the instrument down, ready to abandon the project as a gross failure.

"Geoffrey, what was that wonderful sound?" Marguerite asked when he returned.

"Oh that... that was a broken record I tried out on father's gramophone," he lied.

"Was it one of those zinc recordings of his?" she asked eagerly. "The sound was extraordinary, Geoffrey. I would love to hear more."

"It is just one disc in a useless piece of junk. It was not worth messing with."

"Are you certain? Surely you must be desperate to hear music again too?"

"Perhaps but I am convinced there is nothing else in there. Everything is too warped and far gone to repair." He walked away with a mind to put a hammer through it but when he arrived at the workshop he was struck by the intriguing ugliness of the contraption and at the last minute decided against wrecking it, at least for the time being.

In the oppressive afternoon heat, some six weeks after the rains had ended, Marguerite came staggering along the veranda to where Geoffrey had been attempting to compose.

"Geoffrey, the time has come when you need to help me," she said, clutching her stomach.

"Why, what is it?" he asked, dreading but already knowing the answer.

"The child is coming."

"What do you need me to do?"

"Help me to the lagoon," she said, struggling down the steps.

"Why go there now? There may not be enough time. Surely it would make more sense to stay here where there is a bed?" He grabbed hold of her to prevent her from tumbling down the steps.

"The only place I am going, Geoffrey, is to the lagoon and if you will not take me, I will make my way there alone." Her fingernails dug into the flesh of his arm. "Well, are you going to help me or not?"

"If that is what you want then I am not going to argue. Just wait while I get Father's medical bag and some clean sheets."

"There is no need for sheets. I will be in the water."

"I am begging you to give up on that barmy idea, Maggs!"

"If you had bothered to go through Father's research books and read the passages I marked, then you would realise this is an established practice in many parts of the world."

"Perhaps it is, in clean water but not here in a phosphorus lake fed by a tributary of the Amazon. Who knows what could be swimming around in there?" He could only pray that the armlet would send out the same radiating energy that kept him safe while swimming, or better still that she would see sense and change her mind.

After a slow and at times distressing walk to the lagoon, Geoffrey assisted her into the stone circle and made her rest on the rocky shelf before they entered the water.

"I just need a few moments to catch my breath and prepare, Geoffrey," she said, unpinning her dark hair and tying it back, away from her face.

"Do you intend keeping all those clothes on in the water?"

"Not all of them, no but there is a need for modesty," she said, clutching at the rock as another more severe cramp took hold.

"They are becoming more frequent now," Geoffrey said, trying not to look at her body as he helped her remove the baggy painter's smock.

"We should get into the water. It will not be long now," she said calmly, now dressed only in a thin slip and taking his arm as he assisted her to the water's edge.

"There will be a section of shallow water, no more than two feet deep, where I know you will be safe," Geoffrey reassured her.

Leading her on to the wide shelf of rock that stretched out into the water, he helped her sit down on the edge, then dropped to the lower level where it came up to his waist. Here the water was much clearer and he realised he was standing on the top step of a steep flight of stairs that had been cut into the rock face centuries before, leading down through a man-made fissure and ending up at the blurred shape of the ancient temple of Orpantha.

"Thank you for being here with me, Geoffrey."

"I am here to help in whatever way I can. I know about cutting the umbilical cord, so there is no need to fret about that when it arrives," Geoffrey reassured her, checking that Archie's sheathed knife was firmly attached to his belt.

"I had not expected the water to be so warm," Marguerite said, as they both looked down, trying to understand the source of the unexpected heat.

Beneath them, the submerged temple could now be seen much more clearly than before and it was from there that the warmth seemed to be generated, flowing directly towards them, the source a stone altar carved in the shape of a sleeping dragon. Although Geoffrey knew this image was carved from stone, at that moment it appeared to be glowing, even pulsating because of the ever-shifting underwater currents, as if the creature was breathing. From its shape, beams of amber light now began to radiate upwards towards them, like the rays of the morning sun, gradually isolating each step, in their steady ascent until reaching them just as Marguerite began an intense and extremely vocal period of her labour.

Wary of predators that might be attracted by their presence, Geoffrey was relieved to find that the warmth generated by the creeping spread of amber light felt very much like what he had experienced when he and Lorenzo were underwater, safely enclosed within an invisible perimeter from the lurking caiman and piranha.

At the moment of birth it was unclear if it was the phosphorous element of the water or some other source that was responsible for a radiating light that appeared to encompass the newborn like an amber cocoon as he emerged. The light dimmed slightly as Geoffrey cut through the umbilical cord but he could see that the infant's eyes were wide open, as if the child was able to see everything, his perfectly formed limbs already engaged in the action of swimming, as though he had adapted instantly to the underwater environment.

As Geoffrey lifted the infant out of the water, there was an unearthly, radiant glow from the baby's skin and he knew that this was not just the reflection of the underwater beams of light. Still more shocking was the vivid birthmark of a winged spirit in flight, positioned centrally like a tattoo between his shoulder blades, a mark identical to Archie Westbrook's.

Glancing down at the temple, Geoffrey was awestruck by the transformed beauty of the structure. This was no longer a gaunt relic of aged stone columns but an enchanted temple of worship, where carved images of water-dragons on each of the columns glistened with gold from the reflected light. It was an extraordinary sight, a vision that would remain with him for the remainder of his life.

Helping his sister to the bank, Geoffrey prayed that wherever Lorenzo was, with his power of telepathic observation, he might have witnessed the extraordinary birth of his son.

"He is so perfect," Marguerite said lovingly as Geoffrey handed the auburn-haired infant into her arms once they had reached the bank.

"Now you must rest before you attempt the journey back," Geoffrey said, wrapping a sheet around both her and the child.

"Thank you, Geoffrey, for everything you have done here for me. I knew helping with the birth would be an embarrassment but thank you also for bringing me here to the lagoon. I hope you will agree, now that it is over, this was the right thing to do."

"I could not agree more. It was better to deliver him here than anywhere else. It was meant to be. I understand that now." He made a silent vow that he would protect his sister and her precious child until he could get them safely back home to England.

After resting for a few hours they made their way back to the safety of the compound. Although she was slow and a little unsteady, Marguerite was able to walk back with him, her arm linked with his for support, allowing Geoffrey to cradle the infant.

Compared to the length of time it had taken Rosamund to recover from the miscarriage, his elder sister's recovery seemed to border on the miraculous as she was up and about early the following day.

With a newborn in their midst, the new priority was to keep the infant safe. Yet, perhaps because of the strange phenomena he'd witnessed at the birth, Geoffrey had the sense that the child did not really need their protection, an idea that only increased when he found a green iguana sleeping inside the crib. This was a disturbing sight at first but even as he was trying to work out how best to lift the gurgling infant out of the cot without alerting the sleeping reptile, he saw the baby reach out and caress the creature awake, which then scrambled out of the crib and was gone in seconds.

"You must remove that material from around the crib, Geoffrey," his sister said the following morning.

"I fixed it there to keep the mosquitoes and lizards out."

"Well, for some reason he cannot settle with it there. He kept me awake all night."

"Of course, if that is what you want," Geoffrey said, remaining determined to keep an eye on the child while his sister slept.

At dawn he crept into the room to discover the wolfhound settled at the side of the crib and the iguana asleep inside it, the baby's arm hooked comfortingly around the reptile. Unsure about how to remove the lizard without disturbing either the infant or his sister, Geoffrey decided to leave well alone.

"Have you noticed how he seems to attract so much wildlife?" Marguerite asked the next day.

"Wildlife?" he asked, unsure if she was referring to the iguana.

"Every day this week, two blue macaws have been perched outside the window every morning when he wakes."

"Anything else?" he asked.

"There are a lot more lizards clambering up the walls than I can remember from before. Do you think they are safe?"

"There is nothing we could do about that even if we wanted to, not out here. If you carry on like this you will become a nervous wreck. What you really should concentrate on is coming up with a name for him."

"I was thinking about naming him Edwin – after Grandfather."

"Do you not think that is a bit too English?"

"What do you mean by that? English is what we are."

"Maybe we are but not Lorenzo and he is the father. Why not come up with something a bit more exotic?"

"Why change it to anything other than an English name of my choosing, whatever it is. I am his mother!" she protested.

"Well he needs to be named soon. He is already more than a week old, so until you come up with something definite, I will call him Red."

"You cannot call a child that."

"Actually, I think Red is quite appropriate. It is the colour of his hair, after all."

"His hair is not red, it is auburn."

"Red is close enough; unless you would prefer me to call him Rusty?" Geoffrey laughed at her shocked reaction.

"You can be really insufferable at times, Geoffrey. How could you suggest naming him after the gardener's old dog?" She bundled up the infant and lifted him up.

"I am going to feed him now Geoffrey, so please do not enter the room until I tell you."

"No need to fret about that. I am off out with Bog Boy!" he called after her, knowing the dog's name would irritate her too.

Twice a day, when Geoffrey arrived at the lagoon for his intensive swimming sessions, he would spend time where the birth had occurred to see if the amber light was still illuminating the sunken temple. Most of the time he saw nothing but the distorted shapes of the grey stone columns, except for one occasion, by moonlight, when the water was completely still and he was able to make out the carved altar, glowing with a dull amber light.

One morning when the infant was a month old, Geoffrey was surprised to find his sister at the lagoon just after dawn, drying him off having bathed him in the water.

"I never hear him cry in the night. I thought all babies did that," Geoffrey said.

"Some do but he is quite content in that adorable crib you made."

"I am just relieved that it never fell apart when you put him into it."

"It was an ideal gift, Geoffrey."

"I suppose it needed to be. What else would be appropriate for such a perfectly formed creature as this?"

"Perfectly formed yes but Edwin is not so in every way, possibly because of birthing him here in the lagoon."

"What an odd thing to say, Maggs. The birth could not have gone better… for either of you. So why say that? Unless perhaps you are referring to that strange birthmark at the base of his neck?" Geoffrey said, untroubled as the gurgling infant grabbed hold of his own claw-like hands.

"You noticed that?"

"It would be difficult not to."

"Are you not shocked by it?"

"I might have wondered if it was a tattoo, had I not been there at the birth."

"The shape of the wings is so detailed. I do not understand how this could this have happened. There is no history of anything like this in our family. Grandfather would certainly have made us aware of it, had there been."

"Maybe not in our family but there could be a hereditary birthmark on Lorenzo's side. The mark is extraordinary, I grant you but not unprecedented. Indeed, Archie's family has a similar mark, passed down through their male lineage." Geoffrey tried to remember in more detail the mark he had seen through Archie's torn shirt that night at the opera; from what he could recall the infant's was identical in every way. Which could have made sense if Archie had been the father, rather than Lorenzo.

"That birthmark is not the only defect. Can you see the fine webbing between his fingers?" She opened out one of the baby's hands. "It has also formed between his toes. Could it be the effect of this water? It takes all of my time to get him out, once he is in there."

"For an intelligent woman, you have quite the imagination. When we finally get home you might consider becoming a writer."

"Geoffrey, do be serious!"

"You must have noticed Lorenzo has something similar on his hands? Thicker too, from what I remember but maybe it develops with age and is why he is such an incredible swimmer. His son obviously takes after his father."

"Unlike you I never saw him up close, at least not in daylight."

"That is probably because you had other things on your mind."

144

"It was not like that! Lorenzo was comforting me," Marguerite snapped angrily. "You make me sound like some wanton baggage."

"Whatever you want to call it, all you have to do is look at the result and be thankful it happened."

"God knows I am and more than you could ever imagine." She pulled the journal from the capacious bag that once again seemed constantly attached to her shoulder since the baby's arrival. "I drew this for you," she said, removing a page from the soiled volume and handing it to him. "It is not much of a gift but I hope you will like it."

"Why would I want a gift?" he asked with some confusion, before falling silent as he gazed at the portrait she had lovingly drawn of their mother.

"Happy birthday, Geoffrey dear," she smiled, cradling the gurgling infant.

"Is it really my birthday?" he asked with astonishment.

"It is and the last one of your teenaged years."

"Thanks for this lovely drawing of Mother."

"I thought this would please you. You were always so very close."

"You could not have given me anything better than this, I can assure you." He continued staring closely at the image, unable to resist comparing it with his sister as she sat beside him.

"Then you do like it?"

"Of course I do, truly. I hesitate only because I am trying to work out when this change in you happened. Comparing you to this drawing, Maggs, you could be a younger version of Mother."

"You are allowing your imagination to run away with you, Geoffrey. It is true, I have lost some weight but I am nothing like Mother and I never could be." She smiled modestly, bringing an end to the conversation.

Marguerite and Geoffrey had taken extra precautions to protect the infant from mosquitoes and other flying insects, though reptiles and predators posed more of a threat since the baby's arrival. The more pertinent issue, however, was Rosamund's reaction when she was shown the new arrival for the first time. Within moments she had run away screaming and barricaded herself in her cabin for the rest of the week. When Geoffrey finally gained entry, the slight progress she had been making towards normality had gone completely, leaving her with a wild look in her eyes, totally uncommunicative.

In her more lucid moments Geoffrey would find Rose talking to herself but not in English. Instead she spoke strange words in a weird language, which he realised sounded very similar to what Lorenzo had used during those long hypnotic sessions by the lagoon.

"He is coming," Rosamund unexpectedly mumbled when Geoffrey arrived with her food one morning.

"Who is coming?" Geoffrey asked.

"He," she said reverently, pressing her fingertips against her temples in just the way Lorenzo had done when transferring the violent visions of the hunters' deaths.

"Are you in pain?" Geoffrey began but said no more when she pressed a forefinger against his mouth.

"Aqui hablante," she said with some annoyance, as if distracted from listening to an important conversation inside her head.

"Rose, are you ill?" Geoffrey asked but when Rosamund responded she again spoke rapidly in the same mysterious language, not a word of which he understood.

For some weeks after this strange outburst Rose did not speak clearly in any language at all but continued to mutter unintelligibly while pacing up and down the veranda until eventually she would sit down abruptly and stare expectantly at a narrow animal track leading out of the forest.

One morning, as Geoffrey returned at dawn after swimming in the lagoon, he saw to his amazement not just two blue macaws perched in a tree but an entire flock, squabbling for positions on the nearest bough that overlooked the sleeping quarters of the infant. Nearby were a group of howler monkeys and a dangling tree python, bridging the gap between the boughs to bring it closer to the building.

As Geoffrey stood watching in silence, he could sense the presence of other, unseen, creatures close by, watching where the baby slept and he instinctively made sure that Archie's knife was easily accessible in its sheath. A crashing sound alerted him to something heading in his direction, forcing its way through the dense undergrowth. Within moments a wild boar crashed through the bushes, squealing continually, with an arrow lodged in its neck, the echoing sound prompting the flock of macaws to lift into the air en masse, screeching and transferring their alarm into the other visiting creatures, most of which also bolted.

Balancing his spear in readiness, Geoffrey watched as the boar fell dead a few feet away from where he was standing. Remaining perfectly still he was already prepared for the human threat long before the headhunters emerged through the gap in the bushes. There were four men in the group, ferocious young warriors daubed in tribal paint and each carrying a weapon. Dangling from their belts bobbed the chilling shrunken heads of adults and children and his blood ran cold as the hunters' attention focused on the sound of the baby's crying through the nursery window.

The odds of survival would have been minimal against the band of warriors, even though Geoffrey and the hound had the advantage of being undetected and he tried desperately to come up with a plan of attack. At that moment the decision was taken out of his hands as a huge jaguar, unseen until now, sprang down from a nearby tree on to the shoulders of the warrior beneath, tearing into him with its ferocious claws. Its weight sent the hunter crashing to the ground where the animal sank its teeth into his neck, killing him in seconds, before making a spring-loaded leap towards a second hunter before he had time to react.

With the odds now even, Geoffrey launched himself at the man closest to the jaguar, leaving the dog to attack the fourth native. The confrontation was over almost as soon it had begun, with all four headhunters dead and Geoffrey preparing to take on the jaguar. However, he held back upon realising that the creature seemed to have no further interest in either of its victims and indeed was paying no attention to either him or the hound. The enormous cat, which Geoffrey now noticed had its left ear missing, simply lay down across one of the twitching bodies and focused its gaze on the child's window until the crying had ended.

What he found even stranger was that the wolfhound displayed no signs of aggression towards the jaguar. In that moment of calm it seemed as though a battle to protect the child's safety had been won through an unlikely alliance between the three of them. Both the hound's collar and his own armlet had stopped glowing too, which only confirmed that any threat to the infant was over.

Although Geoffrey never saw the jaguar alive again, he often had the sense that the animal was not too far away and that if he needed to leave the compound for a period of time, he could have confidence that the child was safe under the surveillance of that strong and savage protector.

Chapter Eight
Conflict

Geoffrey secretly persisted with his attempts to master the misshapen instrument and, after a while he could play a few simple chords, which he did only for the enjoyment of the child and whenever Marguerite was not around. He found great satisfaction in being able to transfer a little of his own pleasure in music to the infant who, until then, could never have known what joy the sound could give.

For the past week there had been an alteration in Rosamund's behaviour. She gazed constantly and expectantly along the forest path and had become more obsessive in her gibberish talk. Her figure had thankfully resumed its former, sylph-like shape and her short-cropped hair was now the same length as his. Sometimes he would find her with her eyes closed, the fingers of both hands pressed against her temples.

"I brought you this food, Rose," Geoffrey said, uncertain what reaction he would get once she opened her eyes but this time, Rosamund took hold of his arm gently and led him to the edge of the veranda, where she once more stared along the animal track.

"He is coming, Jeffy," she said, speaking English for the first time in weeks.

"No one is coming to rescue us, Rose, not after all this time. No one knows we are here."

"Orpantha, he knows," Rosamund said confidently.

"Where on earth did you hear that name?" Geoffrey asked.

"Lorenzo," she said with closed eyes, pressing her fingers against her temples once more.

"Why would he tell you that?"

She opened her eyes and stared at him.

"Because… he is bringing you a special gift Jeffy, one that will help you play music again."

"How could I ever play again with these damned claws?" Geoffrey protested, barely able to prevent himself from yelling. "Whatever you think, Lorenzo will never come back again now. He has been gone for almost a year."

"Orpantha, he will come," she said confidently, her calm words only making Geoffrey feel more exasperated than ever.

"Well good luck to him if he can find us here, because no one else can!"

Making his way back across the compound, Geoffrey stopped to look back at his sister, who was once again staring intently along the track. At that very moment there was a movement in the bushes and the dark, hunched figure of the priest appeared astride his big-boned mule, followed immediately by Lorenzo on foot, the monk Drangoo trailing behind. It was with mixed feelings that Geoffrey watched the trio. Knowing the life he had created for his sisters and the infant was about to change completely he couldn't help but feel a sense of resentment at the appearance of such a dynamic usurper as Lorenzo appeared that afternoon.

There was no question that Lorenzo was a magnificent specimen of manhood, his darkening auburn hair down to his shoulders, shining like glistening copper in the sunlight. His pale olive skin emphasised the intensity of the extraordinary green eyes, glistening like emeralds. At that moment none of his attributes affected Geoffrey more than the enviable sight of Lorenzo's perfectly formed hands.

Geoffrey could hear the baby wailing for attention in the back room, not crying as normal but bawling, as if the infant knew his father was here and was calling for Lorenzo's attention. Given the extraordinary powers the young man possessed, it was logical that some of them could have been passed on to the child. However, it wasn't Lorenzo's smiling face that caught his attention, as if acknowledging what he was thinking but the harsh look on Harvey Fitzgerald's ravaged features as he dismounted, which sent chills of fear down Geoffrey's spine.

"Good day, sir," Geoffrey said through gritted teeth, wondering how to get rid of the three men before any awkward questions were asked about the wailing infant.

"Where is the Lady Rosamund?" the priest demanded.

"The whereabouts of my sister are none of your concern, Sir," Geoffrey retorted as Marguerite came silently on to the veranda, unnoticed by the priest.

"I ask you again, Geoffrey… where is the Lady Rosamund?"

"Are all Americans so devoid of good manners they would enter a habitable place without offering so much as a good day to Lord Geoffrey when he greets you, or does that only apply to yourself, Father Fitzgerald?" Marguerite snapped, glaring down at him from the veranda before Geoffrey had time to answer.

"I do apologise, Milady," he responded warily, seeming troubled by her appearance.

"Very well, then I accept. Now perhaps you could elaborate on why you have the need to speak with Lady Rosamund."

"Do forgive me, Lady Claudia, if I appear shocked. Seeing you here… and alive… is, is overwhelming."

"My mother, Lady Claudia, is dead, Father Fitzgerald. You of all men should know that. After all, you helped bury her."

"I am fully aware of that, Milady and yet it is difficult to believe that you are not her. I cannot comprehend how this could be."

"There is no mystery here, I can assure you. I am Lady Claudia's eldest daughter and I have been fortunate to have inherited some of my mother's physical attributes."

"But I understood there were only two daughters stranded here, Lady Rosamund and that lumbering artist, Lady Marguerite."

"For a man of the cloth you are not only devoid of any manners but you clearly cannot understand the English language. I am the Lady Marguerite you so ungraciously refer to. Lady Rosamund is my sister and so, returning to my earlier question, what is it you require from her?"

"I heard a child crying when we approached. Naturally I assumed it was conceived during that repellent incident with those caiman hunters."

"Lady Rosamund's rape resulted in an early miscarriage, from which my sister is still recovering. Therefore, as a man of God, I would not expect you to make any contact with her. The only man she is able to relax with is Lord Geoffrey and now, if you will excuse me, I will attend to any refreshments we can offer before you and your companions continue on your way." She was clearly impatient to get rid of them, a sentiment that Geoffrey was in total agreement with.

"Then where did the sound come from?" the priest insisted. "I recall the native women in Lord Oliver's employ were all deceased. Was I mistaken, or did any of their infants survive?"

"Not one. The child you heard crying is mine," Marguerite responded icily.

"The infant is yours?" Fitzgerald asked with some confusion. "Then you must forgive me, Milady. I had assumed when we met that you were unmarried!"

"And why was that? Because you thought me so unattractive that no man would look at me?" she baited him. Geoffrey remembered her using the same tone with their father when she was at her rebellious worst and wondered if she had the revolver handy, fearing that she could be tempted to use it if they didn't leave soon.

"Milady, I cannot understand how you could have taken your marriage vows out here without the blessing of a priest? There are no others in these parts apart from myself. Might I therefore inquire after the age of the child? By the sound, it cannot be more than a few months old."

"That is none of your concern," Marguerite retorted, turning to leave before the priest strode up the steps, two at a time, to challenge her.

"Well I think it might well be," the priest said, catching his breath as she spun around to face him, her cheeks flushed and her eyes blazing.

"Priest or not, you are not welcome. No one has invited you up here and I want all of you gone, NOW!"

"Judging by your reaction to my presence, Milady, there is obviously an attempt to conceal something. Why would you behave in this manner to a man of God? I mean you no harm. I ask only after this child and am merely curious to see it."

She blocked him from getting any further up the steps, "and I say you shall not. I am in no need of your hypocritical sermons, Father Fitzgerald, neither is my child and I must ask you to leave immediately."

"I am in no mood to be trifled with after our journey here, Milady. If this child is of mixed race is nothing to be ashamed of. Mixed blood is not uncommon out here."

"Something you and my father both know from personal experience. Any man in your compromised position would naturally say so," Marguerite retorted.

"What you might consider my failings as a priest are not in question here, madam. All I am asking for is that you allow me to see the infant. How difficult could that be?"

"I would strongly advise you not to try." She pulled the revolver from her bag and clicked off the safety catch. "My advice on this issue would be that unless you are desperate to meet your own maker any time soon and settle your own issues of infidelity to the Church, then you should take my advice and leave well alone."

"What is it with this family? Why are you behaving like a deranged nun rather than a woman of high rank? If you will not agree to my simple request and allow me to see this child, it then raises the question of whether Drangoo could be the father; if so, it would not be the first."

"How dare you imagine that I would conceive a child with that... that deviant?" she retorted, the expression on her face convincing Geoffrey she was about to pull the trigger and be damned with the consequences.

"Then show me the child and prove me wrong? Recalling the shape you presented when I was last here, no other man but Drangoo would have looked at you twice," the priest taunted, savouring each comment and seemingly intent on riling her even more.

"That is quite enough of your insulting behaviour, you American bastard!" Geoffrey shouted. "I order you now to step away from Lady Marguerite immediately!" He brandished the spear, fully prepared to use it.

"Would you dare threaten a man of God?" the priest snarled. "I will step away when I am ready and not a moment before."

"He is not worth it, Geoffrey!" Marguerite screamed, her raised voice clearly alarming the baby and making it wail even more lustily. "You will go to Hell if you do. He is still a priest."

Geoffrey only now noticed that Lorenzo had gone missing during the volatile exchange and knew exactly where he was when the baby stopped creating and began gurgling with delight.

"Ah… now it becomes infinitely clearer if, as I begin to suspect, this is your brother's child, is it not?"

"How dare you, a man of God, accuse me of behaving in such a diabolical way as that with my own brother?" Marguerite raged, brandishing the revolver again.

"It would not be unheard of in your country, madam; take Lord Byron for a prime example."

"You disgust me… the effrontery to compare a distressed woman's single indiscretion to your own obsessive behaviour with the local women? You who profess to be a man of God, whose own lack of morality created not only Lorenzo out of wedlock but also the Otter and that depraved monk and presumably many others. The only facts here are that you and my debauched father are not so very different, except that he is dead and, at the moment, you are not."

"If Lord Oliver was indeed your natural father," he retorted angrily.

"What are you implying by that remark? Of course he was my father. Why would you imagine otherwise?" Marguerite snapped.

"Simply because Lord Geoffrey has the look of his father, as too does the Lady Rosamund and all of his five children born here had his fair hair, whereas you, madam, have no features resembling his at all." The priest looked around impatiently. "Where is Lorenzo?"

"Lorenzo, him here, Papa." From the moment he appeared on the veranda, cradling the gurgling infant in his arms, Geoffrey knew there was no chance of pretending that Lorenzo was not the father. Their identical hair colouring shone like burnished gold in the sunlight and from the natural bond between them it would have been impossible to imagine otherwise.

"Lorenzo is the father of your child?" the priest said, his mouth gaping.

"That is a private matter and is not up for discussion," Marguerite snapped. "Therefore, because of your insulting behaviour, I must ask you to leave this compound immediately." She firmly removed the child from Lorenzo's arms, despite the infant's protests.

"You expect me to leave here, knowing that I have a grandson, Lorenzo's child?" the priest asked incredulously.

"I have acknowledged no such thing."

"There is no need. They have that unusual hair colour, as did my late wife."

"Do not assume that I am a fool. No Jesuit is allowed to marry." She cradled the bawling infant against her as she strode away.

"Come back here, madam! Do not dare walk away from me!" he ranted uselessly after her departing figure, his mouth gaping, gasping for air as he gripped the handrail. "Get her back here, Geoffrey!" he demanded. "I need to see that child... to make sure."

"Only a colonial halfwit could expect a woman of breeding to come back after being spoken to in such a way, Fitzgerald. My sister is not a dog being called to heel, nor is she a madam. The Lady Marguerite has a title and I would advise that you either use that in future or suffer the consequences," Geoffrey said.

To Geoffrey's surprise the priest made no reply but sank to his knees, reaching out towards a thunderous cloud formation above the forest and offering his open palms into the heavens.

"Blessed be this day, O Lord. My prayers have been answered."

Uncertain what to do and unwilling to just stand there as he prayed, Geoffrey was on his way towards the store cabin when he heard an ear-piercing scream of rage from inside Rosamund's own cabin and immediately set off at a run with the hound at his side and Archie's knife unsheathed in readiness.

"Rose... this is Jeffy, please let me inside," Geoffrey called anxiously, unable to open the barricaded door.

"Step back, Geoffrey," a voice said as the priest appeared behind him like a dark, threatening cloud in his black robe. He clamped Geoffrey's arm in an iron grip before dragging him back to the edge of the veranda. "On the count of three we both run at the door like a battering ram," he instructed and with their combined weight they forced the door just wide enough to squeeze inside.

Once inside the reason for the blockade became clear and to Geoffrey's immense relief he found Rosamund unharmed, although the same could not be said for Drangoo. The monk was pinioned to the door by his torn and bleeding ear. Rose had stabbed it through and impaled him there with her scissors.

"Loco bella, she want kill Drangoo, Papa!" he squealed, struggling unsuccessfully to remove the embedded scissors.

"You twisted imbecile!" the priest snarled, wrenching the weapon from the wood in a calculatedly insensitive movement that immediately caused more screaming.

"What was this monster doing in here… he has been warned about going anywhere near my sister," Geoffrey said, still gripping Archie's knife angrily.

"I no want be here," Drangoo whimpered, trying to stem the blood from his torn ear.

"You are not allowed anywhere near her!" Geoffrey yelled in pent-up fury, as the priest grabbed his wrist to stay his hand.

"Leave this to me, Geoffrey. You will only make matters worse." He grabbed Drangoo by the throat in a chokehold, thrusting him hard up against the wall. "Why are you in here, you monster, if you have been forbidden entry?"

"Bella Rosa make much crying and Drangoo come help, then she make loco!"

"Then explain why the base of your habit is hooked into your belt to expose that unsightly man-handle? This was no mistake, Drangoo, so do not take me for a fool by repeating that lie."

"I not know how it be, Father. Drangoo swear."

"Swear until kingdom come but I know better. This woman is not one of your whores. Come anywhere near her again and I will break your arm in three places. Now cover yourself up and get out of here before I do that regardless!" he snapped, cracking the monk a fearful backhanded blow across the face.

During this violent display towards Lorenzo's half-brother Geoffrey had looked away from Rosamund for barely a moment. The priest inadvertently took a pace towards her, at which she launched herself at him, her nails clawing at his face like a ferocious wildcat before Geoffrey could pull her away, kicking and screaming.

Contrary to everything Geoffrey had assumed about the priest's unfeeling character there were tears welling in those fearsome blue eyes and he felt sure this was not just from the pain she had inflicted, an assault to which he had offered no resistance but from his distress at the alteration of her appearance and her obvious mental instability.

When Geoffrey entered the kitchen later, once Rosamund was calm enough to be left on her own, the place had the appearance of a field hospital in a war zone, where Marguerite was administering first aid to both Drangoo and Fitzgerald.

"Why did you not try to protect yourself?" she asked, putting aside the needle and thread after stitching up a deep gouge on the priest's throat.

"I would not lay a hand on that troubled child. Lady Rosamund has been through enough."

"Then, as a man of God, you should be aware that I pray each night those men will burn in Hell for what they have done to her." Marguerite began to tend to Drangoo's torn and ragged ear.

"More than likely but Lorenzo has assured me their own torment began soon after they departed from there."

"How could he know that?"

"He sees things. That is how," Geoffrey interrupted.

"Lorenzo told you this?" the priest exclaimed with evident surprise.

"Not exactly… he showed me."

"I have no idea what you are talking about, Geoffrey," Marguerite said, breaking her concentration from stitching back the section of the monk's ear. "Perhaps you might continue this conversation outside. I cannot concentrate with all this distraction."

It was clear that the priest had no intention of letting Geoffrey go without a full explanation. As they reached the veranda he asked, "If Lorenzo allowed you to see what happened, where was this exactly?"

"Down at the lagoon, when he was re-awakening my body from the paralysis."

"Tell me… was this in or out of the water?

"Why do you ask? Is this about the submerged temple?"

"You know about this?"

"Lorenzo took me there," Geoffrey admitted but realised that this had been unwise when he saw the startled response.

"That would be impossible. Even if you avoided the underwater predators you could never have held your breath for long enough."

"Then how would I know of its existence, if I had not seen it? If you think me a liar, then why not quiz me on its design and construction?"

It was a bold challenge and one the priest accepted instantly, asking for specific details about the steps leading down to the temple and the creatures etched into the columns. Lastly, he asked about the intricate carving on the altar, all questions that Geoffrey had no trouble answering.

"What you tell me is incredible, Geoffrey," Fitzgerald reluctantly admitted. "That temple is a sacred place and known only to a few, otherwise I would not have doubted your word. So perhaps you could also explain to me how an Englishman, with no prior knowledge of the customs in this region, could have possibly known that the chosen ones amongst the river children must be delivered underwater above the temple of Orpantha?"

"Primarily it was at Lady Marguerite's request and secondly because this was the safest place in these waters for her to give birth," Geoffrey explained but he could tell the priest was still sceptical. "What you should also be aware of…" He hesitated for a moment. "… is that the Lady Marguerite and I both had an identical dream about her giving birth there."

To his surprise the priest took the revelation in his stride. "That would have been my Lorenzo's doing," he said, with the glimmer of a smile that altered his features so completely his face almost mirrored Lorenzo's own.

Once the cross-examination was over Geoffrey went directly back to Rosamund's cabin, where he stayed until the light was fading, making sure the room had been returned to a more habitable state. On his return to the kitchen, although there was no sign that a truce would ever form between Marguerite and the priest, they at least seemed to be tolerating each other's company.

"Where is Lorenzo?" Geoffrey asked.

"He is with Edwin, where he has been all afternoon," Marguerite replied.

"Where is that devilish monk?"

"Where he should be… down on his knees, praying for forgiveness from the Almighty," Fitzgerald said.

"Well he might get that approval from his God but not from mine. If he tries anything like that again with Lady Rosamund, I guarantee that evil swine will be dead before he can offer up another hypocritical prayer," said Geoffrey.

"I agree with those sentiments too," Marguerite said. "I had heard of immorality in the Church but until we were abandoned out here I never imagined that sort of thing could actually happen."

"Drangoo has always had a perverted sense of his bodily needs. It cannot be beaten out of him and God knows I have tried on numerous occasions. I assure you, I will endeavour to keep him under control."

"A womaniser like my father is hardly the best example for someone in need of moral guidance," Marguerite scoffed, as she sterilised the surgical implements in boiling water.

"You might regard me as immoral, madam but I can assure you that it was because of my undying affection for Lorenzo's mother that I broke my vow of celibacy to the Jesuit faith and married her to legitimise his birth."

"So you readily admit to being flawed in your devotion to Christ's teachings?"

"Nothing can distract me from God's work here, other than my physical needs."

"What a disgusting creature you are!" she observed, just as Lorenzo entered, allowing her to remove the wailing infant from his arms.

"With your provincial outlook and blinkered vision, madam, that might be how I appear. However, the fact remains that Lorenzo's birth was legitimate, which is not the case with your own child and that must be corrected immediately."

"What exactly do you mean by that?"

"I would have thought that obvious, to anyone else but you it seems. This child must be legitimised through the sanctity of marriage. Therefore you must marry my Lorenzo."

"I will do no such thing!" she protested hotly.

"Protest all you like and yet I say that you will."

"What if I refuse?" She held the baby defiantly against her.

"Then this child will be removed from you, by force if necessary."

"You cannot do that."

"I can, madam and I will. It is clear that you have no understanding of the dangers that face a child such as this. You are no longer in England where you have unlimited wealth and could protect him every hour of the day. Surely even you must have realised this place is Hell on earth. What you fail to understand is that this child will be at risk if you deny him legitimacy. Living here without it, you risk having him butchered because of his heritage and I will never allow that."

"I have a revolver and I can shoot more accurately than most men."

"... and when you pause to reload, what then? Lorenzo's mother was younger than the Lady Rosamund when she was taken from me and ceremoniously sacrificed because of her tribal heritage. Lorenzo survived through infancy only because he was with me that day and I could protect him. The same must apply to his son. Once the word of this birth has become common knowledge, his life will require constant protection."

"Why is there a need for Lorenzo and I to marry?"

"When my time at the mission is over, I will return to North America… with Lorenzo and with my grandson. Be under no illusions to the contrary, madam, I have no intention of this child being branded a bastard and this marriage will take place, like it or not."

"North America? Are you out of your mind?" Marguerite gasped in amazement.

"Not in the slightest. I still retain a large property in New England and substantial wealth. You may think this contradictory to my faith but I was not yet fully ordained before my banishment here. The child will want for nothing, I can assure you."

"You expect me to agree, not only to this outrageous suggestion of marriage but to emigrate with my child to the United States of America? If you think that, then you must be out of your mind. How could you imagine I would ever agree to such a proposal? I would never consider bringing up my child in that lawless country."

"If you want this child to survive, then yes, you either comply with my offer or I will take him by force. The choice is yours, madam!"

"Are you crackers? Listen to what he is saying, Maggs. You must think this through carefully before you reject his offer," Geoffrey reluctantly acknowledged. For her to snub the offer of marriage to a man like Lorenzo, albeit one made by his father, seemed preposterous when she had never been sought in marriage by anyone that he knew of. If she were so stubborn as to ban Lorenzo from her marital bed, then who else would she ever consider good enough? For a moment Archie Westbrook came into his head but he dismissed the thought.

"I would have thought you would understand my refusal, Geoffrey! This marriage is a ridiculous idea," she retorted.

"Then let me ask you this, madam," the priest insisted. "Do you propose spending the remainder of your life on this unforgiving continent, simply because of your own cloistered perspective?"

"Of course I do not. I have no intention of remaining in this awful place for a moment longer than is absolutely necessary and I certainly do not need the added complication of marriage when I return to England with Edwin!"

"Just how would you propose getting this child out of South America without any paperwork? He was not delivered in a hospital and there is no registration of his birth. All the authorities would have to go on is your word and without a passport or other legal document to prove that you are related – such as a certificate of marriage or of the child's baptism – this infant might easily be stolen. On top of which, the boy barely resembles you. I can assure you, madam, the word of any woman, English or not, carries very little weight in this part of the world."

"You should listen to him, Maggs. It does make sense."

"I would have more chance convincing the authorities at the British Consulate than producing a scrap of paper from some hypocritical priest... especially one with his own son born in wedlock! His so-called marriage document would be thrown out of any court in the land."

"Not necessarily, madam. Lorenzo is legally my son by the law of adoption. It was a practical way to prevent him from being taken from me by the Church or the authorities on our return. Although, in the eyes of God, Lorenzo is my son through marriage, the necessity of arranging this adoption has legitimised him, allowing me to pass on his ancestral name and estate."

"I have respectable contacts in Pernambuco who would help."

"Do you honestly imagine that your contacts there would accept a fallen woman back into their society? Once they know you have borne an illegitimate child there will be no help offered from that quarter, I can assure you. I have seen it many times before. It would be a degrading experience, madam, the impact of which might lessen over the years but will never be forgotten."

The weight of his argument had clearly given Marguerite pause to consider.

"If I agree to your proposition of marrying Lorenzo, what then?" she asked guardedly.

"Once the ceremony is over and the marriage contract has been signed, the child will be baptised. With that and a notification of his birth, I will set off immediately for Coyacuche, where I can arrange for the paperwork that you and the infant will need for any travel arrangements."

"It seems that you leave me no option other than to agree to your proposal," she said with resignation.

"All you have to do, madam, is to take a long look at my Lorenzo. I must say that this proposal would hardly constitute a prison sentence, for any sane woman!"

"Looks are not everything, Father! Surely love must count for something, even by your own warped standards."

"No but appearances help. You cannot honestly think I wanted my son to be anchored down by a woman of your age? A beauty you might be now, madam but that will soon fade in this climate and with it any physical attraction. One night of mutual passion hardly constitutes a basis for love, so in that at least you and I are proven equal."

"What are Lorenzo's sentiments regarding this proposal?"

"The boy will do what is right, madam. You have a son together and from what I have seen he cares about the child deeply. A woman in your position cannot ask for more than that, surely."

The wedding ceremony, such as it was, took place the following day in a forest clearing where gigantic trees arced gracefully above the couple. Lorenzo wore the same ill-fitting clothes he had first appeared in at the compound, whereas Marguerite was a breathtaking replica of their mother, wearing a long silk underslip that emphasised her now remarkably slender figure. In one hand she carried Lady Claudia's rosary and prayer book, in the other was a spray of pale flowers. From her earlobes dangled the glittering blue sapphires. Although Marguerite had wanted Rosamund there for the occasion it was considered too risky, so Geoffrey stayed close by on her veranda, holding the baby, where he had a clear view.

Once the ceremony was over, Geoffrey and Drangoo barely had time to witness the marriage certificate before Marguerite snatched it from them and waved it at the priest.

"This must be amended immediately, Father Fitzgerald. This date here is incorrect. Lorenzo and I are the same age," Marguerite huffed.

"No, madam, he is not. Drangoo was my first born, with a woman of Coyacuche. It is he who is twenty-seven. My Lorenzo may have the athletic attributes of a mature adult and the inherent wisdom of the ancients but he is much younger."

"Then how old is he?" she asked with unconcealed astonishment.

"My Lorenzo is twenty. He would have been nineteen when you took him into your bed, madam. Perhaps you would do well to dwell on that information from your somewhat compromised position on the moral high ground you tend to favour!"

The growing tension between Marguerite and Fitzgerald took an even worse turn at the child's the baptism. At the makeshift font, instead of baptising the infant Edwin, after their maternal grandfather, before either of them knew what was happening the priest christened him Zacharias Fitzgerald. Geoffrey was convinced that had the revolver been to hand his sister would have shot the man where he stood.

"How dare you go against my wishes? You vile insensitive creature!" Marguerite ranted, causing the baby to wail loudly, which in turn set Rosamund pacing about her cabin, hurling against the wall anything that was not fastened down.

Chapter Nine
Turmoil

The frenetic confrontation had given Geoffrey a headache and he was anxious to have some time to himself but he had barely got clear of the bungalow when Marguerite called after him.

"Where are you going, Geoffrey?"

"As far away from here as I possibly can. I am moving into the store cabin, away from this constant shouting."

"You must stay here, Geoffrey. Father Fitzgerald and Drangoo will be leaving at first light."

"They are both going?"

"The priest has decided they will reach Coyacuche much more quickly by river than by trekking overland."

"That does not make any sense. They will be battling the current most of the way."

"That is why they are both going, so there is no reason for you to leave." She was clearly distressed by the thought of him moving further away.

"Do you honestly think those two are the only reason I am going?"

"What else could it be if not for them?"

"Maybe because I have no intention of spending any more time than I need to in a bungalow with such thin walls."

"Why does that matter, Geoffrey? That store cabin will be so cramped for you. Surely you are better off here in your own room."

"If you think I fancy the prospect of being kept awake every night with the grunting and groaning on the other side of the wall, then you are drastically mistaken. I am moving up there with Bog Boy. Rose will be safe enough too, now that you have a husband to look out for you both. I will send a postcard if I get lonely," Geoffrey said peevishly.

"Very well… have it your way but if you intend staying up there, you must take things from the bungalow to make it more homely. Is there anything I can get for you?"

"Yes there is, since you ask. I would like Mother's photograph from the garden party."

"Why not take the drawing I did of her for your birthday I thought you loved it?"

"Of course I do but Rose fell in love with it too. I have framed it for her and hung it over her bed to help her sleep."

"Then you will have Mother's photograph, as soon as I can find it. Is there anything else? One of the easy chairs perhaps, or a small table; the one you work on up there is so rustic."

"It suits my requirements. What I would like is her miniature prayer book, with the ivory cover," Geoffrey said hesitantly.

"Why would you want that? It is so small you might easily lose it and that would be a shame; it has been in the family for generations."

"I will take good care of them both."

"Then I will get Lorenzo to bring them over for you."

"No need… I will collect them later," Geoffrey said, not wanting to face him.

"It would be no trouble, I assure you."

"Maybe not for him but it would be an inconvenience to me."

"Then be prepared to be inconvenienced, Geoffrey, whether you like it or not. Lorenzo has something to give you."

Barely an hour had gone by when Lorenzo appeared on the veranda, as silently as a ghost.

"You must show me how you do that," Geoffrey said icily, unnerved at first by his sudden appearance but then more so on realising how much he had grown during Lorenzo's long absence. It made him somehow comfortable to find that they were now the same height, even though his developing physique could never compete with Lorenzo's.

"I come bring these," Lorenzo said, handing over the photograph of Lady Claudia and her tiny prayer book and also offering him a misshapen package wrapped in a piece of beautiful cloth, tied with vine.

"What an extraordinary fabric this is. It looks almost Venetian." He fingered the fine gold thread, woven into an indigo design on the violet and crimson cloth. From the glazed look in Lorenzo's eyes it was clear he had no idea what Geoffrey was talking about. "Where is this from?"

"Mi madre… it Lorenzo mother, she wear in temple."

"Then you must have it back, if you have kept it all these years."

"No, this for Jeffy, other, it for Zack… Edwin," he swiftly corrected himself with a winning smile, to which there was no response other than for Geoffrey to unwrap the gift.

"What the hell are these?" Geoffrey asked in horror, staring at the two sets of articulated wooden fingers.

"Them for make music." Lorenzo reached over in an attempt to attach one set to his wrist but Geoffrey shook him off angrily.

"Keep your bloody hands off me, you perverted bastard. Are you going out of your way to make me feel more of a freak than I already am?"

"Jeffy, him no like?" Lorenzo asked with astonishment.

"LIKE THEM?" Geoffrey screamed, knocking them out of Lorenzo's hands. "I HATE the bloody things. Take my advice and leave here now, while you can, before I am tempted to run you through and make my sister a widow."

"Lorenzo, him no mean harm. He want give back música."

"Piss off, you insensitive bastard and take those bloody things with you," Geoffrey screamed, kicking the fingers across the floor towards him.

"These Lorenzo make for Jeffy," Lorenzo said defiantly, leaving them where they lay as he turned to leave.

"Then they can damned well stop there and get eaten by termites for all I damn well care!" Geoffrey called after him.

It was almost dark when Geoffrey calmed down and picked up the fingers from the floor to examine them and in the lamplight he could fully appreciate the amazing craftsmanship. Needless to say, as he began to acknowledge the amount of time and effort Lorenzo must have spent on them and the guilt of his own unreasonable behaviour, Geoffrey had a very unsettled night.

On the following morning Geoffrey put the two sets of fingers into one of the secret drawers of his father's bible box. In the other, he placed his mother's photograph from the garden party with the prayer book. Finally, he pinned Archie's portrait over his bed before he set off with the hound but in the opposite direction from the compound.

When he eventually returned and made his way down only Marguerite was there, hanging out laundry.

"Have they gone?" he asked.

"If you had been here, instead of retreating into the store cabin in a tantrum, you would have known that Father

Fitzgerald and Drangoo set off first thing this morning. Apparently the rains are already overdue. If they begin while they are away it could take more than a month before they get back. If the rain holds off, they could return here in less than two weeks."

"Did Lorenzo go with them?" Geoffrey asked, praying he had, since he felt that only time would heal the rift between them.

"Lorenzo insisted on staying. If you are looking for him, he will not be back for some time. He is with Edwin at the lagoon."

"He will not want to speak with me anyway. We had a row last night. I came down to apologise."

"Arguing seems to be second nature to you these days, Geoffrey. I realise that you are no longer the same boy who came out here and have developed rapidly into a young man but even so, would it be impossible for you to be a little more tolerant?"

"Could you honestly expect anyone in their right mind to be comforted by those grotesque things Lorenzo brought over for me? I am fully aware I will never be whole again but I am trying my very best to adapt."

"I have no idea what you are talking about, Geoffrey."

"Those wooden fingers! Surely he must have shown them to you, or at least have mentioned them to you."

"No, he did not. What did you say they were?"

"They are attachments to replace these missing fingers of mine. Now do you understand why I got so angry? If he was not so bloody perfect, I would probably not be so aware of what I am lacking."

"Lorenzo is a magnificent specimen but he does not have the same talent for music that you have, Geoffrey."

"Did have, you mean."

"You have an extraordinary gift for composition. Once we are away from here, the gift you have been blessed with will return, perhaps more powerfully than before. No one could be the same after the experiences you have endured; they have changed all of our lives forever and even Lorenzo is not perfect."

"You are only trying to make me feel better. Of course he is perfect. Even I can see that and I am not the artist you are."

"Well for one thing he eats with his fingers and his skin is rather coarse. Have you not noticed the webbing between his fingers?"

Geoffrey made no reply, not wanting to embarrass either of them by acknowledging that he was aware of almost everything about Lorenzo. Treading carefully as he moved away, he almost tripped over a rush mat and a wooden-block pillow, close to where he had once slept on the veranda. "Why did you allow Drangoo to sleep out here? It is too close to Rose's cabin."

"That is where Lorenzo has chosen to sleep. He cannot rest properly in any bed," she said awkwardly.

"When will he be back?"

"I cannot be sure. Why not go over there and make your peace? It would help if we can avoid more unpleasant atmospheres now that the priest and Drangoo have gone. Edwin gets noticeably restless whenever people are angry."

"If you think it will help," Geoffrey said. On reflection, if Lorenzo was staying he was keen to get any unpleasantness over with as soon as possible.

As expected, he found Lorenzo in the lagoon with the infant, squealing with delight and bobbing up and down from under the water like a playful dolphin.

"See, him much happy in water!" Lorenzo greeted him, carrying the struggling child to the bank.

"Then why is he so unhappy now?" Geoffrey asked as Lorenzo sat beside him, comforting the child.

"Lorenzo no want him stay in water," he said.

Geoffrey examined the tattoo-like birthmark between the child's shoulder blades.

"Do you have this same mark, Lorenzo? It is amazing," Geoffrey asked, wondering if, as with Archie, the distinguishing mark had been handed down from the father.

"Lorenzo, him no have. Zack him much importante." He pulled the wet hair away from the base of his own neck to show there was no mark there.

"This does not make any sense. Why would Archie Westbrook, a dear friend of ours, have an identical mark, while you do not? You are Edwin's father, not him!" Geoffrey said, staring into his dark, hypnotic eyes as they spoke.

"Who this Archie? Why him have same royal brand like Zack?"

"He is an Irishman; we met in Pernambuco when we first arrived in South America. Apart from that I have absolutely no idea why he would bear the same mark as your son."

"This same man you have in drawing, Jeffy?" Lorenzo asked.

"Yes, the same man."

"Where your Archie now?"

"Presumably he is somewhere in Southern Ireland, at least until his father recovers."

"This Archie, him, he come here?"

"That is hard to say, although I suspect he would, if he knew what has happened to us. He was very taken with Rose when we arrived here and I think she was pretty keen on him."

"And him like Jeffy too?"

"I doubt that very much. We parted on bad terms, rather like you and I did last night. I would be surprised if he has given me a second thought since we left."

"Lorenzo would much like meet this man you like, Jeffy, see mark for myself."

"I did not say that I liked him," Geoffrey protested.

"Jeffy no need. Archie watch over him sleep," Lorenzo said with the knowing smile that Geoffrey found so irritating.

"You do talk a load of bollocks!" he snapped.

"Why Lorenzo make sad?" Lorenzo asked, placing the infant on the ground.

"I am not sad. Not in the least," Geoffrey protested but he knew any denial would be useless if Lorenzo pressed his damp fingers against his temples and he felt the crackling energy begin inside his head.

"Why Jeffy much sad with what Lorenzo, him make?"

"Those articulated fingers were a remarkable gift, Lorenzo, truly and I should have been more appreciative of the workmanship when you gave them to me. I was a fool for being so bloody rude last night and for that I sincerely apologise."

"No, it be Lorenzo idiota, him think they easy for wear."

"I promise I will try them on when I am ready but I cannot do that yet. I need more time to accept what I have become… that I am no longer whole."

"Why Jeffy want live far away from Lorenzo?" he asked as they made their way back to the compound.

"Why does everything need to revolve around you, Lorenzo? I'm staying up there because I prefer to be where it's quiet and I can write down music and for no other reason," Geoffrey lied. The thought set him wondering if he should perhaps begin work on another composition as made his way up the rickety staircase to the store cabin.

"Then I much happy for Jeffy" Lorenzo said, looking after him curiously.

During the two weeks after the priest's departure the humidity became almost unbearable. Ominous dark storm clouds lingered overhead for days on end and jagged bolts of lightning illuminated the entire compound, with horrendous crashes of thunder that seemed to pre-empt the end of the world but not a single drop of rain fell.

"This cannot be normal," Geoffrey announced to his sister after another sleepless night.

"Who knows what the weather should be like here, Geoffrey? Edwin does not appear to be in the least affected by this humidity and these mock storms, nor Lorenzo." Marguerite busied herself changing the infant's makeshift nappy.

"How come I am not surprised by that, when Lorenzo struts around wearing nothing more than a belt? It is not a decent way to behave."

"Come now, Geoffrey, none of us are dressed appropriately. Look at yourself in the mirror if you doubt me."

"Very well... I only worry how Rose might react. She is used to seeing me without a shirt but that is allowed. I am her brother."

"Lorenzo would never disrespect Rosamund by not being fully dressed. He cares about her; even you must see that."

"Of course I do but what if this awful humidity pitches Rose over the edge and she races over here brandishing a knife, what then?"

"The weather must break soon and then everything will get back to normal."

"How can you stay so logical?"

"We must trust in what Father Fitzgerald said about the rainy season. There is nothing anyone can do that will alter the weather pattern. It has to rain eventually."

"With that the rivers will swell to bursting and that will bring more caiman closer to the compound and all the debris along with it, just like last time."

"Unlike then, we have Lorenzo with us. Surely you must feel safer with him here?"

"We did manage before."

"Then we did not have Edwin."

"When the priest returns I cannot imagine he will allow you to get your own way with that name, not if he was christened Zacharias instead of Edwin."

"I am confident Lorenzo will support my choice in this. He is Edwin's father."

"And Fitzgerald is his. You have seen how he dominates him."

"Edwin is my child and whatever that priest wrote on those documents, that is my son's name!" she shouted, before her voice was lost in the violence of thunder crashing immediately overhead.

After a troubled night's sleep in the sweltering humidity, Geoffrey awoke with his head filled with disturbingly erotic images of himself and Lorenzo by the lagoon, uncertain what had actually happened between them, what was a blurred memory of the past and what might be romanticised fiction. He felt even more tired than he had on the evening before.

The air was heavy and oppressive when he descended the stairway just before dawn and staggered, bleary-eyed, into the shower, in the vain hope of cleansing his troubled thoughts away. The tepid water seemed darker in colour than he remembered, although in the early morning light it was hard to be sure.

For a second or two Geoffrey had no idea what was happening, as the coils of a green boa constrictor wrapped themselves around his chest. As the squeezing began he realised too late his stupidity in not lighting the oil lamp to make an inspection of the area before he entered. Because of the pressure it was impossible to shout for the hound or reach Archie's hunting knife, lying with his crumpled trousers on a stool near the door.

In his blind panic Geoffrey was unaware of anyone entering the ramshackle building until the serpent's grip suddenly went slack and the dismembered head hit the floor, spurting blood up his legs. Dazed and barely able to breathe Geoffrey stumbled outside and collapsed onto the soft carpet of leaf mould.

"Why Jeffy no make light?" Lorenzo asked, leaning over him with concern.

"I was tired and like a fool I never thought," Geoffrey gasped.

"Why no sleep?" Lorenzo asked, attentively examining the angry red pressure marks on his scarred torso.

"Nothing that would concern you," Geoffrey lied, unwilling to admit even to himself how vivid the dreams had been, particularly as the source of his confusion was now leaning over him.

"Why Jeffy make lie?"

"I did no such thing!" Geoffrey protested angrily, struggling to sit up.

"You say bad sleep it not you and Lorenzo?" he said, staring intently and holding a gaze from which Geoffrey was unable to look away.

"Not exactly that," Geoffrey said as the familiar buzzing began in his head.

"Why Lorenzo make fear?"

"Because… because of the thoughts I have been having. Stop messing with my head, you bloody freak!" Geoffrey shouted.

"You no want me do this?" Lorenzo asked.

"For pity's sake, leave me alone. I cannot think clearly with you staring like that and stop cramming these… these illicit thoughts into my head. Unlike you, I am only human!"

"Lorenzo go swim… you come, make feel better?" Lorenzo said, gesturing towards the lagoon.

"I am not sure that I should… well, maybe," Geoffrey said reluctantly, knowing that his young life would never be the same if he accepted.

After keeping out of the way for almost two days and desperately in need of a shower, Geoffrey reluctantly came down from the store cabin as the light was fading, praying that he would not meet Lorenzo. He had almost made it when he was confronted by Marguerite.

"Geoffrey, where on earth have you been? I have been worried sick about you."

"There was no need… I, I have been working on a new composition," Geoffrey lied.

"This is wonderful news, Geoffrey but why would that prevent you from eating?"

"I just got carried away. Time flies by without you knowing."

"If you had not appeared by this afternoon, I would have come up there to get you. Father Fitzgerald and Drangoo will be arriving soon and I need your support."

"You have Lorenzo. He is your husband."

"A husband who will not even share my bed; instead he chooses to sleep alone on the veranda. Sometimes I wonder if he ever felt anything for me at all."

"He must have. You have a child together and you are beautiful, like Mother."

"Then why would he only offer me tenderness a year ago when I was in need of comfort before our marriage but not now, if I have changed for the better?"

"That would be a question for Lorenzo and certainly not for me."

"These past few days he will barely look at me, let alone speak."

"Well that is nothing new. His grasp of English was never that good at the best of times." Geoffrey was relieved that for once the downside of this exchange did not come from him.

"I am being serious, Geoffrey. Did you and Lorenzo have a falling out? Because that is how it seems, with you moving up there to the store cabin when you could be down here in the main bungalow."

"It would make it impossible to compose if I did. I am staying put for the time being at least; although I am hungry," he said, which thankfully ended the inquisition.

Not wanting the embarrassment of being around when Lorenzo returned, Geoffrey agreed to get more supplies from the cave in readiness for the arrival of the priest and Drangoo but first he really needed to wash.

"Maybe you should wait until Lorenzo returns and then he can help."

"There is no need. I will go once I have showered."

"You cannot use that place again, Geoffrey. You must wash in the stream from now on. The water coming out of the shower is almost pure mud and it seems the water supply feeding it has dried up."

"That never happened before."

"Well I can assure you it has now. If you shower under that, you will be dirtier when you come out than before you went inside."

Returning to the storeroom, Geoffrey prised open the lid on the first of the crates he had recovered from the trading post, only immediately to be attacked by a colony of angry ants. Slamming the lid shut, he was stung twice before he could nail it down tight.

Depressingly, he soon found that the second and third crates had clearly been broken into and resealed while at the trading post, leaving only a few empty tins rattling around inside. In the fourth and final crate there was one tin of dried milk, six rusted cans of bully beef and seven of baked beans. Apart from these unopened items it was clear that nothing was edible. With the rainy season imminent the situation was desperate situation, as they would soon be marooned in the compound for the next couple of months. With growing despair he concluded that, realistically, the only way to get any food to see them through that period would require him to return to the trading post.

With despair he remembered the struggle it had taken to bring these partially empty crates back to the compound and the prospect of returning to negotiate with the devious Misqualla was a nightmarish thought but there was no alternative and the situation had to be addressed as soon as possible.

He reported the bad news to his elder sister.

"When Father Fitzgerald returns, I will ask him to remain here while you and Lorenzo take the dugout to the trading post for supplies," she suggested.

"I can manage perfectly well on my own," Geoffrey said, still determined not to spend any more time in Lorenzo's company than was absolutely necessary.

"That makes no sense at all, Geoffrey."

"It would if I set off right now with the Otter," Geoffrey shouted above the rumbling thunder. "Once this lot is unleashed, the river will be impossible to navigate."

"Precisely and that is why you need a man with you, not a child."

"So what you are proposing is that I have to sit it out until that objectionable priest returns? It has been almost two weeks since Fitzgerald left here. God only knows when he will return. It could be months before we see him again."

"He will return soon with the documents; if not for our sake, he will do it for Lorenzo and Edwin's safety. Father Fitzgerald is a father and grandparent, who I sense would do anything to protect his own, as would I, as a mother."

"You make it sound as if the end of the world is nigh, not just an impending rainy season," Geoffrey said.

"Normally I would not worry but there is something about the way Lorenzo spends every waking hour with Edwin, as if every moment with him could be the last," Marguerite said. It was an observation that made Geoffrey more anxious than ever to set off.

It was barely light when Fitzgerald and Drangoo returned to the compound on foot. The priest was bleeding badly from gouges along his right arm and the stub of a broken spear protruded from his left shoulder. Drangoo followed closely behind, a satchel slung across his shoulder containing the precious travel documents.

"What happened?" Marguerite asked as she carefully removed the broken spear, dressing the wound as efficiently as a practised surgeon. It was clear the priest was suffering badly but throughout the process he showed barely any reaction to the pain.

"Headhunters, further north from here," he said through gritted teeth. "I can assure you the group will not be bothering anyone else but I strongly suggest that you keep your revolver loaded in readiness for any others who might appear."

"Do you think this spearhead might have been poisoned?" Marguerite asked as she examined the wound.

"Had it been, I would not be with you now, madam and the labours of my excursion to Coyacuche would have been all for nothing." He rested a scarred hand on the battered document bag on the table.

"So do you have all the documents you require?" Geoffrey asked, hoping his own passport was still in his father's bureau where he had left it.

"Everything is in order for Zacharias to enter the United States legitimately."

"Then I should have them for safe keeping," Marguerite said, preparing to cauterise the wound. The stench of burnt flesh sent chills along Geoffrey's spine, recalling the nauseating smell that had penetrated his barely conscious state as his fingers were being removed. Yet still the priest did not flinch.

"What you ask would not be in the child's best interests. There are no duplicates."

"Then what better person to leave them with than his mother; unless you do not trust me?" She thrust the glowing iron rod, steaming, into a bucket of water.

"I trust no one, madam, other than Lorenzo."

"Then why object, since Lorenzo will be remaining here with me?"

"I do so because Lorenzo has been distracted of late." He began tapping his temple feverishly. "There have been no clear messages sent through about the child during my absence, only troubling thoughts about turbulent floodwater. You can trust me on this issue, madam. These documents will be safer kept at the mission, rather than here."

"Then, as you have already suggested, Father, we should come with you."

"That would not be safe, not with the rains imminent. Now the river level has dropped so low we must travel overland and the journey will take more than two weeks on foot. It would not be safe for an infant with so many predators and headhunters about."

"Are you suggesting we should remain here until after the season is over?"

"No I am not, madam. Lorenzo will bring you and the child to the mission by canoe once the main deluge is over and the river has returned to a normal level. I will leave Drangoo behind to help out until then."

"I am damned if I will allow that to happen. You and I both know the Lady Rosamund would be at risk if you leave that revolting pervert here," Geoffrey challenged.

"It is a risk I grant you but Drangoo is strong and you will need his assistance in the canoe to collect supplies from the trading post. The water level is extremely low in sections and the canoe will need to be hauled into deeper water."

"Lorenzo will accompany Geoffrey in the dugout, so there is no need for Drangoo to remain here," Marguerite insisted.

"You should reconsider, madam, before dismissing this proposal. The Lady Rosamund can be violent. How could a lone woman protect this infant with Lorenzo gone?"

"A perfect reason why that monk should not remain here."

"Not if Lorenzo remains here with you and his son. The child presents no fear to the Lady Rosamund and he must be protected at all costs. He may not bear the royal mark but my Lorenzo is fearless and he would protect his son to the death if any headhunters happened upon you, a probability that should not be ruled out."

There was nothing Geoffrey or his sister could say that would change his mind, especially as they realised in the end that his arguments made sense.

The following morning, Geoffrey and his sister were left alone to talk over the proposed plan while the priest prayed with Drangoo in a lean-to at the rear of the compound.

"Do you understand what he was saying about the messages Lorenzo was sending?" Geoffrey asked, although his own experiences gave him an inkling.

"You should not be concerned about everything he says. Father Fitzgerald is an old man and you saw the state of him when he arrived. I am surprised anyone of his age could have survived such an attack. His mind must have been playing tricks. Either that or he simply dreamt there was some form of telepathic communication."

"Maybe, although I would not be too sure about that," Geoffrey retorted, surprised that she would question Lorenzo's extraordinary powers, particularly after they had shared the same dream about the birth.

"Reading someone's mind is impossible, Geoffrey. Trickery of that nature might be acceptable at the Theatre Royal in Derby but not here in this wilderness. It is sensationalism for entertainment value and nothing more."

"That is a load of tripe and you know it. We have both seen and experienced things here that neither of us can truly explain."

"I refuse to argue about this, Geoffrey. You have an overactive imagination, probably due to all of those *Boy's Own Papers* you read so obsessively."

"Very well… then perhaps you can explain what he was saying about the royal mark of Orpantha?"

"I admit Edwin has an unusual birthmark but I will not allow that awful man to see it. He is planning something and I do not trust him. The sooner we can get Edwin back home to England the better."

188

"Agreed but even you must admit that birthmark is a bit more than unusual. What bothers me is that is it identical to the one Archie has."

"You cannot in all honesty believe the mark Archie Westbrook has is identical to my Edwin's?"

"If I am right, then it opens up a fearful can of worms."

"Meaning what exactly?" she demanded.

"Archie said the mark was hereditary and could only be passed down through the male line of the Westbrook family," Geoffrey said.

"Then since Lorenzo and Archie Westbrook are not remotely connected, that proves those marks are entirely a coincidence."

"Maybe not, if what the priest hinted at when we first met was true." If those suspicions did prove correct, it would most certainly provide a reason why the unlikely marriage between his parents had ever taken place.

When the priest mounted the temperamental mule later that morning, the snorting animal was once more brought instantly under control the moment he was seated on its back and Geoffrey reluctantly had to admire Harvey Fitzgerald's grim determination to overcome every obstacle that stood in his way. Seeing his agility in mounting the mule bareback, without any aid, he truly had no idea how old Lorenzo's father actually was.

"Drangoo may not be the best marksman but he can shoot adequately if necessary," the priest called down from the mule. "Therefore I am leaving my Winchester rifle with him as a precautionary measure but only for your journey upriver."

"I know we have already discussed this but Lorenzo would be a much more suitable travelling companion for my brother," Marguerite said.

"Please do as I ask, madam and allow my Lorenzo to remain here with you and the child while Geoffrey and Drangoo get the supplies from the trading post; that is if you value Zack's safety."

"What are you implying?" Marguerite said.

"I would have thought it clear enough, madam. Admittedly Lorenzo has known every section of these treacherous waters from birth but then so does Drangoo. We are all aware provisions need to be negotiated for as soon as possible and there is no one better suited for such negotiations than Drangoo. They must set off tomorrow at daybreak. Once the rainfall begins, it will be almost impossible to reach the trading post against the force of the current."

"Oh, very well... have it your way if you must!" Marguerite retorted, then paused as before returning into the bungalow. "Why is Lorenzo not here to help resolve this?" she hissed at Geoffrey as she passed.

"Have you any idea where Lorenzo is?" Geoffrey asked the priest. As he spoke he felt his eyes lose focus and gripped tightly onto the handrail as a familiar but still unsettling sizzling sensation entered his head.

"You will find him at the lagoon but take heed of the warning offered by a parent. I know the type of man you are, even if perhaps you do not but rest assured, the force of this whip will shred every inch of flesh from your back if you try to engage my son in anything unnatural."

"What the hell do you mean?"

"If you need it spelled out, it is apparent that you have strong carnal desires towards the male species in preference to women."

"Go to Hell, you geriatric old fart! The sun must have addled that twisted old brain of yours to accuse me of something like that!" Geoffrey silently dreaded that his sister might have overheard the accusation.

"Protest all you want, Geoffrey but understand that you have been warned. If on my return I discover that you have prevented my Lorenzo from fulfilling his chosen destiny of immortality, I will take great pleasure in breaking every bone in your body and feeding it to the piranha, piece by unnatural piece."

"You profess to be a man of God and yet could suggest such a thing about me, you evil bastard!" Geoffrey raged.

"You may see me only as a priest but what you fail to understand is that I am but one link in a chain of survival for these mighty forests. Your carnal awakenings cannot and will not be allowed to interfere with the predicted coming of Orpantha." The older man leant down from the mule threateningly, a well-honed bowie knife clasped tightly in his hand.

"What man of God would willingly kill an unarmed man?" Geoffrey retorted sick to the stomach about what he'd been accused.

"One who would do it willingly, if you interfere with the vision Lorenzo's mother received at his birth," the priest hissed. "A dormant gene of Orpantha will soon be reborn through Lorenzo and thereby fulfill an ancient prophecy in his son."

"Which he already has, with Edwin," Geoffrey challenged.

"A healthy son, yes he has but one who was born without the royal mark and not conceived with the Lady Rosamund."

"Rose! You expect my sister to have Lorenzo's child after what she has already been subjected to?"

"That is how it was foretold and how it will come to pass."

"Whatever outrageous ideas you come up with, I swear to you now, if Lorenzo goes anywhere near my sister I will kill him myself before he can lay a hand on her and that goes for any renegade priest too!" Geoffrey raged.

"Harm one hair on Lorenzo's head, you piss-elegant little shit and you will be dead before you hit the ground," the priest snarled back, savagely reining in the rearing mule before urging it into a gallop. "You would do well to take heed of that warning, Geoffrey," he called over his shoulder. "I will be back again!"

"And I will be waiting here when you do… with a spear aimed at your lying throat!" Geoffrey yelled after the black, billowing robes as they became enveloped in a cloud of dust.

After the sound of pounding hooves had died away, it was a while before Geoffrey could think clearly. All too soon Marguerite appeared on the veranda.

"Has that despicable creature gone at last?"

"Yes, he has."

"What were you arguing about? I could hear you yelling from way back in the kitchen."

"It was nothing much. You know what he is like… Fitzgerald has got annoyance down to a fine art."

"There must have been something that triggered such a volatile response, Geoffrey?"

"It was about Lorenzo, something about him needing to fulfill his destiny and conceive another child."

"How dare that man intimate such an outrageous thing to anyone? My body is not a factory," Marguerite said hotly, looking into the compound inquiringly. "Where is Lorenzo? He should have returned with Edwin before now. It is time for his feed."

"The priest said he was at the lagoon. I can go there if you wish."

"Yes I do; but before I forget, do you still have any of that fish glue you used on the crib?"

"There is some left in the store cabin, why?"

"The spine on my journal is coming apart in this humidity. I am concerned some of the pages will fall out. Would you take it up there before you go? It is on the grand piano."

"I thought you needed Edwin back?"

"Of course I do. I just want to make sure it is safe and out of harm's way. Drangoo has a nasty habit of interfering with everything and I do not want those grubby hands fingering through my illustrations. They must all be kept in pristine condition if Violet Dobson is going to get them into print."

"Then I will take them up to the cabin now. Have you still got Don Julio's satchel handy?"

"I hid it on top of the bookcase. It is too high up there for Drangoo to reach." She followed him into the living area where, after reaching it down, he placed the journal carefully inside.

As expected, he found Lorenzo at the edge of the water where the baby was once more splashing about happily.

"Marguerite would like you to bring Edwin back for his feed," Geoffrey said, keeping his distance.

"Lorenzo, him no go, Zack he much happy here swim."

"I can see that but you should take him back now. There was an argument with your father before he left and she is not in a good frame of mind at the moment."

"Lorenzo come, if Jeffy, him swim?"

"Very well," Geoffrey reluctantly agreed, "but only if you agree to come back directly, otherwise my sister will be sending out a search party." As he stripped off the prospect of a swim grew more appealing and he waded out into the lagoon but swam around for a shorter time than he would have normally, before returning to the bank with Lorenzo and the infant.

"Lorenzo much sorry, Papa him say much bad." He looked troubled.

"You know about that?" Geoffrey asked but seeing the intensity of Lorenzo's eyes he remembered the sizzling impulses inside his head and understood.

"Much bad soon happen Jeffy, when it time for Lorenzo to go."

"What bad things? You cannot leave, Lorenzo, we need you here."

"It no me. Lorenzo him much want stay."

"Then do that. Tell that insane priest he can go to hell!" Geoffrey ranted but at Lorenzo's distressed expression and with tears welling up in his eyes, he instinctively leaned over and embraced him.

"It no possible Lorenzo him stay."

They stood locked in the embrace at the edge of the lagoon, Lorenzo confessing his darkest fears and the intensity of his premonitions of death and the afterlife. Neither of them

194

was aware of a figure in the bushes until the hound gave a warning growl.

"Someone was watching," Geoffrey declared nervously, breaking away to put his clothes on. "We need to make a start and head back. You should get dressed too, Lorenzo. My sister will create like hell if you turn up naked."

Geoffrey kept Archie's hunting knife unsheathed in readiness as the hound charged ahead of them through the bushes. When the high-pitched sound of a man's scream sounded close to the compound they both set off at a run. By the time Geoffrey arrived in the clearing, Lorenzo was already there, holding the infant under one arm and restraining the dog with the other, to prevent it from reaching Drangoo on the veranda where an ill-tempered Marguerite was tending his injuries.

"This animal is dangerous, Geoffrey. Are you waiting for someone to get killed before you take notice?" Marguerite handed the monk some iodine to put on a savage bite to his calf.

"Bog Boy would not attack anyone without good reason," Geoffrey said defensively. Cradling the infant, Lorenzo went inside the bungalow without saying a word.

"This poor man did not stand a chance when that creature charged after him into the clearing. I saw everything from here."

"He was being protective."

"Protective of what exactly when you were nowhere in sight? Can you honestly equate savaging a man's leg with being protective?"

"Yes I can, otherwise Bog would have torn out the damned monk's throat. What I do not understand is what that pervert was doing there anyway?"

"Drangoo was simply returning from an errand. I asked him to remind you to bring Edwin back here, which is what I asked you to do earlier!" she snapped, handing the monk a roll of bandage and a safety pin.

"If you sent him to get us, then how come I never saw him?" Geoffrey said, wondering just how long he had been spying on them in the bushes.

"No doubt you and Lorenzo were too occupied with each other to see anyone else."

"What are you suggesting?"

"I am suggesting nothing, Geoffrey, just stating the fact that Drangoo returned here with some rather disturbing information about you and my husband."

"So he *was* spying?" Geoffrey raged, fearing what interpretation of the scene the monk might have returned with.

"Not in the least; he was merely presenting the facts as he saw them," Marguerite retorted, her cheeks flushed with anger, her mouth grim.

"Then you had better spit out whatever it was, because it seems you are bursting to tell me."

"Well, since you ask, can you deny that Drangoo saw you and Lorenzo both naked, locked in an embrace… well, can you?"

"I have no reason to deny that, why should I? We embraced and nothing more. Whatever that pervert was implying, I assure you nothing happened. I would swear it on Bog's life! The reason that we were not dressed was because we had been swimming. It was simply an expression of reassurance, nothing more!"

"Then why do you look so guilty, Geoffrey? Perhaps you could also explain to me why you would need to embrace Lorenzo in the first place?"

"Physical contact was just my way of comforting him. Lorenzo is not the superhuman we have always assumed; he has feelings too and he is deeply troubled about the outcome of the imminent rainfall." Geoffrey paused, unwilling to burden her with the darker elements of what Lorenzo had confided in him.

"What could trouble someone who was born out here? Lorenzo must be used to the changing seasons, the way we are to ours at home. That cannot be the reason for what Drangoo saw. There must be another reason," she scoffed.

"Well, since you ask, Lorenzo has got it into his head… that he has seen his own death."

"That is impossible."

"Lorenzo has visions, as you well know and I am convinced he meant every word."

"Whatever the cause, that does not explain what happened between you. Gentlemen do not embrace each other… particularly when undressed."

"I have already told you. That was only because we had been swimming together when he confided in me."

"Can you swear that is all it was?"

"How many times do you want me to go through this? It was an expression of comfort, nothing more. Nothing would have happened, not this time, Edwin was there," Geoffrey said.

He realised his mistake immediately.

"This time…? Then I was right, something has been going on between you. I knew it! Do not bother to deny it, Geoffrey, it is written all over your wicked face. You never were a good liar. The last thing I would have expected of you is to become like Father, except your perversion is with Lorenzo and if anything that makes it even worse. I am ashamed to call you my brother!" she screamed, clenching her fists as though she was about to strike him.

"I do not love him," Geoffrey said, uncertain of how to stop the tirade of abuse that he knew would follow.

"This is not about experimenting with a boy of your own age from the village."

"Maybe not... but he is barely a year older than I, if what Fitzgerald said was correct!"

"Regardless of that, Lorenzo is a father, with responsibilities... He is my HUSBAND, damn it!"

"I did not intend for anything to happen and neither did he. It just did."

"How long has this... this disgusting episode been going on?"

"It only happened once... I think, maybe twice."

"You only think! What you have done is abhorrent. You are disgusting, Geoffrey. Thank God Mother is not alive to hear this. You should be ashamed even admitting it."

"Well I am not. Take a good look at me and the claws you have left me with. Who in their right mind would entertain the idea of being intimate with someone who looks like this, except for Lorenzo? He saw the real person beneath this disfigured body and he comforted me when I needed it most."

"Do not take me for a fool, Geoffrey. Something that intimate does not just happen by chance."

"Then how was it for you on the night Edwin was conceived?" Geoffrey taunted.

"What we did was the natural course of events. What you have done is not only unnatural, it is also against the law. You could be imprisoned!"

"The only law out here is one of survival and if my immense gratitude for the long hours of care Lorenzo spent in restoring this wrecked body of mine is not worthy of my affection, then I do not know what is. I will not deny I have feelings for Lorenzo but whatever they are it was never love, just a strong attraction and, believe it or not, the thought of betraying you, of all people, in that way disgusts me too but then I am the one who has to live with it."

"I hope you burn in hell for this, Geoffrey!" She stormed off inside and would no doubt have slammed the door behind her, had it not been just a bead curtain that snagged her hair on the way through, which made her even angrier, if that were possible.

Chapter Ten
Disaster

The preparations for the trip to the trading post were swift and decisive, if also somewhat volatile as a result of his sister's adamant refusal to allow Geoffrey to even speak with Lorenzo. Her husband's reaction, however, was just the opposite, weathering the blistering storm of accusations by responding with either shrugs or a shake of the head. When he did speak, it was only to insist that Geoffrey took the wolfhound with him for protection.

"When you have decided what is happening, we will be waiting in the dugout," Geoffrey muttered, making his way to the staging with the dog close at heel.

Marguerite finally appeared, her attire more like a grizzled hiker than anything remotely resembling a woman of breeding. Particularly notable was the shortened length of her dress and a pair of their father's scuffed, calf-length boots but more intimidating than either was the grim set of her mouth, her cheeks red with anger.

"Is everything loaded?" she demanded.

"There is enough tarpaulin to make a shelter, if that is what you are asking. Where is that idiot Drangoo? It will be dark soon."

"Drangoo is not coming," she snapped, getting into the canoe unsteadily. "I will be going with you instead."

"You...? That makes no sense at all."

"Drangoo is not coming with you because he is terrified this animal of yours will attack him again."

"Have you given any thought to Edwin? Surely he needs you here with him."

"It is time Lorenzo faced up to his responsibilities and finally realise what it means to be a full-time parent," Marguerite said bitterly.

"What about Rose? You know damned well she will not be safe with that monk roaming around."

"For the time being your lover will be moving into her cabin with Edwin. You can sort out your alternative sleeping arrangements when we return!" she barked, taking up the paddle.

"For pity's sake… I am sorry, Maggs. It was an error of judgement on both our parts and you have certainly made your point but for now, if you won't change your mind, we must concentrate on the journey ahead, so will you please let the whole unsavoury business drop."

"Are you going to cast off?" she responded icily and barely spoke for the remainder of the day.

If Geoffrey had hoped for a thaw in her attitude towards him over the following days, he might as well have been alone in the canoe for all the conversation they exchanged. They paddled in this fashion for more than three days, with Marguerite barely speaking, even at mealtimes, until on the morning of the fourth day Geoffrey awoke from a disturbing sleep in a panic and immediately confronted her with his fears.

"We have to go back immediately, Maggs. I had this awful vision last night."

"Do not be ridiculous. We must be over halfway by now. Even you must appreciate those provisions are essential for our survival."

"I do not give a fig about that… we must go back now, before something dreadful happens at the compound," Geoffrey said in desperation.

"Presumably this concerns Lorenzo?"

"Partially, yes but only through the images of destruction he transferred to me."

"Do you take me for an even bigger fool than you already have? Images cannot be 'transferred'."

"If you had seen what I did, you would not question my motives."

"Your motives will always be questionable after what you have done," she snapped, turning her back on him.

"How many times do I have to admit that what we did was wrong but for Pete's sake do not allow what happened in the past to cloud your judgement. Just hear me out."

"Is that not what I have been doing for days, listening to your feeble protestations?"

"This is not about anything like that."

"Then what is this about exactly?"

"This warning vision was urging me to return immediately. I have seen the terrible things will happen to everyone in the compound if we do not return in time."

"What you had was just a nightmare… like the grotesque images you and Lorenzo have forced into my own dreams. You always suffered from nightmares as a child and this is just another one of those episodes."

"This was no dream, I swear. It was a telepathic communication. These images were sent as a warning from Lorenzo."

"Do you think for a second that I am remotely interested in hearing you mentioning his name all the time? I am sick of it, do you hear me? I do not want to hear anything you have to say about that pervert I was forced to marry."

"You would not say that if you had seen these images: torrential rain and horrific flooding of the compound. We would not be at odds with each other like this, squabbling over past events. We would be heading back there as quickly as we could."

"There is no sign of rain, nor has there been for months. If you expect me to turn tail and head back again, just because of a nightmare, then you are greatly mistaken." She held out the palm of her hand. "See… not a drop!"

"For Christ's sake will you listen to me… you do not understand the significance of this vision. This was a message from Lorenzo, a cry for help that we cannot ignore."

"We are not going back until we have the canoe full of supplies and that is all I have to say on the matter." She clambered into the canoe, waiting impatiently for Geoffrey to dismantle the canvas shelter and pack it into the dugout with the mosquito net and cooking utensils, with no offer of help.

After the heated exchange they continued much as before, in virtual silence, towards the trading post, three more days of paddling through the lowered water level with barely a word exchanged.

Towards the end of the second day there was some evidence that violent storms were raging somewhere up ahead. The skies had darkened considerably with frequent electrifying flashes and thunderbolts and soon after they were confronted by an unexpected surge in the water level, carrying with it the shattered trunks of felled trees that were heading towards them at an alarming rate.

"We need to find shelter on the bank, Maggs," Geoffrey shouted, paddling furiously against the surging waters, visibility down to only a few feet ahead in the driving rain that had swept in with the storm.

Once they had dragged the dugout as high as they could up the embankment, Geoffrey hauled out the tarpaulin and rigged up a makeshift shelter.

"How did you know about this place?" Marguerite asked grudgingly.

"This was an overnight stop when I came back with Misqualla."

"That means the trading post must be quite close?"

"Normally I would expect we could reach it in a day but with all of this floating debris on the river I am not so sure."

During all of their time in the rainforest Geoffrey had never witnessed such a terrifying storm as this. Crashes of thunder and continuous lightning began soon after they made camp and continued throughout the night, accompanied by violent winds that tore down most of the canopy and only the corner of a flapping section beneath which they huddled together to keep them from getting soaked.

At daybreak the torrential downpour had eased off but a blanket of heavy rain had set in, soaking Geoffrey through in seconds as he made his way down to the canoe. It looked more like a horse trough than any mode of river transport and after bailing out several gallons of rainwater he decided it would be suicidal to launch the dugout back onto the river, particularly as the rain gave no sign of abating.

"You should dry off before breakfast," Marguerite greeted him, her earlier bitterness seemingly forgotten as she stirred the last of the baked beans in the blackened saucepan.

"There is no point. I need to reattach this canopy while I can."

"You will only have to take it down again before we set off."

"Normally I would but with all of this debris on the river we would get less than half a mile before the canoe gets holed and we are dragged downriver with it."

"Surely it is not that bad."

"Take a look and see for yourself." Geoffrey began making their shelter more secure while Marguerite put an oilskin sheet over her head and sloshed down to the river's edge.

"It looks awful," she agreed on her return. "How long should we wait?"

"Until this rain eases off, I suppose but I have no idea when that will be. Lorenzo would have known," Geoffrey added without thinking and the silence from his sister descended once more like an invisible wall between them.

They sat out the rest of the day in mutual discomfort beneath the canopy, eating the remainder of the bread Marguerite had baked for the journey, before she settled down for the night in one corner, covered by the oilskin, while Geoffrey and the hound curled up together in the other.

"Maggs, you had better come and see this," Geoffrey said, waking his sister gently in the early hours.

"What is it, what has happened?" she asked, following him down to the river's edge.

"What do you make of this?" Geoffrey was staring blankly at the water, which was as still as a millpond, with no movement among the flotsam and shattered trees that would have previously churned past them in seconds. It was as if there was suddenly no current at all.

"This does not make any sense, not after the storm last night and with the water level already so high. By now the river should be swollen and ready to burst its banks and yet there is barely any movement at all. It seems to have stopped flowing overnight," Marguerite said anxiously.

"Then we should get a move on and reach the trading post while there is still time, before whatever has dammed up the flow eventually bursts." Geoffrey returned to the shelter to collect his bag of trading goods and whistle the hound back from its hunting and they set off immediately.

"What about the awning, Geoffrey? You cannot leave that behind; we will need it."

"There is no point. We can shelter here on the way back. I will remove it then."

The further they went upriver, the lower the water level seemed to have dropped and by the time the trading post was visible in the distance the bottom of the dugout was catching on higher sections of the riverbed. It was late afternoon when they arrived at the docking area where, because of the low water level, the staging was much higher out of the water than before, making it awkward to tie up.

Once Geoffrey had clambered on to the decking, he helped his sister up the slippery rocks until she was able to grab a handhold on the framing.

"I suppose I should have asked before now... what did you bring to trade, Geoffrey?"

"Father's telescope, a pair of binoculars and the silver-handled magnifying glass that Misqualla had an eye on; those and a few items that we no longer need," Geoffrey said. He was suddenly aware that she was now wearing their mother's sapphire earrings. "Surely you cannot be thinking of trading those in?"

"Of course not. If they are on me they will be safe. I would never trust Drangoo not to go through my things, especially now that Lorenzo will be preoccupied with Rosamund and Edwin."

"You could have left them in Rose's cabin. They would have been safe there."

"Not if Rosamund had one of her tantrums and started throwing things. Trust me, Mother's earrings are much safer where they are."

"It will be like waving a red rag at a bull when Misqualla sees them. They are so beautiful and Mother loved them so much, so I do not understand why you would risk losing them. Why not keep them hidden in your pocket for the time being at least, until we are on our way back?"

"They are safer in my earlobes than anywhere else. If anyone tries to take them from me I will shoot them without hesitation. You know I am perfectly capable of that; and besides, I have taken the precaution of bringing along other items of jewellery to trade."

"Why trade anything belonging to Mother, not when I have brought all this stuff of Father's? At least none of that has any sentimental value. Just allow me to barter with Father's stuff first, before you show anything of Mother's."

"Misqualla is a crafty operator and will want every single item we have in exchange for those supplies. Remember I have dealt with him before. Rest assured, I would never part with any of Mother's jewellery unless it was absolutely necessary; that is why almost everything I have brought along for trading belonged to Father's mistresses. Most of it is convincing paste but there are a few precious gems amongst them."

"What you need to remember is that Misqualla and I did not part under the most genial of circumstances, so I hope you have the revolver with you right now."

"Of course I have, that goes without saying. It is also fully loaded," she said calmly.

"Then with Archie's hunting knife and my spear we should be able to fend off any unexpected attack," Geoffrey said, remembering Misqualla's collection of well-armed bodyguards.

"Do not think because of this that I have forgiven you, Geoffrey, because I have not and I probably never will."

"Why would that matter? Once you go to North America with your new family you will never see me again anyway. Besides, I will have better things to do at home, taking care of Rose in whatever property Mother has left me in her will, rather than having to worry about having your good opinion," Geoffrey retorted, gathering up his spear as they began climbing the wooden steps set against the cliff face.

Once they had reached the top it became obvious why their arrival had gone unnoticed. There was frenzied activity taking place to shore up a section the trading post's roof. Looking like a gleaming blur of polished ebony through the downpour of driving rain, it was a seemingly futile attempt to re-erect the collapsed central part of the building.

Seated like royalty beneath the only sound section of the structure some distance away was the familiar figure of Misqualla and beside him, his companion with the gold armband. The moment he became aware of the recent arrivals, Misqualla's high-pitched screams of outrage even penetrated the squalling rain.

Undaunted, Geoffrey had his spear balanced in readiness, while at his side the wolfhound's hackles were spiked like an Elizabethan ruff, its teeth bared and snarling as they moved forward together, perfectly synchronised as the coordinated killing machine they had become.

"Wait here, Maggs, as a back-up. If we get overpowered, make a run for it."

"I will do no such thing!"

"Then have it your own way. Just wait here, unless I call," Geoffrey commanded as he and the dog moved steadily forward.

"Why you want kill Misqualla?" the owner shrieked amid a frenzied waving of muscular arms, the collection of bracelets jangling up and down with every theatrical gesture. "It no enough you injure my Masqutoo, make my bambino no good warrior?" Misqualla's saucer-like eyes rolled in all directions as Geoffrey and the hound moved ever closer.

"We are not here to kill anyone, Misqualla," Marguerite called from behind them. "We came here in peace."

"Like hell we did!" Geoffrey hissed, wanting nothing more than to plunge the spear into Misqualla's trembling throat until he felt his sister's restraining touch on his shoulder.

"Then why come?" Misqualla screeched.

"We are here to trade for supplies, nothing more," Marguerite said calmly, stepping forward.

"What Missy bring Misqualla for trade?" His voice grew more confident as he eyed the dangling sapphires greedily.

"If you so much as lay a finger on those earrings, you will be dead before you hit the ground, you fat freak!!" Geoffrey threatened, stepping into line with his sister, the hound at his side, snarling.

After the initial stand-off, at his sister's request Geoffrey reluctantly agreed to remain outside the trading post to make sure that no one else entered, while Marguerite went inside with Misqualla to trade for whatever items they needed. It took until dusk to conclude the bartering and by the time she returned to where he was sheltering she was ankle-deep in mud.

"I have marked everything we need to be crated up. It will be loaded into the dugout in the morning."

"Did you have to part with everything we brought?" Geoffrey asked. An intense rumble of thunder rolled over them, not too distant and getting closer.

"It was the harem jewellery that caught Misqualla's eye. There was no interest in anything of Father's except for the magnifying glass."

They found respite from the rain in a makeshift stable housing a few scrawny hens, an old sow suckling three piglets and an underfed, overworked mule that had flies buzzing around the deep weals and sores across its back from constant beatings.

"We need to get some rest before morning. Was there any offer of shelter for the night? I have nothing here I can rig up for us against this downpour." Geoffrey covered his ears against another sequence of deafening thunderclaps.

"All I could think of was getting out of there."

"Maybe tomorrow we can make a deal for this old mule. It is almost dead on its feet."

"What would be the use, Geoffrey? It is not a stray dog we can take back with us in the dugout."

"You cannot expect me to just leave it here."

"Do be realistic for once. We have no alternative. I just wish it could be otherwise."

"There must be something we can do?"

"We are not at home in Ashbourne, Geoffrey. There are more important issues to contend with. Before we leave in the morning, it is imperative that I locate Misqualla and negotiate for a block of salt I forgot to purchase."

"Have you got anything left to trade with? That freak will never budge if not."

"I kept these back, just in case," Marguerite said, producing a second pair of earrings from her bag, paste jewellery that sparkled like cascading diamonds in what remained of the daylight.

"Great but take my advice and do not wear mother's sapphires when you show them to her, otherwise those will look like what they are."

"I am not taking these off, Geoffrey, whatever you say."

"I do not understand why not. They will be perfectly safe in my pouch."

"I am not prepared to do that and that is my final word on the matter. It is far better that we concentrate on finding somewhere decent to sleep before it gets too dark and we cannot see anything at all. We must rest. We have a lot a paddling ahead of us tomorrow."

"Well I suggest that we stay in here overnight. It is too dark now to go searching for any alternative shelter. Besides, I did a bit of negotiating of my own while you were inside and swapped a bolt of mosquito netting for my old penknife with one of the natives before he mentioned it to Misqualla and the price tripled."

"I cannot believe that anyone in their right mind would have traded anything for that rusty old knife," she said with amazement.

"It was the blue enamel casing that caught his eye. The blade is not much use I grant you but I doubt he will ever use it anyway."

"Then why would he trade for it?"

"Probably to wear it around his neck as a decoration; I cannot imagine there is another like it in the entire rainforest."

That night, as Geoffrey was about to rig up a makeshift bed from crates at either end of the stable, he stopped, barely able to breathe for the stench from an empty stall next to the mule.

"Do not come over here, Maggs, whatever you do."

"What have you found?"

"Another mule that must have been dead for more than a week" He covered his nose before approaching the rotting carcass. "Just stay where you are while I drag it outside."

"You cannot do that on your own."

"All that's left is virtually skin and bone," Geoffrey said optimistically but he was still unable to move it more than a few feet.

"Now will you let me lend a hand?" Marguerite said. Attaching another rope around the hooves, together they dragged it clear of the building.

Once he had got his breath back, Geoffrey dragged the crates together and added a thick layer of straw to keep them as high as possible from the ground, a precautionary measure against snakes and rigged up a thick cover of mosquito netting over each one.

Although the bed was hard and uncomfortable, Geoffrey fell asleep within moments and didn't wake all night. Not even the crash of thunderclaps and crackling of lightning could wake him from that unnaturally deep and disturbed sleep.

He awoke in a panic with a blinding headache, fearing the worst. When he eventually staggered to his feet the wind was howling. The rain, slashing diagonally into the shelter, had saturated the netting and soaked him to the skin. Only then did he come to his senses and realise that he was not at the compound, where his nightmarish visions had taken him. Needing time to readjust his thoughts, he leant against the mule's stall, running back over the sequence of tragic events he had witnessed, events seen through Lorenzo's own eyes, as if Geoffrey's mind had been transported into Lorenzo's head.

The visions had begun with his mother's face, looking up at him from the portrait photograph taken at the garden party in Ashbourne, the comforting image he kept on his bedside table. Moments later the photograph was held up by a hand that also held his mother's miniature book of prayer bearing the family crest on the ivory cover. None of this made any sense until he saw Lorenzo's face reflected back from a wall mirror as he emerged from the store cabin and on to the veranda where the Otter was sheltering as a storm raged around the compound.

"You stay. No leave," he heard Lorenzo's voice say.

"Why Lady Rosa she no come, Lollen?"

"Lollen, him go find," the voice said, before he felt himself stepping into the thunderous downpour. "Otter no follow... comprende?"

"Si, Lollen, I here."

Trapped within Lorenzo's body, the disconnected movement made him as giddy and nauseous as if he were on a cakewalk at the fairground. As Lorenzo began moving quickly across open ground towards the cliff steps the sensation was worse than any nightmare, a prisoner within another's body, unable to use his own limbs.

As they neared the cliff edge he could see clearly a raging torrent below, surging through the compound where his mother's cabin had once been. The building was almost obliterated by the turbulent water, as too was his father's laboratory and the connecting breezeway linking it to the bungalow would have been unrecognisable had it not been for the shattered columns projecting above the surface. Even as he watched, the mass of water surged through with terrifying force, carrying with it a mass of uprooted trees and debris that had partially dammed the narrow canyon. Now an unrelenting torrent gushed overland, smashing and crushing everything in its path, tearing down more of the ancient forest and propelling fallen trees like battering rams into the compound with a terrifying roar.

He struggled to detach himself from the petrifying visions as he saw Rosamund trapped under the partially collapsed roof of the veranda, her dress impaled by a section of splintered timbers from the tilting roof. There was nothing Geoffrey could do except watch as more sections of the splintering cabin slowly disintegrated about her.

What was equally unnerving for Geoffrey was that there was no sign of the infant other than the partially submerged crib just a few feet away from his sister's outstretched arm. Even as he watched, the crib was dragged into the water as a section of floor split apart from the disintegrating veranda and had soon disappeared from sight.

With the speed at which Lorenzo was moving, Geoffrey knew that he would soon reach the steps leading down into the compound, until a rifle shot rang out and he lurched forward, stumbling and dropping to his knees a few feet away from the very edge of the cliff. Yet within seconds Lorenzo was back on his feet, staggering towards the steps.

Through Lorenzo's eyes Geoffrey briefly saw the blood oozing from the gunshot wound to his thigh, before he turned to face the would-be assassin. Drangoo was fumbling to reload the rifle in the torrential downpour, the clip of bullets slipping from his hand before they fell into the squelching mud.

Screaming with hatred, Drangoo charged like a maniac through the blinding rain towards them. Gripping hold of the rifle barrel, the monk made a vicious swing at Lorenzo, the weight of its butt striking with almighty force so that it shattered his shoulder on impact, pitching him over the cliff edge and into the raging torrent.

Through Lorenzo's eyes, Geoffrey could only watch with horror as they were swirled around amid a mass of colliding logs, animal carcasses, fragments of bungalow walls and shattered furniture as Lorenzo battled valiantly against the ferocious undertow. Somehow, despite his injuries, his remarkable abilities underwater enabled him to avoid being crushed and to eventually reach Rosamund's stricken position.

When Lorenzo surfaced, Geoffrey could see how little of the bungalow remained. The main part had been battered and crushed by uprooted trees, leaving only a fragmented section of the living space. Even as he watched through Lorenzo's now blurred and watery vision, the floor beneath the grand piano began to splinter and break apart, carrying with it the few remaining pieces of furniture that floated momentarily before being swept away.

It was only when Lorenzo had struggled on to what remained of the veranda where Rosamund was still trapped that he glanced up and Geoffrey saw that Drangoo had descended what remained of the steps and had the rifle shouldered and aimed directly at them. Preoccupied with taking the killer shot, the monk was unaware that the upturned piano was being swept in his direction, until it smashed into the wooden steps immediately beneath him and tore out the entire section, toppling him off balance. As he clung desperately on to the lower step, a shattered piano leg became snagged in his robe and dragged him with it, floundering behind the huge instrument. Moments later, another surge of water impaled the body of the instrument on the jagged trunk of a tree, overturning the piano with the monk still attached by his habit. He screamed to the Almighty for help, a sound that was accompanied by a jarring, musical discord as the instrument was dragged beneath the water, taking Drangoo with it.

The replay of Geoffrey's nightmare ended abruptly with the crack of a revolver being fired, a sound that prompted him into action. Trying to ignore the throbbing pain behind his eyes, he staggered past Marguerite's empty bed and into the rain, wading through the squelching mud that came up over his ankles as he made his way towards the building. To his relief he saw Marguerite backing cautiously out of the door, aiming the revolver at the darkened interior. However, once was able to see more clearly she appeared to be in a great deal of pain, her right earlobe was badly torn and bleeding and the sapphire earring was missing.

"Come one step closer and I will fire!" she cried, her voice barely audible above the sound of howling wind. Breaking off, she turned, lowering the weapon as everyone from inside the building rushed out, her words drowned out by the most terrifying noise Geoffrey had ever heard.

Leading the group was Misqualla. Beside him was Masqutoo, who allowed the deadly machete to slip from his nerveless fingers as he stood looking towards the river with his mouth gaping as the rumbling, distant at first, came ever closer until it became almost demonic while the ground beneath their feet trembled as if the world itself was about to shatter into pieces.

The trading post's elevated position high above the river offered little protection as a gigantic wall of water surged towards them, carrying aloft most of what had stood in its path. Uprooted, ancient trees crashed past them on a vast body of water almost at eye-level, while tons of debris came veering over the cliff edge, spearing sections of the already unstable structure and felling it to the ground like splintering matchwood.

Geoffrey knew at once that this terrifying spectacle of nature at its most violent was the reality of the glimpse into the future Lorenzo had transmitted to him. Within an hour the devastating surge would hit the compound and there was nothing he could do to prevent it from happening. Regardless, he knew he had to get back and help in whatever way he could, even though it would take days.

"We have to go back right away, Maggs," Geoffrey shouted, grabbing her by the arm and unthinkingly leading her towards the steps where the dugout had been moored but beneath them the entire lower section of the docking area had been either smashed into fragments or swept away in the floodwater, along with their dugout and every other vessel moored there.

"The boat has gone, Geoffrey! What can we do? There must be some other way to get back," Marguerite screamed hysterically, pushing past him to reach the steps before she slipped and fell to her knees, twisting her ankle.

"It is impossible to get down there without breaking your neck. There are no more steps after this top section and that is barely holding together." Even as he spoke the entire section collapsed, the steps splintering apart as they crashed into the rock face before being swept away by the swollen river.

"I have to get back… Edwin is in danger!" she cried.

"Lorenzo will make sure he is safe. No one knows this place better than him and he can swim like a fish," Geoffrey reassured her, although Lorenzo's visions led him to fear it would be impossible for any of them to survive such a force of nature.

"Please… we cannot stay here, we have to get back!" she urged, grabbing his arm for support.

"We cannot leave without provisions."

"We have to leave now… immediately!" she protested.

"You cannot go anywhere with that twisted ankle. Maybe I should go on ahead and you follow later; I can leave you the hound for protection," Geoffrey suggested, realising he would make better progress alone.

"There is nothing on earth that would prevent me from going with you."

"Then we must make preparations. For a start, we have to take some of the goods you have traded."

"Geoffrey! We need to leave now!" she screeched manically.

"Be practical, Maggs. We cannot survive without food. It will take over a week to reach to the compound on foot."

"Surely we can procure another boat? There must be something that can get us there faster."

"Not unless we can haul a log up here and hack out a canoe. We have no alternative but to get back on foot and for that we will need that mule," Geoffrey said decisively.

It was soon apparent that Misqualla and her muscle-bound accomplice were gone and after a short confrontation with one of the remaining bodyguards, who seemed more intimidated by the ferocious teeth of the wolfhound than either Geoffrey's spear or his sister's revolver, most of the goods Marguerite had purchased were exchanged for the mule and its panniers, along with two hens, a worn military backpack and a small tarpaulin. After Geoffrey had crammed whatever he could into the backpack, he packed some tinned provisions into the mule's panniers and because of his sister's injury made room for her to ride on its back.

"Do hurry up. Is it absolutely necessary to repack everything?"

"Can you not see I am doing my best to make room for you?"

"What is the use? The poor creature is weighed down enough without adding my extra weight."

"We have no choice. If you had not twisted your bloody ankle in the first place, then you would not need to ride and I would not be loaded down like a packhorse," Geoffrey said, though he regretted it immediately.

"I suppose I could manage with a walking stick; although I did see some crutches hanging from one of the shelves."

"I will go and look."

"If you do, then take the revolver. You could be outnumbered."

"There is no need for that. It will be hard cheese for anyone who tries anything," Geoffrey said, striding off through the mud with Archie's knife in one hand and his spear balanced lightly in the other, the hound close at his side.

Once inside the collapsed structure Geoffrey soon located the crutches, one of which was splintered under a fallen shelf and although he had been prepared to negotiate with Misqualla's one-eyed henchman for the other the crutch was offered to him as a gift after a warning growl rumbled in the hound's throat.

Because of the flooding it would have been impossible for them to follow the river, so their only alternative was to go further inland in the hope of finding a route through the forest.

"What makes you think there will be a trail this far inland?" Marguerite said.

"It makes sense; not everything would have been brought here by canoe. There is a village built on stilts not far down the river; if we can reach there, we might even be able to get hold of a canoe," Geoffrey said, remembering his journey with Misqualla. "If we take the first track we come across, that might well take us there."

They eventually reached a worn trail going in the right direction but it wasn't long before they came to a flooded section that would have been impossible to cross in the fading light.

"So what happens now?" Marguerite asked in frustration.

"We have no option other than to wait it out until the water subsides."

"But that could take days… even weeks!"

"Not necessarily. The ground must be really dry after being so long without rain. It should soak away before long."

"You cannot be certain about that."

"Maybe not but it is the only option we have."

Geoffrey tethered the mule and prepared to unload.

"What are you doing? We cannot stay here. We have barely gone any distance at all, Geoffrey!"

"There is nothing we can do anything until morning. You need to rest your ankle while you can. Have you got anything that might help?"

"Perhaps," she said, opening her bag and removing a bottle containing a small amount of clear liquid, with a label that looked almost as worn out as Geoffrey felt at that moment.

"Witch hazel; I brought it along just in case. There is not much left."

"Then use what you have, there is no point saving any if it works," he said.

Once Geoffrey had rigged up a shelter and was about to set a fire to heat up a tin of baked beans, practicality hit home. "Bugger… we don't have a tin opener!"

"I still have an old army knife of Father's I brought with me to trade. There are lots of odd gadgets on it. There might be one amongst them," Marguerite said, rummaging through her bag.

"Is one of them a hoof-pick?" Geoffrey asked.

"I thought you wanted a tin opener?"

"Yes I do but I just hoped there might be one of those as well, if it is ex-military. The mule is limping badly and there may be something wedged it its hoof. If not, I suppose I can prod around with a stick." Geoffrey took the knife from her, firstly opening out the primitive tin opener and then a lethal-looking spike. "Where on earth did you find this? I swear I went through all of Father's things before we set off but I never saw this."

"It was in the laboratory drawers. Misqualla was not interested in trading for that, only the paste jewellery." She tore the corner off a blank page in her journal, sticking it over the torn section of her earlobe with the last of the witch hazel, then began strapping up her ankle with a strip of material from her muddied skirt.

"And one of mother's sapphires, it seems," Geoffrey said, stabbing the opener viciously into the tin of beans.

"You should check on the mule before the light goes completely, while I get these heated up over the fire," she suggested.

Geoffrey checked on his sister several times during the night and each time found Marguerite staring across the floodwater at the continuation of the submerged trail where it entered the forest. When dawn broke, although the water had receded quite a lot, Geoffrey was determined not to set off until lunchtime.

"Why not load the animal now, Geoffrey? The water will only come up to waist level and the mule will be fine," Marguerite snapped irritably.

"It is not the water level that concerns me but what might be in it," he retorted. He hoped she was not going to be so unrealistic for the entire journey.

"Well you can stay here if you want but I am not prepared to wait indefinitely. Edwin will be in danger and we need to get across this water now."

"We are both staying!" Geoffrey said. The wolfhound had returned from hunting with an animal carcass, the remains of which he grabbed and threw into the still water, where within moments the surface erupted into a battleground as two small caiman fought for possession.

After that experiment, Marguerite had no alternative but to bide her time and wait for another three hours until the water was low enough for them to cross. Even so, the sight of a large water snake coming directly for them suggested that the odds of survival on the long trek ahead were decidedly against them. Although Marguerite and the hound had already reached dry land, Geoffrey and the mule, hampered by its heavy load, were still in the water but Geoffrey was already prepared and speared the reptile in the throat, just as its head reared up in readiness to strike.

"Bravo, Geoffrey!" Marguerite said, ashen-faced. "How you have managed to acquire such a skill is beyond me but I am so glad that you have."

It seemed almost impossible to make any headway, leading a loaded mule over saturated ground and through huge pockets of water that were often deceptively deep, until they found a worn track through the forest on higher ground. When the trail became less distinct Geoffrey allowed the hound's tracking and survival instincts to guide them to the safest route.

It was also gratifying during those first days on foot to observe the companionship that developed between the dog and the mule. At first it had proven an obstinate beast, its stubbornness delaying them on many occasions but as the days went on the animal made more steady progress with the hound trotting along at its side.

How long before we reach the village?" Marguerite asked when they made camp on that second night.

"It cannot be far. It only took half a day by boat. I just hope the natives are friendly enough to exchange a canoe for this old mule."

"Failure is not an option, Geoffrey. It would take weeks to get back on foot."

"I agree but it will not be an easy task. I cannot imagine they will have any spare dugouts after the flood."

"What if they refuse to help... what then?"

"Forge an alternative deal, I suppose," but Geoffrey was unable to come up with an immediate solution.

"What could we offer that would tempt them?" she persisted, hanging onto one of the mule's panniers for support as she hobbled along the track.

"Maybe if we agree to leave the mule, along with everything we have packed into the panniers, they might consider loaning us a dugout and a paddle-man on the condition it would be returned to them afterwards."

"Would that work, do you think?"

"It seems a reasonable enough request to me but then I am not a native, am I?"

He was unsure of anything at all as the extent of flood damage to that section of forest became apparent. Here the force of the water had uprooted dozens of giant trees and carried them downriver, leaving others shattered or uprooted. It was like the aftermath of a war zone.

"Are you certain this is the place?" Marguerite asked when they reached the end of the trail three hours later.

"It must be," Geoffrey said despondently as he surveyed the shattered remains of the stilts that had once supported the native homes, all but a few of the posts swept away by the uncontrollable power of the torrent.

"This is awful; there is no one left here."

"None of them could have withstood the force of that water," Geoffrey said, hoping to find an overturned dugout they could re-use but seeing nothing.

"If there are no canoes, Geoffrey, then what can we do now? We must get back... we have to."

"The only way is to continue on foot, that is, unless we come across another village on the way but we are not going anywhere until you have rested. You look done in."

"I will be fine, once I rebind this ankle."

"Very well but after that I think we should take this other track." A narrow trail led inland towards higher ground but still appeared to be heading downriver.

"Do you think it will take us to the compound?" Marguerite asked as he helped her on to her feet.

"You are asking questions I cannot answer. I have never been here before. All I can tell you is that it is heading in the right direction and there is less foliage to contend with. On the lower ground you would never make it through the denser areas on that ankle and neither would the mule. I guess we have about four hours of daylight left before we need to make camp, so we must push on."

"Mother would be so proud of you, Geoffrey, dealing with this dreadful situation and taking everything in your stride," Marguerite said, with genuine affection, for now forgetting her anger.

"I suppose it is a case of do or die," Geoffrey said. He was quietly pleased not only that she was allowing him to take the lead but that the Lorenzo situation had, at least for now, apparently been relegated to the back of her mind.

The trek through the forest over the following three days was uneventful but as the trail seemed to be taking them deeper inland, with no sightings of the river, whenever the well-trodden path split off into others it was agreed they would follow the track nearest to where they knew the river would be flowing.

"This cannot be right, Geoffrey. We seem to be going even deeper into the forest."

"I realise that but at least we are going in the right direction."

"Maybe we are but I am sure that we have been veering away from the river for a long time. We will never find a fishing village this far inland. We must get back as soon as we can. God alone knows what might have happened at the compound if that giant wave had not diminished before reaching them," Marguerite said with fear in her eyes.

"This is the right way, I am sure of it," Geoffrey said, handing her his battered old compass.

"Are you sure this is working?" She frantically tapped the glass.

"I am as sure as anyone can be that we are going in the right general direction. All of these tracks will lead to a village eventually. We just have to pray that wherever we end up the natives are friendly."

"Well I am fully prepared to use Father's revolver if they are not."

At dusk on the fourth evening the trail opened out at a clearing overlooking the river. This was a point where two tributaries converged and the flooding was still very much in evidence.

"Do you recognise where we are, Geoffrey?"

"Not exactly but I am positive we are further downriver than I had hoped."

"How is that possible?"

"That trail we followed inland must have cut out a few bends in the river; if so, it could have taken a huge chunk off our time in getting back."

"Are you sure, Geoffrey?"

"I cannot be certain, not with the landscape so altered." Geoffrey squinted in the fading light at an incongruous but oddly familiar shape amongst the boughs of a tree on the opposite bank.

"What are you staring at?" she asked as he deliberately moved to block her view across the river.

"A damaged tree, nothing more," Geoffrey lied, trying to get his sister away quickly before she could recognise their father's wrecked grand piano, impaled on a branch of the shattered tree. Dangling from its frame was Drangoo, or what little there was left of him beneath a swarming army of soldier ants that were picking his remains clean and the remnants of his torn robe, fluttering from one of the broken piano legs. As horrific as this scene was, what was worse was that it confirmed that the terrifying images Lorenzo had transmitted on that fearful night were accurate and he dreaded what other horrors would be awaiting them at the compound.

At mid-afternoon the following day they took a well-needed break after climbing to an elevated position where it was possible to see the river again, snaking ahead into the distance.

"Is that a native village over there?" Marguerite asked, pointing out an open area below them.

"I cannot see anything," Geoffrey said, his attention diverted by a warning growl from the hound, the hackles on the back of its neck fanning out.

"Down there," Marguerite said, still oblivious to any threat.

"Never mind that, have you got the revolver handy?" Geoffrey whispered.

"It is in my bag, why?"

"Then get it out now and load it." Geoffrey said, balancing the spear in readiness.

Almost before Marguerite had slipped off the safety catch a group of seven headhunters broke through a gap in the bushes with their recent trophies from what appeared to have been a tribal massacre, heads dangling grotesquely by the hair from two carrying poles supported between four of them.

Although the hunters had clearly been unprepared for a confrontation so close to their own village, three of them immediately charged, brandishing bloodied machetes with terrifying, warlike screams. Within seconds, the poles transporting the jostling heads were also dumped on the ground as the other four joined the attack.

Before the hunters were able to get close enough to strike, one of them dropped dead with a bullet hole between the eyes. Another was felled, screaming, tugging to free Geoffrey's spear as it went clean through his chest, impaling him against a tree as he coughed up blood with every weakening effort. Meanwhile the hound had dragged a third native to the ground by his throat.

This deadly response threw the other four hunters into momentary confusion before they regrouped and charged in a second wave. A bullet through the heart stopped one before the second, wielding a machete, was stopped by two consecutive bullets moments before he could embed the weapon in Geoffrey's skull. Turning to confront the next attacker, Geoffrey plunged Archie's hunting knife deep into the man's eye-socket piercing his brain, killing him instantly. The surviving hunter, seeing the odds changing so quickly, hobbled away screaming through the bushes, bleeding profusely from a severe bite from the wolfhound.

"Do you think any more will be coming, Geoffrey?" Marguerite asked, calmly reloading the revolver. "I only have five bullets left."

"Then you had better make every one of them count."

"We should leave here as soon as possible."

"I am well aware of that but we cannot go anywhere until they are all buried."

"You plan to bury these monsters?" Marguerite asked incredulously.

"Not them. It is the heads of their victims that must be laid to rest."

Geoffrey scouted around for a suitable area for the burial.

"How can you remain so calm? The very idea is making my skin crawl."

"I have done it before and felt all the better for it." He began digging a hole with Archie's knife.

"How could you have done this sort of thing before without my knowledge?" She turned away from the gruesome sight as he buried the first of the shrunken heads.

"A while ago now, the day Bog Boy and I became acquainted."

"But… but you told me those wounds you suffered were inflicted by a thorn bush and an animal?"

"That was only partially true. Some headhunters did the rest."

"Why did you not say anything?"

"It would only have alarmed everyone and by then the danger was already over," Geoffrey said matter-of-factly, continuing with the burial.

"How many hunters were there?"

"Three. I threw them off the edge of the cliff and let the caiman do the rest." Geoffrey was more occupied with digging another hole than answering questions.

"What about these bodies?" she asked, looking at the dead hunters.

"We leave them where they are. Condors are always out scavenging. What we need to do now is to get away from this track and try to find some other way back."

"That might take even longer and we need to get back as soon as we can!"

"I agree but if we continue along this route it will eventually take us down into the village where these men came from and we would never get back alive. So I propose that we make for higher ground, away from the flooding. There must be other tracks leading down to the river."

"Could there be other villages, nearer the compound?"

"I would think so. Some of the women in Father's harem must have come from close by and those natives we found when we first arrived must have come from a local village to work for him. If so, there might well be a trail from there, leading to the trading post."

Chapter Eleven
Dread

After they left the track to avoid meeting more hunters, Geoffrey soon realised that forcing a passage through the forest with a packed mule was even more difficult he had anticipated, even with the aid of a headhunter's machete.

"Surely there must be some other way of avoiding the village?" Marguerite said when they stopped to rest.

"All we can do is press on. Eventually we must cross an animal track that will hopefully go in our direction."

"Then why have we not found one? We have tramped quite a distance from the village."

"Animals are not stupid; they have an instinct for self-preservation. I doubt if any creature would go near human habitation by choice. We should come across one soon," Geoffrey said, with more confidence than he actually felt.

"I just hope you are right." She unhooked a second machete from the mule and worked with him, slashing a passage through the dense foliage.

For the next hour they continued hacking through the undergrowth until, to their relief, they came across a track. It did not lead in the exact direction Geoffrey had wanted but instead veered diagonally back the way they had just come. However, nearing exhaustion and having no real alternative they agreed to take a chance.

The trail descended a steep incline then hooked sharply away in the original direction towards the compound. Looking back, they soon realised the narrow escape they'd had. The jagged rock face rose immediately above them with its eroded cliff edge where, had they continued in the same direction, they would surely have plunged to their deaths.

By morning on the following day the track had dropped down to river level. Because of the recent flooding it was not only difficult to locate the path and negotiate the ankle-deep mud but also to keep up a decent pace.

They had been making slow progress for about three hours when they came upon a water-filled dugout, wedged firmly in the branches of an uprooted tree.

"This could be a life-saver, Maggs," Geoffrey cried enthusiastically, hacking off some of the boughs with his machete.

"... but Geoffrey... it might be damaged and sink."

"Not if it is holding water. What we both need to do now is start bailing it out."

"Even if we do get it emptied, we could never move that weight on our own. We should press on. There might be another close by."

"Or not... What we have here could work well enough. All we have to do is release it. Why not lend a hand, because I am not going anywhere until we try."

"What you are proposing is impossible, Geoffrey. Why not accept that and waste no more time here? You and I could never move this tree trunk in a million years."

"If the Ancient Britons could erect something like Stonehenge, then surely we should be able to slide a dugout over this mud, especially with the mule to help," Geoffrey said firmly and made no comment when his sister began helping to bail out the water with a battered saucepan.

It took the remainder of that afternoon to hack the dugout free of the tree and for Geoffrey to adapt what little rope they had into a harness, by which time it was almost dark so the project was abandoned until the following morning.

Despite the weight of the canoe, once the mule had been harnessed and encouraged by the wolfhound, they were eventually able to launch the vessel into the water.

Building a makeshift ramp from a pile of logs, Geoffrey tried to coax the mule into the dugout.

"Are you out of your mind?" Marguerite complained. "We cannot take that animal with us."

"Well I am damned if we are leaving it here."

"Geoffrey… Be practical."

"That is exactly what I am being. The mule will be dead before nightfall if we do not take it with us."

"We cannot waste any more time before we set off. Launching this canoe has taken almost two days already."

"If it were not for this mule, we would never have got the bloody canoe into the water to begin with and if we had not, the two days you are prattling on about would have probably extended into another week if we'd had to wade through this damned mud all the way to the compound."

"Geoffrey, please reconsider," she pleaded.

"For God's sake Maggs, do shut up! The mule is coming with us – get used to it!"

Finally, Geoffrey tried putting the hound on board first and because of the clear companionship between the animals, it then took little encouragement to get the mule into the dugout. Once they were all aboard, struggling with every ounce of strength he pushed the canoe further into the water before he jumped on board himself.

The final push to reach the compound was a Herculean task. After a sleepless night with Marguerite unable to rest and pacing about agitatedly, they cast off again at daybreak. By the second afternoon of intense paddling their hands were bandaged heavily with whatever wrapping they could find, not only to combat the pain but also to keep the swarming flies away from the blisters.

As they came closer to their destination, the dread in Geoffrey's heart grew with every passing hour as they picked their way through the aftermath of the flood. As if in a single stroke by the hand of the Almighty, huge swathes of the ancient rainforest had been levelled by the immense surge of crushing water cutting across the land. Behind it were left mounds of vile-smelling debris and animal carcasses, dammed up against what remained of the shattered trees.

There was an unnatural stillness in the air as they neared the compound. No sounds of howler monkeys or screeching macaws, the familiar battery of sound that would normally have greeted them. Instead there was only silence and foreboding. That morning the air was humid and oppressive, threatening an imminent storm. In the distance was the ominous rumble of thunder.

As they rounded the bend, Geoffrey knew at once that his worst fears of the devastation foretold through Lorenzo's thought-transference were indeed a reality. Almost nothing remained of the compound that had been their home for so long.

Marguerite was on her feet in seconds, her mouth gaping like a landed fish in silent disbelief, her features the colour of marble as Geoffrey manoeuvred the canoe alongside what little remained of the landing stage. When they finally came to a rest, she began screaming Edwin's name like something demented, scrambling from the canoe and wading frantically through the water until she was able to clamber out, knee deep in stinking mud, forcing a way through towards the shattered ruins.

By the time Geoffrey had secured the dugout and coaxed the mule onto the remains of the docking area, Marguerite had already reached the framework of what had been the staircase but, because the bottom section had been washed away, it was impossible to reach the store cabin.

"There is nothing left, Geoffrey!" she screeched as tears streamed down her face, falling to her knees in the mud.

"Do not give up hope, Maggs. They might have taken shelter in my cabin," Geoffrey said, helping her up.

"The staircase has gone! Lorenzo should have been here when we arrived. He would have known we were coming. He promised faithfully to take care of Edwin." She began staring wildly around the devastated area. "Most of the bungalow and Rosamund's cabin have been completely swept away, Geoffrey," she whimpered, twisting wildly about her, as if expecting them to appear from the ruined building, whose base was marked only by the sections of corner posts rearing up through the layers of the packed, grey slime.

"We need to check out my cabin before we imagine the worst," Geoffrey said but the wrecked section of the staircase confirmed the images he had seen of it being swept away, taking with it the grand piano, Drangoo and the Winchester rifle. His only hope lay in Lorenzo's supernatural ability to remain submerged underwater and he prayed that he had been able to utilise it to rescue his infant son and Rosamund from certain death.

Leading Marguerite by the arm, Geoffrey forced a pathway through the mud until they reached the sloping section further along the cliff as they followed the winding track up to his solitary cabin. Even though he kept telling himself they could all have survived, he could not blank out the vision in which the crib had been barely inches from Rosamund's outstretched hand before that section of the veranda had been swept away in the torrent.

By the time they reached the top of the steep gradient Marguerite was verging on hysteria, her breath coming in short, sharp gasps as her legs buckled and gave way. "Wait for me, Geoffrey!" she croaked, slapping the damp ground with the palm of her hand, unable to stand.

Geoffrey paused at the sight of the body of a jaguar, recognisable from its missing left ear, its hindquarters viciously scarred by a hunter's machete. It was also clear from the posture of the animal's carcass and its savage expression that it must have been killed while attacking. Its claws were fully extended, its teeth bared and it had undoubtedly fought until the final spark of its life was extinguished. There were several knife slashes to the head and throat and the killer thrust was embedded so deep into the jaguar's chest the weapon would have been too difficult for the hunter to retrieve.

As Marguerite forced herself to her feet, Geoffrey noticed a torn strip of black material caught on one of the animal's broken canines.

"Edwin... Edwin!" Marguerite cried in desperation, her voice high-pitched and desperate as she pushed past him into the clearing. "Lorenzo... where are you? Is my baby safe?"

"Do not go inside the cabin without me!" Geoffrey called, racing after her as she entered.

The first thing he noticed was the amount of blood splattered across the floor and pooled against the leg of his narrow bed. There were also scarlet smears on the mattress and even more on the pillow and he began to scour the cabin for fear that his sister might unwittingly come across the Otter's headless body. Marguerite began wailing hysterically, ranting wildly about setting off in search of her son, something that would be impossible in the current downpour and there was nothing Geoffrey could do to console her. Rejecting any attempts of comfort, instead she sat huddled on the floor of the veranda, her bare arms clasped tightly around her knees, her dark, straggling hair hanging like rats' tails, dripping with water.

Distressed and frantic with worry, Geoffrey wandered aimlessly through the cabin, looking at everything but seeing nothing until he stopped at the wall mirror, where Lorenzo's reflection had looked out at him. Curiously he went over to his bedside table, where the oil lamp, box of matches and his copy of *Treasure Island* were exactly where he had left them but the photograph of his mother and her miniature prayer book were gone.

Another oddity was that a long drawer had been removed from his bamboo chest and the contents dumped on his bed for no apparent reason. He had no idea if anything was missing, or why the drawer had been left empty on top of the chest. Nothing made any sense – even the brutal attack on the jaguar didn't add up. All he could hope for was that if the Otter had indeed been here, as in those nightmarish visions, the boy had escaped before the vicious killer responsible for these unrelated acts had found him.

Marguerite was inconsolable that night and unwilling to accept the evident loss of her son. Unable to sleep, Geoffrey could only stay with her, illuminating as much of the area as he could with one of his father's hurricane lamps as a relentless search of the areas surrounding the compound began and went on until dawn. Their quest continued every day for a week, beginning at daybreak and not ceasing until it became impossible to see after the oil supply ran out. It was only then that she would stop and pick at whatever food her brother put before her.

"You really must try and eat, Maggs," Geoffrey urged.

"There will be time enough for that when we find Edwin," she replied, pushing the uneaten food aside. "We must set off again at first light."

"Try and eat something, for Pete's sake… You cannot go on like this," Geoffrey urged but she would have none of it.

"I am not hungry. You eat it, Geoffrey."

"I will not eat if you do not." He had hoped the guilt would encourage her to eat but instead she stood up, ready to leave. "What are you doing?"

"I need to reload the revolver. You have seen how the caiman are preventing me from searching further along the bank."

"We have no more ammunition. What we had would have been swept away in the flood."

"I purchased some at the trading post. Not even those caiman are going to prevent me from doing what I must."

"… but Maggs… the flood was more than two weeks ago. You have to be practical. Nothing could have survived out here for that length of time, not without food and water."

"Edwin is out there, Geoffrey… he is alive. I am his mother and I would know deep in my heart if he was not!" she screeched, tearing twigs and trails of lichen from her hair.

At daybreak on the following morning, Geoffrey's heightened sense of hearing alerted him to the sound of natives jabbering urgently some distance away. To begin with it was unclear where the sound came from but that changed with the first sound of gunfire. Isolating where the second shot came from he raced downhill towards the river with the hound alongside. Reaching the dock, the first thing he saw was their recently acquired dugout being paddled away downriver with the body of a dead native sprawled over the side, his arms trailing in the water. Nearby, another man was floating face down in the river closer to the staging, visible only before the carcass was dragged beneath the surface by a black caiman.

Until then, Geoffrey hadn't noticed Marguerite standing at the very edge of the water, reloading the gun but with no time to fire off another shot before the canoe was paddled out of range and rounded a curve in the river.

"Watch out for predators," Geoffrey said as he reached her, taking her by the arm and pulling her further back on the bank.

"We must get after them, Geoffrey. We cannot allow them to get away with our only means of searching further along the river for Edwin." She shook herself free.

"There is no chance in Hell we would ever catch them on foot," Geoffrey said.

"There must be a way to catch them. There has to be!" she said frantically, her eyes wild and staring.

"If you wait here, I will take Bog Boy and see if I can cut them off," Geoffrey said, in an attempt to appease her.

"You cannot fire a revolver Geoffrey, so I will come with you. I will not hold you up."

"Unless your ankle gives out again. To get there ahead of the dugout means a steep climb up the canyon. Be practical, Maggs. You would never make it but the hound and I just might."

"How will you confront so many of them?" she called, following him regardless.

"I can manage well enough with Archie's knife and my spear and the hound and I working together as a team." He paused briefly to restrain her. "Wait for me here. If you follow me you will either be in the way or likely get killed!"

"Then I will wait for you here," she said but his instincts told him otherwise. Beside him the bullet holes and congealed blood were still engrained in the wooden mooring post where Valdez had been assassinated.

"Rest up in the cabin while you have the opportunity. We can begin searching again in the morning, with or without the canoe."

After a short diversion to the cabin to collect the hunting knife and one of his spears, Geoffrey set off after the dugout. Although the climb was steep, it wasn't long before he became aware that he hadn't been the first to take that path. A trail of recent mule droppings and a discarded piece of heavily bloodied cloth convinced him this must have been the route taken by the ruthless hunter who had butchered the one-eared jaguar. If so, he rather hoped he would soon come across the hunter's own rotting carcass.

On reaching the top of the rocky outcrop, Geoffrey came upon a broken horseshoe and from the sharp gouges in a recently exposed section of sloping rock below the track, where the moss and grass had been torn away, he could only assume the animal had plunged over the edge into the floodwater channelling through the gorge below and had probably taken its injured rider along with it.

This potentially satisfying conclusion was only short-lived as he came across more of the bloodstained material

240

under a deep shelf of rock where the hunter had clearly taken shelter, leaving behind the charred remains of a fire. The blade of a blackened knife suggested the killer had attempted to cauterise his wound but a trail of dried blood indicated that this had not succeeded. It ended with a smear on the bark of a tree further down the side of the gorge, at which point, reaching a fork in the trail, Geoffrey had to divert along the branch that led down to the river.

Although by cutting across country Geoffrey had got ahead of the dugout, it was instantly clear that there was no chance that he and the hound could reclaim it. There were four men paddling with two others armed with spears, bows and sheaths of arrows. It would have been suicidal for him to even attempt to ambush and so he reluctantly decided to abandon the project. With it went their only means of reaching Father Fitzgerald at the mission, unless of course that had been washed away also.

Geoffrey had agreed to help his sister's continuing search to give her some peace of mind but now so much time had passed since the flood he knew no unprotected child could have survived with so many predators hunting food. Now they no longer had a canoe to search for the boy he thought that perhaps he could make her see reason and begin to accept the fact that Edwin would never be coming back.

It was almost dark when Geoffrey and the hound returned, hungry and exhausted but on reaching the cabin he found it empty. Trying not to panic after searching the compound, he made his way cautiously down to the dock area with an oil lamp in one hand and Archie's hunting knife in the other. In the fading light he then made his way along to the lagoon where he found her seated cross-legged in Lorenzo's stone circle, staring blankly across the water where phosphorescent fish leapt out of the water, catching hovering insects.

"You came back," Marguerite said slowly, barely turning her head as he approached. "I waited for you at the dock for the longest time."

"I did not get the dugout back. There were too many of them to challenge," Geoffrey said, squatting beside her.

"Then you should have allowed me to go with you."

"It would not have done any good. It was a terrible climb, even without a twisted ankle. My calves were aching like hell by the time we reached the top."

"I still think I should have gone along too."

"I refuse to argue about this… so why not come back to the cabin and eat? You cannot go on like this every day, barely eating."

"I am not hungry."

"At least come back and rest," Geoffrey said; if there was one renegade hunter in that area, there might well be others.

"There is no point going back there Geoffrey. I cannot sleep until I find Edwin and, before you ask, I could not eat anything anyway."

"Then let us go back and come up with a plan on how best to search for him in daylight. If you will not do this for yourself then do it for me. I need to sleep where we are reasonably safe. God alone knows what is wandering about down here in search of food. I can barely keep my eyes open. That dash up the canyon has just about finished me off."

"Very well but only on condition that we set off again at daybreak," she said, reluctantly getting to her feet.

Waking before dawn, Geoffrey made his way to his father's

store in the rock face. He was relieved to see that, because the door was so tightly fitted to the entrance, the remaining tinned produce hadn't been washed away with the floodwaters.

Returning with three cans of baked beans and a tin of bully beef for when they returned, Geoffrey went to wake his sister. She had already left but getting the wolfhound to track her he found her searching through a devastated area of the uprooted forest close to the river. Thus began another day of intense searching, rooting through the smashed furniture from the cabins, littered at random in the mud among shredded items of his mother's linen that fluttered from the jagged remains of bushes and trees. Having spent the entire day alert for any attack, it was only as they headed back towards the compound, exhausted, that Margaret suddenly screamed.

"Geoffrey, look out!" She fumbled inside her bag for the revolver as a huge caiman crashed through the undergrowth and lunged at Geoffrey, its jaws gaping expectantly, so close that he could feel its breath, acrid and nauseating on his face.

Without hesitation, Geoffrey rammed the well-honed spear hard into the upper jaw of the monster, with such force that it pierced straight through, pinioning the writhing creature to a tree where, seconds later, it was dead from a single shot to the skull.

Exhausted but unable to sleep, Geoffrey spent most of that night making a replacement spear, using the deadly sharp arrowheads he'd saved from the most recent encounter with headhunters. Before they left, he padlocked the mule securely into the lean-to alongside the cabin.

"Have you left any food for the animal?" Marguerite asked.

"There is plenty; Father used that place to store grain. That mule has more food to dine on than we do."

By the end of the day, apart from more fragments of the compound's buildings, they had found no trace of human life. Even so, Marguerite refused to give up hope, continuing to search until dusk.

Late on the morning of the next day, their search was brought to an abrupt halt when they discovered the crib Geoffrey had carved, covered in grey slime and snagged high among the tangled roots of an uprooted tree.

"Pray God he is not in there?" Marguerite cried, scrambling towards her brother and knee deep in mud.

"The crib is empty" was all Geoffrey could say, emotionally drained after steeling himself to look inside.

"Let me see... let me see!" she screeched, her fingers gripping deep into his arm as he hauled her up the mangled roots.

"We do not know for certain that he was in here."

"Then where is he, Geoffrey? Where is he?"

"I only wish I knew." Geoffrey looked around at the devastated area of uprooted trees, animal carcasses and the remnants of structures projecting up through the steaming mud. "No one could have survived this, no one."

"You cannot say that, I would know... I would know if he had not, here, deep inside!" She pounded her heart. "I am his mother, Geoffrey, I would know that," Marguerite choked, tears streaming down her face. "Edwin has to be alive... I cannot live without him." She clung to the roots for support, calling her son's name over and over until her voice was hoarse.

It took over an hour before Geoffrey was able to free the crib, which he took back to the cabin. For the following two weeks he accompanied his sister on her fruitless search, realising that he had to come up with a logical reason to dissuade her from continuing with this obsession before she went raving mad.

"We cannot carry on like this, Maggs. It has been almost a month since the flood and you need to accept the fact that if Lorenzo, with all of his skills in the water, did not survive, then neither could Rose or any infant."

"I refuse to accept that, Geoffrey. I cannot forget him… and I will not, whatever you say!"

"Believe me when I say that I am only trying to be objective. Tomorrow I will go to the burial site and I will make markers for all three of them, just in case and you should come with me too."

"You cannot ask me to do that." She began wringing her hands in distress.

"Maggs, you must have somewhere to grieve if all else fails."

"It is different for you, Geoffrey, preparing to accept that Rosamund and Lorenzo will never return but I will never do that, not for Edwin."

"He is not coming back, Maggs. You need to accept that."

"Never… I never will, whatever you say. He is alive… he needs me. I am determined to find him, whatever you damned well think!"

At daybreak, Geoffrey was woken by Marguerite striding past where he was sleeping on the veranda.

"Where are you going so early?" he asked groggily.

"Where else would I go, if not to continue to look for Edwin?"

"You really cannot hope to find him after all this time," Geoffrey said.

"Quite frankly, I do not give a fig about your logic, Geoffrey. If he is anywhere out there I will find him on my own. I do not want you there. I will be safe enough with the revolver."

With Marguerite gone, Geoffrey made good use of his time alone at the burial ground, constructing an intricate cross, taller than himself, that was woven together from pieces of bleached river-wood he had been stockpiling over recent weeks for this specific purpose. He bound them together with lengths of copper wire from the storeroom before sinking the cross into the ground, then wove a Christ-like figure from lengths of vine before attaching this to it. Remembering the unexpected appearance of headhunters at this remote spot, Geoffrey made two improvised spears that he incorporated into the figure, weapons that could easily be detached if needed.

At the base he built a rockery from whatever pieces he could move. Once these were in position he planted a wild garden of ferns and a single, scarlet orchid among them, completing the memorial barely moments before his sister appeared.

"Oh Geoffrey… I did not expect to see anything like this," she said with unconcealed admiration.

"What did you think I was doing up here?"

"Not anything like this. This memorial for Mother is truly inspired. It is beautiful."

"I have been thinking that, when we eventually return home, perhaps with your knowledge of plants we might recreate a tropical garden as a memorial to them... under glass, of course. What would your thoughts be on that as a project?"

"I cannot be sure," she responded, guardedly.

"I thought that we could take back seeds and maybe a few cuttings from here when we leave and you could get them to germinate in the hothouse." He thought it strange that she didn't agree readily, in view of her knowledge of flora and fauna and the natural ability she had in getting anything to grow. "Do you think it a bad idea?"

"No, on the contrary, it is a lovely concept and a credit to you but apart from at Kew I have never seen anything like the variety of blooms that grow here, at least not in England. For an ambitious project like that, you would need to arrange to import plants and not just seeds or cuttings." She looked appraisingly around them at the varied plant life, her eyes a little less dull than before.

"Then you think we should go ahead and do it?"

"There is no sense in planning anything, Geoffrey; there is barely enough food to sustain our survival here for much longer. The project you are suggesting could take weeks, even months."

"I realise that well enough, not without more supplies anyway. Besides, it was only an idea."

"An interesting one nevertheless," she said thoughtfully.

"Whatever happens, we need to leave for the mission within the next three weeks if we are to stand any chance of ever getting home," Geoffrey said.

"And how do you propose we do that without a canoe?"

"Use the alternative: take the mule and trek overland."

Marguerite was gone for most of the next day and when Geoffrey returned with a catch of harpooned fish his sharp hearing alerted him to the hushed sound of strange voices on the other side of the clearing. Since his sister was not one of them, it was clear their sanctuary had been invaded.

With the spear balanced in readiness, Geoffrey and the hound crept silently through the bushes to confront the intruders.

There were two white men on the veranda, both clearly shocked by his unexpected appearance. The older of the two was urging the younger, heavily bearded man not to venture out into the clearing, sound advice the younger man chose to ignore, either through bravado or crass stupidity since it would have been apparent to anyone that he would be dead in seconds if he made a single false move.

Taking in every possible threat, Geoffrey saw a rifle leaning up against the doorframe, barely a stride away from the older man but this could only be reached if he chose to risk that move, which he must know would resulted in the younger man's death, or even his own.

Feeling the warning heat generated from the hound's woven collar against his bare thigh, Geoffrey tightened his grip on the spear in readiness to embed it in the older man at the slightest movement towards the rifle. He still kept his eye on the cautious approach of the bearded man who, although coming closer, appeared less of a threat.

As the younger man stumbled, an intricately woven chain around his neck became visible, almost identical to both Geoffrey's own and the hound's collar, worked with similar lengths of copper hair that, like his own armlet, appeared to be faintly glowing. More disturbingly, unlike any adversary they had confronted before, the man continued to approach, despite the threat of the spear pointed directly at his throat.

Had Geoffrey been aware of the shocking transformation that had taken place from the innocent adolescent he would have presented just two years earlier, he might have begun to understand the terrifying apparition he and the hound presented that day. Now he appeared more like a merciless savage than anything remotely resembling an English aristocrat.

Crammed on his head was a makeshift hat plaited from palm fronds, which made it difficult to see his face. His lean, muscular body, partially visible within a dirty linen waistcoat, was horrifically scarred; even worse was the gruesome mutilation of his hands. His long fair hair had been bleached white by the sun, so that he might have been an albino or a throwback from mixed-race parentage. Even up close it would have been difficult to estimate his true age from the scarred, sunburnt body.

The bearded man attempted to question Geoffrey using fragments of Spanish, Portuguese and French, resorted lastly to English and speaking clearly with slow deliberation.

"I mean you no harm," he began, indicating the plaited band around his own neck. It was clear that he was trying to appear calm, until the moment his gaze focused on the silver and bone-handled hunting knife tucked into Geoffrey's belt.

"How the hell did you get hold of my knife, you heathen bastard?" he challenged, as if forgetting the spear that was levelled at his throat.

Although it was now clear that at least one of the men spoke English, Geoffrey chose to say nothing, unsure which of the two he should focus on. The older man was shouting instructions to his bearded companion but Geoffrey's keen hearing had alerted him to someone else approaching. Now worried that a third intruder might join them, Geoffrey watched their movements with equal intensity, calculating who would make the first move and consequently he picked up only fragments of what the younger man was saying.

"Answer me, you bloody moron, where did you get it?" the man yelled menacingly, still seemingly undaunted by the deadly weapon aimed directly at him.

"Señor Archie, move… I can take him down from here," the older man now called, grabbing the rifle and shouldering it in readiness to take the shot.

"Keep out of this, damn you. I want answers!" the bearded man responded angrily, not taking his eyes off Geoffrey for a second.

It was an audaciously familiar stare, a challenging eye-to-eye contact that gave Geoffrey the chills. Deep down he began to feel he had seen this man before.

The wolfhound was crouched in preparation to attack but Geoffrey instinctively restrained the animal by placing a hand on its neck. "Bog Boy, stay," he commanded softly, continuing to balance the spear in readiness.

"Bog Boy…? Who the hell are you?" The man glowered, as if some deeply buried realisation was beginning to dawn.

"Get clear, Irishman, now. I have him in my sights!" the older man cried, clicking off the safety catch and squeezing the trigger.

"For God's sake no… I know him!" the bearded man cried, stepping recklessly into the line of fire just as the rifle went off. He gasped out "Jeffy?" as he reeled forward from the impact of the bullet.

As the shot rang out Geoffrey turned to hurl the spear at the older man, impaling his left arm into the upright post of the veranda, the rifle clattering onto the wooden floor. Although his immediate impulse was to see if the man at his feet was either dead or still breathing, his primary concern was that he no longer had a spear, so he moved swiftly to the opening through which the approaching person would soon appear. The footsteps had stopped advancing after the crack of gunfire.

With Archie's hunting knife poised in readiness, Geoffrey waited silently as his keen sense of hearing picked up the sound of laboured breathing and a few moments later the safety catch of a handgun being released before his sister appeared through a gap in the bushes.

"Who are these men, Geoffrey?" Marguerite asked, keeping her distance and staring at Captain Giorgio's impaled arm with no sign of sympathy or any offer of help. Instead, without even a tremble, she levelled her revolver at him.

If she had expected the injured man to quake with fear, the effect was the exact reverse. Bellowing like a raging bull and with seemingly superhuman strength combusted through excruciating pain, the Captain began screaming abuse at the top of his lungs before snapping the shaft of the spear with his right hand. Within moments he had wrenched his arm free in a fearsome display of power. Yet once the pierced forearm was freed, it was as if Giorgio's strength was exhausted as he sank to his knees. Whimpering with agony, he poured a dash of neat whisky from his hip flask on to the wound before binding it with his neckerchief, a feat he achieved with one hand and his teeth. It seemed he was aware of nothing but his injury until a shadow made him glance up and he found himself staring into the barrel of a revolver.

"Do not kill him, Maggs!" Geoffrey called out, stooping over the crumpled figure at his feet as she pressed her pistol to Captain Giorgio's temple.

"Are you hurt, Geoffrey?"

"No I am not but this man here is and it looks serious."

"Did that hunter attack you?"

"On the contrary, he stepped in front of the bullet to save me," Geoffrey called back, still astonished at the man's behaviour.

"You must be mistaken, Geoffrey. No one would do that if you were about to harpoon his companion."

"I am under no illusion about what happened here. I just know what he did." Geoffrey began to examine the lifeless body at his feet. "He addressed me in English."

"That is a help at least. Who are you… and what are you doing here?" she demanded of Captain Giorgio. "We have nothing here worth stealing any more."

"I no good Inglese speak," Giorgio mumbled.

"You seem to understand it well enough… Who are you?" she repeated coldly.

"Giorgio Papas, captain of boat. We come in peace. Not want harm."

"So why did you shoot that other brute?"

"I no want harm Señor, him good man, him get in way."

Not taking her eyes off him for a second, Marguerite kicked the rifle out of his reach.

"Are you sure that you are unharmed, Geoffrey?"

"I would have been if this fellow had not taken the bullet instead." Geoffrey was relieved to see some signs of life as he prodded the injured man with his sandaled foot. "That bastard over there was aiming at me, not him."

"What shall I do with this creature?" Marguerite asked, releasing the safety catch of the revolver.

"You no kill Giorgio, I good Catholic same as… same as you, Lady Rosa. I grandfather!" Giorgio pleaded, grimacing with the agonising pain.

"What did you call me?" Marguerite demanded, clearly unnerved at hearing her sister's name so unexpectedly spoken by this would-be assassin. "Why did you mention Lady Rosamund's name? Well go on…? Answer me, you, you murdering foreigner!"

"Do not kill him, whatever you do," her brother urged. "They both seem to know something about us. This one here with the beard; I'm sure he called me by my name just before he took the bullet."

"He called you Geoffrey?" she asked in amazement.

"Not exactly; it sounded more like Jeffy."

"Then you must be mistaken. Only Rosamund and Lorenzo ever called you that." She turned to resume her interrogation of the man staring down the barrel of her revolver. "Now… I will ask you this only once, otherwise I will squeeze the trigger. Who in God's name are you and who is that man you shot? What do you want with our family?"

"I am Captain Giorgio Papas, from Karaka," he mumbled, spitting out a mouthful of blood and neckerchief fibres. "Me hire boat for bring Señor to this place, he no go back until he find la bella Rosa here, she Inglese Lady."

"Then who is your companion and why did you kill him?"

"Signor, him no dead… he good Catholic, same as Giorgio. If him die I no get pay and Giorgio burn in hell for kill," he said wretchedly, staring at the bearded figure on the ground.

Tearing off a sleeve from the man's shirt, Geoffrey jammed the material up against the open wound to stem the flow of blood.

"Is he dead?" Marguerite called out.

"Not if I can stop the bleeding. Can you give me a hand to bandage this up? It is one hell of a mess. The bullet went clean through."

"I cannot leave this other brute alone. He might try something else." Only when Geoffrey had sent the hound over to watch over the wounded captain did she come to his aid.

"We should get him inside and do something to help, otherwise he will die. This wound looks ghastly," Geoffrey said, although he took some comfort in seeing the bleeding had eased.

"I doubt that but if he does survive this wound will take some time to heal."

"Then we should get that other fellow out of our way, otherwise we will never get this man inside to stitch him up," Geoffrey said, whistling the dog to heel.

"What shall we do with him?"

"Lock him up out of the way."

"How can you be so calm about this, Geoffrey, when these brutes tried to kill you?"

"Only the one I speared tried that. This one was different. He tried to reason with me before he lost his temper for some reason. For now I suggest we lock him up in the lean-to with the mule."

"You no keep Giorgio in this place, I no animal!" he complained bitterly as Geoffrey pushed him inside.

"Stay quiet, you wicked bastard, unless you want me to finish you off for good," Geoffrey threatened, slamming the door and barring it securely before hastening back to help his sister carry the injured man inside.

However unexpected the appearance of two white men in the compound might have been, it occurred to Geoffrey as he watched Marguerite remove her hat, just as elegantly as she would have done back home in the presence of other Europeans, how inappropriate her clothing must have appeared, an outfit that would have outraged all of Edwardian society back home in England.

Having gradually discarded any restrictive clothing since their abandonment in the compound, Marguerite had taken to wearing a pair of sturdy boots that had once belonged to their father and a cut-off, knee-length underslip that had belonged to her mother. Her dark, lustrous hair was coiled neatly into the nape of her neck, kept in place with her mother's silver-mounted wooden combs, emphasising the remaining sapphire earring that shimmered in the sunlight like a droplet of ice.

Having laid out the injured man on the bed, Geoffrey began removing the bloodied shirt in readiness for Marguerite's return. Cautiously tearing open the back of the man's shirt he exposing not only the bullet wound but also the unmistakable birthmark, identical to the one that Edwin had been born with.

"Oh my God... Get over here quickly, Maggs, you need to see this!" Geoffrey yelled. "He has the mark! I know who this is. He is too young to be Archie Westbrook's father, so it can only be him... Archie has only damned well found us!"

"Archie went back to Ireland and what would he be doing out here, so far from Pernambuco?" she said, examining the mark between his shoulder blades.

"It must be him look at this birthmark."

"This cannot be, Geoffrey… This birthmark is identical to Edwin's; even its position is the same. How is this even possible?"

"They must be related; it is the only explanation. This mark is hereditary in Archie's family and is passed down only through the male line."

"But Archie is not Edwin's father. Maybe you misheard." To his surprise she took a swig of whisky from the bottle as he cleaned the bullet wound and after they turned him over she took another long draught while Geoffrey cleaned the blood from his chest.

"Old Betsy is not sounding too happy about having company back there," Geoffrey said, becoming aware of a frantic crashing from inside the stable.

"What are you talking about?"

"The old mule, can you not hear the row she is making next door? She must really object to having that old captain forced on her."

"Well that is one thing we agree on. Can you get in there to stop it kicking the wall? This exit wound is frightfully ragged and it is impossible to concentrate with all that noise." She began threading a needle as the sound of crashing increased and then stopped as abruptly as it had begun.

"I will see to it right now."

"Do not be long, Geoffrey. I need you back here to get these lamps alight and hold this man down if he wakes, otherwise these stitches will come apart."

"I will be as quick as I can," Geoffrey said. As he removed the locking bar he was conscious of how menacingly quiet the stable had suddenly become but was unprepared for the savage blow to the back of his head which felled him like a falling tree.

When Geoffrey finally opened his eyes, Marguerite was kneeling beside him. "Geoffrey, what happened? Look at me and try to remain focused!" She helped him to stand. "Your head is bleeding."

"Someone hit me from behind," he said groggily.

"Did you see who?" She looked around, holding the revolver.

They opened the door to check on the captive but after pushing the mule out of the way there was no sign of Captain Giorgio, only a gaping hole at the back of the stable.

"I think we have found the culprit," said Geoffrey.

"I should have shot the swine when I had the chance." Marguerite examined the cut on the back of Geoffrey's head. "This is going to need stitches."

"Then it will have to wait." Geoffrey grabbed hold of his remaining spear.

"Very well but you are not going anywhere until this is bandaged." Wafting away the swarming flies and in spite of his protests she bound up his head with the remains of Archie's a makeshift bandage.

"You will need that for Archie."

"There is more clean linen in the chest. I will tear that up."

"How long was I knocked out?" he asked anxiously.

"Maybe ten minutes. No longer than fifteen."

Geoffrey's attention was engaged elsewhere, staring above the shattered trees as belching plumes of black smoke began spiralling upwards.

"He is over there… he is getting away," Geoffrey cried, focusing on the clouds of belching smoke in an effort to distance himself from the throbbing pain in his head. He must be using green wood to stoke up the boiler and get the engine started."

"How could anyone abandon his injured companion like that?" Marguerite asked.

"Well most certainly not him, not if I can bloody well help it!" Geoffrey raced down the steep incline towards the wrecked docking area, the hound bounding after him, arriving just as Captain Giorgio hastily cast off the mooring rope, leaving it trailing behind in the water as the steamer spluttered into life and began inching slowly away from the bloodstained mooring post where Valdez had been executed.

Determined that he would not escape, Geoffrey sprinted diagonally away from the river and uphill to cut the corner and wait until the labouring steamer came chugging around the bend. He waited on a rocky outcrop where, had Giorgio looked up, he would have seen him immediately but the captain was struggling, one-handed, in a desperate attempt to keep the fire alight and build up steam pressure in the ancient boiler. Since most of the wood was saturated from the flooding it was almost impossible to keep the blaze going. When Geoffrey's voice rang out he looked up and almost collapsed at the terrifying image of a menacing wild man, his head crudely bandaged and with the ferocious wolfhound at his side, standing on the cliff edge just a few feet above with spear in hand. There was little room for manoeuvre since a spreading mass of flotsam had forced the steamer to pass closer to the bank than it would normally have done.

Later, after Geoffrey had returned with the Captain Giorgio, roped and shackled, it was apparent that Archie was fighting for his life.

"You must prepare yourself for the worst, Geoffrey. I cannot see how anyone could survive this awful wound without proper medical attention."

"There is still hope," Geoffrey said, indicating the woven chain around Archie's neck that was now glowing faintly. "This is the same as what you and I both have, woven from Lorenzo's hair. See how it pulsates?"

"For goodness' sake Geoffrey, how can that be of any help? Now do sit down and remove that bandage. I need to stitch your scalp before it becomes infected. We can discuss Archie Westbrook later."

"Surely it would not hurt to consider the logic in what I am saying, instead of just steamrollering over the possibility as is your wont!"

"Of course I would take heed of what you have to say Geoffrey, were any of it based on logic or science rather than these schoolboy fantasies. Why do you always allow your overactive imagination to come up with such ridiculous ideas? The biggest flaw with your crackpot theory is that Lorenzo and Archie Westbrook have never met."

Although Marguerite tried everything to prevent infection in Archie's wound he soon developed a raging fever and they began to fear he would never regain consciousness.

"We must do something, Maggs," Geoffrey said in desperation. Archie came all this way to find us and we cannot just let him die."

"We have virtually nothing available, Geoffrey, you know that. Did you find anything useful on the boat?"

"There were two bottles of whisky and a roll of old bandages but no medical stuff   but they do have a stock of food on board that could last us a few months."

Over the days that followed Geoffrey tried scouring his father's books for any clue about how to treat Archie's ailment but he found nothing.

It was Marguerite's idea to sit with Archie through the night but she offered no resistance when Geoffrey insisted that he should take over. She continued to prepare all of the invalid's meals, feeding Archie with bully-beef broth and a constant supply of fluids but insisted on leaving the room while Geoffrey changed his underwear and remained outside the cabin until Archie had been thoroughly washed down.

Although the idea of cleaning another man's body had initially been a difficult prospect for Geoffrey, by remembering how Lorenzo had cared for him when he was unable to wash and feed himself he steeled himself to deal with whatever was needed. It somehow helped that he had rejected his sister's suggestion of shaving off Archie's beard, since the man he was caring for appeared more like a stranger than the charismatic Archie Westbrook he had come to idolise and he was able to get through all of the necessary ablutions without too much embarrassment.

On the nights when Marguerite would take over, knowing Geoffrey was exhausted, he slept with the hound on the veranda but was often awoken by her tearful sobbing. Realising the cause was the uncertainty of Edwin's fate, he chose to leave her alone with her grief.

After ten days Archie's fever took a turn for the worse and he began to thrash violently around in the cot. Geoffrey took over and stayed with him throughout every night, hoping that his sister would be able to rest more. Her behaviour had become completely unpredictable, at times logical and over critical but at others it reminded him of how Rosamund had behaved in the early days after the rape, a disturbing similarity that had Geoffrey keeping a watchful eye on her.

It took three more days before there was any hint that Archie would emerge from the coma but after another four he opened his eyes and began to show some reaction to the outside world.

At daybreak on the third of those days Geoffrey was woken by his sister, shaking his shoulder.

"Wake up, Geoffrey, Geoffrey... wake up!"

"Whatever is the matter?" he asked groggily, rubbing sleep from his eyes.

"There is nothing the matter. I am just informing you that I will not be here for a while."

"What do you mean by that? Where are you going?"

"I have absolutely no idea. I just need to get away from here. I cannot abide being cooped up in this cabin any longer. There is so much I need to get done."

"I thought you were going to help me look after Archie?"

"Why... because I am a woman?" she huffed, cramming the straw hat on her head with undue emphasis. "I have been doing exactly that for the past two weeks and I am sick of making that disgusting broth. Now it is your turn and you can also get that irresponsible foreigner to be more useful around here. This is not an hotel and I am not his blasted servant, whatever he might think."

"What precisely do you want the old man to do?"

"Nothing at all for me, so I would suggest that you make the best use of him while you can. I have decided to go ahead with that idea you had a while ago, beginning this morning. I will explain more how that lapsed Catholic can help when I return."

"What was it I said?" Geoffrey asked, sure it would be somehow connected to Edwin. "Are you going to tell me what this is about? What could be so bloody important to make you leave at this hour? It is barely light."

"Since you ask, I will be making a start on collecting rare plants for that tropical garden you suggested," she said, as calmly as if she had proposed digging up a handful of flowers from their estate back in England. "Needless to say, these would need to be housed in a structure with controlled heating system. I have sketched a winter garden in the journal, to be constructed at the estate in Ashbourne, facing south. From there it would command a perfect view of the Palladian Bridge, which, if you remember, was always a great favourite of Mother's."

"I thought you had rejected the idea," Geoffrey said, barely able to contain his own renewed enthusiasm for the project.

"Obviously not... that is why I need to make a start immediately. It will take some time to locate and pot up the more unusual species. However, once Archie has recovered and is well enough to travel, enough storage space must be allowed for the collection."

"What makes you think you will find anything growing so close to here?"

"Because of what has survived here after the flood. There are some species I doubt even Kew Gardens have any record of, let alone on display. I have already sketched some of these varieties into my journal; I would show you had I the time."

"I would offer you my assistance but you know me... I hardly know the difference between a dandelion and a dog daisy," Geoffrey smiled.

"Whatever bulbs and roots I return with each day will need potting up into containers, woven baskets preferably, which brings me to your question about what to get that shifty foreigner to help out with."

"Good idea... I can get him to work with me on that, with Bog's help. He is petrified of the hound and will be no trouble, not with the dog breathing down his neck."

"Then perhaps you might begin today." She stepped out into the rain with a digging tool in her hand and the capacious bag, unusually empty, slung diagonally across her chest.

Chapter Twelve
An Unresolved Conclusion

It had been two weeks since the raging fever began and, apart from force-feeding Archie through a tube with the liquidised bully beef concoction, along with crushed mango juice and plenty of fresh water to replace the fluids, all Geoffrey could do was pray that he would eventually recover.

On some days Archie would barely move for hours, mumbling incoherent words and occasionally kicking spasmodically but then unexpectedly he would thrash about wildly on the cot, screaming loudly in what Geoffrey took to be Gaelic. Because he had to spread-eagle his own body across the writhing figure to prevent him from causing any more injury to himself, Geoffrey was convinced that most of it was insults and curses directed at him.

During this period Archie's body temperature began to fluctuate drastically, alternating from burning hot and sweating profusely to uncontrollable shuddering, his skin ice-cold to the touch. Because there were no blankets or covers to pile over him for warmth, the only option Geoffrey had was to get into the cot with him and he prayed his sister wouldn't come in and get the wrong idea. However, on reflection he realised that she had been deliberately avoiding being in the same room with Archie, except under cover of night.

It was during one of these wild, convulsive sessions that Archie's eyes opened wide, glazed and staring crazily at the portrait of himself pinned above the bed.

"Archie... Archie, listen to me and try to understand. This is something Lady Marguerite sketched of you in

Pernambuco. You are safe here," Geoffrey said, barely able to keep the writhing body pinned down on the cot.

After a further three days Archie's movements seemed more coordinated and the blank stare was replaced by a more intense gaze but still he either chose not to speak or was unable to and another four days passed in silence. Marguerite was still avoiding entering the room, concentrating her efforts on gathering a huge quantity of plants.

"For Pete's sake, Maggs, not more plants! The boat will sink without trace if you load it up with any more," Geoffrey complained, trying to work out how many more containers would be needed to get the latest batch of plants potted up.

"I cannot replicate what we have here in a memorial garden without the correct flora and fauna. Even you should understand that!" she ranted, throwing down the trowel in anger.

"I do, you know that. Why not take a break and come inside for a moment. If Archie sees you it might jog his memory and help him to speak again."

"Maybe but not today. There are other things I need to do first."

"Like what exactly?" Geoffrey said, with unconcealed frustration.

"It is no use glaring at me, Geoffrey. I am not going in there and that is final. I have no time for this. I have already told you that I need to collect more plants and whatever seeds I can harvest. If the plants do not survive the journey, at least there will be an alternative."

"That is no reason not to come inside and speak to him."

"Was I not clear enough? No, I will not!" Marguerite snapped, bringing an end to the conversation.

The next day she passed him on his way into the makeshift kitchen they had rigged up in the stable.

"Will you come with me today, Geoffrey?"

"Why, where are you going?"

"To the burial site. I need to replenish the plants on Mother's grave."

"Why the urgency today? I still need to help Archie wash himself down."

"Since you have so clearly forgotten, it is Mother's birthday. That is why she must have more flowers." Her slim figure was backlit by the midday sun and Geoffrey could see Captain Giorgio ogling her from nearby.

"Are you sure it is today?" Geoffrey asked with some confusion, not only unsure of what day it was but the month too.

"Naturally, otherwise why would I have mentioned it? Are you coming?" she asked impatiently, avoiding any eye contact with the leering Captain.

"Of course, you know I will, I just need to let Archie know where I am going first. Why not come in and speak to him?"

"I have my reasons; and while we are on the subject, I do not want that man prying into our affairs; more importantly, I do not want him knowing anything about Edwin," she said harshly, turning her back on him.

"Is that why you are avoiding him?" Geoffrey challenged.

"You know exactly why I will not go in there, so why ask?"

"If you think I have the ability to read what is going on in that mind of yours, then no, I do not."

"Then let me explain… I cannot bear to look at the same birthmark Edwin was born with on another man's back. It is a freak of nature and nothing more. We are not related to Archie Westbrook in any way. Is that not reason enough?"

"No, not really."

"There would be no point in questioning him about it, not least since that would bring Mother's morality into question and presumably Archie's father's also. Therefore I must ask you to respect my wishes and say nothing. Do I have your word on this?"

"Since you put it like that, then naturally I will. If you want to go up to Mother now, then I will be there as soon as I can. Just make sure that you take the revolver with you."

"I have it in here," she called over her shoulder, tapping her bag.

It was soon after Geoffrey returned to the cabin that Archie spoke directly to him for the first time since their confrontation. Although his voice was weak and a trifle shaky the question he posed was clear but it was a difficult one to answer.

"Where is she?" Archie asked. "Lady Claudia. I need to speak with her on a most urgent matter."

"She is not here," Geoffrey said, trembling as he heard his mother's name.

"Then where can I find her?" Archie persisted.

"Mother is at the burial site" was all Geoffrey could bring himself to admit, which he regretted immediately.

"Then you must take me there. What I have to say cannot wait a moment longer."

"That would be impossible, Archie. It is too steep a climb in your condition and you are not strong enough."

"Then might I inquire if Lady Claudia will be returning here this evening?"

"No, she will not," Geoffrey said, unable to bring himself to tell him the truth "Why do you ask?"

"I have information concerning my father and I have not seen her since I was brought inside with my injuries," Archie said. It was clear he was troubled by some important issue.

"You need to rest, Archie. You had a really bad infection after you were shot. You cannot risk another. It could finish you off next time."

"Then that is a risk I must take." Archie struggled to sit up and righted himself on the edge of the cot.

"Archie… you are behaving like a bloody fool. How the hell do you expect to get up there if you can barely walk?"

"I was not expecting to go on foot. When I first arrived I thought I saw a horse stabled next to the cabin."

"We have a mule but no horse."

"Then would you mind if I rode it up to the burial site?"

"If that is what you want, then by all means go ahead; it is your neck not mine but old Betsy can be grumpy unless the hound tags along with her."

"Then I would like to set off now," Archie said, attempting to get off the cot.

"What the hell are you doing? You cannot even stand on your own; let me help." Geoffrey grabbed his arms to prevent him from toppling over and saw a look of horror pass fleetingly across Archie's face.

"What happened to your beautiful hands, Jeffy?" Archie asked, taking hold of the mutilated claws as Geoffrey helped him stand.

"I would rather not say. It is a long story and one I do not enjoy speaking about."

"I apologise; it was not my intention to offend."

"You have not. It is just too complicated to go into right now."

"Then I will leave you to decide whether or not to tell me," Archie said gently as Geoffrey assisted him onto the veranda.

"I appreciate that, Archie, thank you."

Once Geoffrey had managed to get Archie outside the cabin Geoffrey haltered up the mule, worried that Captain Giorgio was now nowhere to be seen.

"What is all this?" Archie asked, as Geoffrey helped him on to the mule.

"A collection of rare plants my sister has suggested we take back to England."

"Would it be imprudent of me to ask after the Lady Rosamund?"

"That is a question I am unable to answer, Archie. The fact is, we have no idea where my sister is at this time." Geoffrey hoped that Archie would leave the matter there, at least for the time being.

"Then I assume this admirable collection of plants must have been selected by the Lady Marguerite? From her absence here, would I be correct in assuming that she is still collecting?"

"At the moment no, she is not; we already have enough, if not too many. My sister is at the burial site with Mother," Geoffrey said, sticking with half-truths to avoid further explanation until they reached the site, where he hoped that seeing his sister would help unravel the confusion in Archie's mind.

"Where is Captain Giorgio? Should he not be here?" Archie asked.

"He cannot have gone far, not hobbled," Geoffrey said, looking around for any sign of the captive.

"What do you mean, hobbled?"

"We had a few problems with your companion after you were wounded. It was impossible to watch him all the time and so he was hobbled."

"What... you actually hobbled the man as if he was some bloody animal!" Archie protested.

"Yes I did, since you ask and I was happy to do it. My sister has been troubled by the captain's attitude ever since he arrived. He treats her as if she was his servant and I don't like the way he looks at her either."

"That is your reasoning, is it? To shackle Captain Papas like a criminal because he does not offer Lady Marguerite the respect her title dictates back in England? This is the backwaters of South America, for God's sake, not Chatsworth Park."

"Don't we bloody well know it! Besides, had you seen the way he leers at her, you would agree about curtailing his movements. The hobble allows him to move about freely enough but he can't run off in the boat."

"Is that what this is all about? You would hog-tie the man like a pig ready for market because you think he would take off in his own boat. Giorgio would never abandon us here."

"Yet that is exactly what he tried after you were shot."

"All you needed to do was disable the engine," Archie grumbled.

"To begin with, I would not have the foggiest idea where to start. I am not a damned mechanic," Geoffrey snapped. Before he could say any more there was a muffled gunshot and at the same moment Geoffrey spotted the remains of the hobble on the ground near the veranda.

"Did you hear that? It sounded close," Archie asked, reining in the mule.

"I think it came from the burial site."

"Then we should get on up there. They might be under attack," Archie said.

"If she was, it would all be over by now." Geoffrey tried to remain calm.

"How can you be so sure? It was only a single shot."

"That is all it would take," Geoffrey said grimly. What he did know was Giorgio wasn't nearby, so if he wasn't already on the boat he feared the reason for the gunfire.

"You will have to follow as best you can, Archie. I need to get up there fast," Geoffrey said, whistling the hound to heel before sprinting uphill with the spear clutched tightly in his hand.

Gasping for breath, Geoffrey found his sister leaning against a tree. There was a savage gash across her cheek and her mouth was swollen and bleeding. The strap of her light garment had been torn off and she made no attempt to cover her exposed breasts but made a valiant effort to cover her thighs with what remained of the torn fabric just as Archie arrived on the mule. Her right shoulder, her arms and both knees were badly grazed. Her legs and body were smeared with grass and mud and covered in cuts that were bleeding badly.

"Where is the evil bastard?" Geoffrey snarled, balancing the spear in his hand.

"In hell by now, exactly where he belongs," Marguerite said, covering herself as best she could as Archie clambered awkwardly down from the mule and approached her unsteadily.

"Whoever did this, milady, he will pay dearly," Archie said.

"Your disgusting companion already has. The wretched creature is dead."

"Captain Giorgio was responsible for this diabolical act, Lady Claudia?" Archie asked with astonishment.

"Leave her be, Archie... this is not Lady Claudia."

"You confuse me with my mother, sir. I am her daughter, Lady Marguerite."

"Do forgive me, Milady... Were you able to shoot the wretch?" Archie asked, tight-lipped and fuming.

"I used the only weapon available and to good effect."

"Then are you sure he is actually dead?" Archie asked.

"I am and now it would be greatly appreciated if you would allow me some time on my own. It has been quite an ordeal," Marguerite said shakily, moving painfully to sit on a rock some distance away.

"Where is he, Jeffy?" Archie asked.

"Over here, take a look." Geoffrey aimed a kick at Giorgio's lifeless body, propped up against the base of the woven figure on the cross.

There was a deep bleeding furrow across Giorgio's scalp where the bullet had missed entering his forehead by only a fraction. Frozen in death, a look of sheer terror was recorded in his features. His blank, unseeing eyes stared down at a broken spear protruding from his chest where it had been thrust mercilessly through his heart.

From the deep gouges raked across Giorgio's face and arms Geoffrey knew that his sister had not given in easily and must have fought him off like a tigress. There were three separate areas that had been churned up like a rugby pitch and because his trousers were still crumpled around his ankles his genitals were exposed, making it clear that in dismounting from the rape he had tripped, thereby allowing Marguerite the opportunity to grab one of Geoffrey's spears from the woven image and ram it hard through his chest. Why she had not fired off a second shot soon became clear as the bloodied revolver was found wedged tightly under a rock, the place where the violent assault must have begun.

To begin with Marguerite refused Archie's offer of his shirt but after her brother pointed out that he wasn't wearing one either, she relented and was able to use her own torn garment to cover her naked thighs.

"We should go back to the cabin, Geoff. Your sister will need time on her own to get over what just happened but she can't stay here; it's far too dangerous to be alone," Archie said.

"I will allow you to escort me part of the way but no further," Marguerite responded. "I intend going by myself to the lagoon where I can wash off the stench from that disgusting animal and I can only do that in clear, fresh water."

"You go on ahead without me. I will be down shortly," Geoffrey said, resetting the plants on his mother's grave that had been disturbed by the struggle.

When Geoffrey rejoined them a while later, his sister's hair, still wet, had been combed away from her face and was tied back with string. She was wearing a cut-down dress that had once belonged to their mother and their father's boots. The dangling sapphire earring glittered as she jabbed viciously at her soiled garments, smouldering on an open fire.

"You have been longer than I expected," Archie commented when Geoffrey joined him on the veranda.

"There were things I had to do that could not be left."

"I can only presume by that that you mean Giorgio's body?"

"Indeed."

"Did you bury him?"

"No, I did not, since you ask... I pitched his disgusting carcass over the cliff. What little there is remaining of him will probably be floating down the river as we speak."

"You did what!" Archie exclaimed.

"I threw his body over the cliff. What did you expect?"

"Holy Mary... that is barbaric," Archie declared.

"Bollocks, Archie Westbrook. You have your head screwed on the wrong way if you think that what I did was not an appropriate end for that piece of filth. What would you have done if he had raped someone that you cared about? Given him a burial at sea?

"No, I damned well would not. If you think that of me, then you don't know me at all. In the same situation I would probably have done exactly what you did but that doesn't make it right. Giorgio Papas was a Catholic."

"Then let him take that issue up with his maker... if he ever gets that far!" Geoffrey snapped, grinding his teeth with annoyance.

"Might I inquire after the Lady Claudia, now that we are alone?" Archie asked more gently.

"Mother was killed by hunters soon after we were abandoned here. It was at the same time I lost these fingers,"

Geoffrey said, offering up his hands. "As you saw, she has been laid to rest in the burial ground."

"And what of the Lady Rosamund, where is she?" Archie asked tentatively.

"My sister did not survive the flood," Geoffrey said, not wanting to go into any more detail.

"I do not understand. The Lady Rosamund must have survived. She was there after the swimmer saved my life. It could only have been her voice."

"What? Did you actually see her?"

"No, I did not. It was just her voice that I recognised."

"Did she call you by name?"

"Yes, except that she called me her cousin," Archie said.

"That makes no sense at all. You must have been confused if you had just been dragged out of the water. What else do you remember about what happened and who was this mysterious person who saved you?" Geoffrey asked.

"It is a long story and I'm sorry I can't be more specific, the reason being that I only saw him underwater. All I can tell you is that he was an incredible swimmer. I plaited this chain I wear from strands of his hair that I found after he saved me but for some reason I can't get the damned thing off now!" Archie fingered the cord around his neck.

Geoffrey spent a week watching his sister's every move before he was sure that this latest ordeal hadn't driven her completely insane. Even so, on some occasions her mood swings seemed to border on madness, particularly when she was in Archie's company.

"Are you feeling any better today, Archie?" Geoffrey asked, potting up more of the plants.

"Not well enough to navigate the shallows but give me another week and I will be fit enough to handle that boat.

"I can always lend a hand," Geoffrey said. He had no idea how he could be of use but felt he should offer.

"I am counting on it, at least until we transfer into something larger. If you will forgive me for asking, you never did explain the reasoning behind all these plants."

"We hope to establish a memorial winter garden dedicated to Mother and Rose once we have returned home," Geoffrey said, realising how excessive the quantity of specimen plants must appear. "Will we need a larger boat because of the quantity of plants?"

"Partly but before you go off at the deep end you must also be aware that legally that old tub still belongs to Captain Giorgio's family and despite what he did I am morally obligated to return it to them. Having said that, we will need something more substantial than a shallow-draught steamer to get us safely back down the Amazon."

"How could anyone in their right mind consider themselves morally obligated to a rapist's family?"

"Because they are innocent of Captain Giorgio's actions and that is why it must be done," Archie said firmly. "However, what I propose must stay between you and me and when the time comes to hand over, you must keep Lady Marguerite away. She must never be in contact with his relatives."

"Have you spoken to my sister about the volume of plants she insists on shipping back to England?"

"There is no need; we should manage well enough. Lady Marguerite has been through quite enough. I would never want to upset her by refusing to take any of them on board."

"We will never get them all on board, not with all three of us, plus Bog Boy and Betsy the mule." Geoffrey lowered his voice as his sister approached with yet more roots in need of potting.

"Of course we cannot leave the mule behind. That would be unthinkable," Archie said.

"There is no need. The animal can remain here with me!" Marguerite announced, depositing her latest collection at Geoffrey's feet.

"What do you mean by that?" Geoffrey asked.

"You heard me well enough, Geoffrey. You have always known that it was never my intention to get on that boat, not without Edwin."

"Edwin?" Archie asked, perplexed. "Who is this person, milady? Why have you never mentioned this man's name before?"

"You were never informed because it was none of your concern, Mr. Westbrook but since you ask, Edwin is my son and I will not leave here without him!"

"You have a child, out here in this godforsaken place?" Archie asked incredulously.

"Edwin has been missing since the flood but Maggs is convinced he is still alive," Geoffrey explained.

"But that happened weeks ago. Was the child alone?"

"We cannot be sure, since Lorenzo and Rose went missing at the same time."

"Who, might I ask, is Lorenzo?" Archie asked, clearly confused.

"Lorenzo is my husband. Edwin's father," Marguerite said. "He idolised our child and would never have allowed anything to happen to him."

"Normally I would agree with my sister but even a powerful swimmer like Lorenzo could never have survived that onslaught of water. No one could," Geoffrey stated.

"Whatever you choose to think is immaterial Geoffrey. I am staying here!" Marguerite insisted, her face ashen.

"But Lady Marguerite, it seems reasonable to assume that your brother's logic could be correct. You can't remain here on your own, not after waiting so long for them to return. You must allow me to escort you back home to England, where you can recover," Archie urged.

"And I say I will not. I am not a package to be returned to the Dales, however good your intentions might be, Archie Westbrook. I will tolerate no interference from anyone in my decision to remain here and that is my final word on the matter."

"Then we shall both remain with you, until such time as you are agreeable to make the return journey home with us," Geoffrey said adamantly.

"Then you can do as you damned well please because I can assure you both that will never happen," she snapped, slamming the door and leaving them to make up rough cots and sleep in the stable.

Throughout the night he could hear her pacing the floor and weeping. The next morning she was barely able to stand and returned indoors, retching into a bucket and making no attempt to go searching for plants until midday had passed.

Her aggressive mood of the previous evening continued and she would barely respond to any of Geoffrey's concerns about her health or accept his apologies for having inadvertently upset her through the suggestion of returning home.

As the week progressed she showed no interest in anything but the collecting more plants, eating only sparsely and always alone.

"I honestly have no idea how to get through to her, Archie," Geoffrey said, after again being denied access to the cabin.

"What happened to her with Papas would unbalance any woman. Just being within earshot will help, knowing that you are close by."

"If we could make our way back to Coyacuche, surely there would be a woman there who could help her through this?" Geoffrey paced the veranda. "I cannot stand by and allow this awful incident to affect her sanity too. Not after seeing what Rose suffered."

"You never did say what occurred with Lady Rosamund."

"No I did not and for Rose's sake I never shall," Geoffrey said adamantly.

"Then I respect your wishes, Geoffrey. I will not bring up the subject again."

"Geoffrey…? You have never called me that before. Are you unwell?" Geoffrey said, stopping to study him more closely. "Why did you not say anything? That wound has started bleeding again."

"I know… but it will eventually stop." Archie rested his head against the veranda post for support.

"I do not understand why, when it was healing so well. Did you bang it anywhere?"

"It must have happened when I fell out of bed in the night."

"Then why did you not say anything before now?" Geoffrey said, assisting him to his feet.

"What are you doing, Geoff? I am fine resting here."

"You will be better once you are on the boat and I have redressed this wound. After that you must stay there and rest on a proper bed."

"What if Lady Marguerite should need you?"

"I will return with the dog once this wound is taken care of. We will be comfortable enough on the veranda; we are both well used to sleeping out."

Throughout the following week, Geoffrey made sure that he was never far from his sister, helping her bring even more plants back to the cabin. Even so, she still didn't speak a word, passing him by as though he didn't exist and bolting the door behind her when inside the cabin.

Archie's condition was worsening and his wound showed no sign of healing. His temperature had rocketed, suggesting an infection had set in and leaving Geoffrey no option other than to clambering in through the window to retrieve some medication when he thought his sister was asleep. Instead he found himself staring down the barrel of the revolver.

"Get out of here, you bastard!" Marguerite hissed.

"You have to allow me inside. Archie is sick and I need anything that can help," Geoffrey pleaded. Her only answer was to release the safety catch on the revolver with a loud click.

When he returned to the cabin later, his makeshift bed had been cleared from the veranda and left upturned in the mud. The only item on the floor was one of Grifka's books in which a page of natural remedies and cures had been marked. Armed with this, Geoffrey retreated into the stable with a hurricane lamp, reading through the information and following cross-references to diagrams in a fold-out section at the back of the book. He paid particular heed to warnings on the exact dosage, since any overdose could prove fatal.

Armed with the book, at dawn Geoffrey made his way through the dense foliage towards the lagoon, where he suspected some of these plants could be found. It was no easy task scouring the recently flooded area for anything remotely recognisable. After an hour of intense searching he located one of the few remaining bushes with flaming red leaves and bright orange berries and another hour was spent picking whatever was growing on the thorny bush. With bleeding hands he continued the search until by late morning he had found an exact match to a leaf of the plant Grifka had drawn and after slicing the plant off at the stem as instructed, he returned to the steamer. It was not a moment too soon. Archie was crumpled up on the floor, most of the bandaging torn from his chest, exposing the weeping sores to a horde of buzzing insects.

Following the instructions in the faded print, Geoffrey lit a small fire and while the berries were simmering in water, he carefully pummeled each stem into a fine jelly that he pasted over both the entry and exit wounds. He covered them with a broad leaf similar to the one Lorenzo had used and bound them securely in place with a flat-stemmed vine. Once the berries had dissolved into the water, Geoffrey hung the container in the river to cool, before measuring out an eggcup full, which he forced Archie to swallow. The Irishman offered little resistance and was soon sleeping soundly.

Returning to the cabin, Geoffrey left Grifka's book on the remaining lounger where it was clearly visible before retiring to the stable. It would be safer not to try to speak to Marguerite in case she had the impulse to fire off a few shots at him through the closed door.

By dawn the book had been removed from the lounger and his sister was gone from the cabin. There were occasions when she could be seen pacing the river's edge, or on others as a dark silhouette on a high cliff, staring up and down the river, her eyes shielded from the sun. This pattern of behaviour continued for a fortnight without a word exchanged between them, broken only by the addition of more plants, left on the veranda for Geoffrey to pot in woven baskets.

By the end of the first week there was a marked improvement in Archie's recovery and by the end of the second he was eating and able to walk unaided. Throughout this period Geoffrey used any spare time in spearing fish, gutting and cooking them and gathering whatever fruit he could find. Wary of the reception he would receive from his sister, he would leave her a covered meal, wrapped in a piece of mosquito net for when she returned.

The ever-increasing quantity of pots that would need to be transported on the limited space available on deck was a growing cause for concern. Geoffrey was pacing the deck one evening when he narrowly avoided colliding with Archie.

"What on earth is troubling you, Geoff… you've been rather distant for days now?" Archie asked and Geoffrey had no option other than to explain the dilemma.

"Apart from leaving most of her collection behind when we sail, there is no possible alternative," he concluded.

"There's one option I can think of, provided you could come up with the materials."

"What would that be?"

"Between us we could rig up a mezzanine floor above the deck. That would allow enough space for any amount of plants."

"Even were that possible, up there the plants would either shrivel up in the intense heat or dry out for lack of water."

"Not if they were shaded with a palm thatch and if we could find a way to irrigate them," Archie suggested.

So a plan was formed. Archie could offer only limited assistance as the exertion of erecting the supporting poles stretched his wounds, which started to bleed again. However, over the following weeks the mezzanine began to take shape and the canopy of palm fronds provided shade. The remaining challenge of how to water the plants without clambering amongst them every day was eventually resolved when Geoffrey found a reel of rubber garden hose and a siphon pump in the storage cave. With one end of the hose fitted to the pump at the rear of the boat and with a spare section trailing in the river, the main length of hose was pierced at regular intervals and attached to the palm canopy and after a few initial setbacks this proved to be a practical method of watering the plants.

"My mobility is much improved, Geoff but I need some way of building up my strength," Archie said when Geoffrey returned with his latest catch.

"Now the mezzanine is finished, we can begin tomorrow if you can make it as far as the lagoon."

"Be logical, Geoff. While there's nothing I would prefer more than that, it would be crazy to go swimming in these infested waters," Archie protested.

"Not for the likes of you and me, Archie. Until we began work on the boat, I swam in the lagoon every day."

"That is impossible… no one could survive in these waters for long, not with all the predators."

"There are in plenty, as you say but none will ever come near enough to attack. Not while you're wearing this as protection." Geoffrey fingered his woven armlet. "You have the same thing woven around your neck."

"You can't be sure of that."

"Then answer me this. Do you not feel the warmth that is generated from the band whenever you are in danger?"

"How would you know that?"

"Because I saw it glowing on the day you confronted me at the cabin. The same thing happens with this armlet and the hound's collar. I realise this must be difficult for you to comprehend. It was for me to begin with but for whatever reason these bands somehow generate a shield of protection in the water."

Although swimming did help Archie improve his strength, being immersed in water for any length of time reduced the effectiveness of Grifka's gel. The supply of berries was almost at an end, so that Geoffrey had to extend his search further afield than he would have liked. Marguerite's moods had worsened considerably and as Archie's wounds were refusing to heal he knew he had to get them away from there as soon as possible.

The rape was never mentioned by his sister but he was convinced that this was one of the reasons for Marguerite's darkening moods. Though three months had now passed since the assault, such an incident combined with the loss of her son would have made any woman lose her sense of reason. One afternoon he came upon her perched precariously at the cliff edge but not making another futile search of the river for Edwin as he might have expected. Instead she was motionless, muttering incoherent words of hate, the solitary sapphire earring dangling motionless beneath the brim of her worn hat.

"Maggs...? You must come away from there. You might easily fall," Geoffrey said gently but keeping his distance, uncertain of her reaction.

"Go away and leave me, whoever you are!" she hissed, barely turning her head but moving far enough for him to see the revolver clenched in her hand, caked in dried mud.

"This is Geoffrey, Maggs, your brother," he said. "I did not mean to startle you."

He was about to step closer when he heard the safety catch click off.

"Liar... Take one more step nearer and I swear you will be dead."

"For Pete's sake look at me, Maggs...! Surely you know me?" Geoffrey cried with desperation as she inched even closer to the edge.

"LEAVE ME... !!! I have to do this," she screamed, tilting her head skywards in futile preparation before stepping forward over the edge and into space.

"You cannot do this... Edwin and I need you!" Geoffrey shouted in desperation, lunging forward to grapple with her, dragging her backwards on to the ground where he was able to wrench the revolver from her hand but not before she had dealt him a severe blow to the temple.

In a daze he half-dragged her back to the cabin and pushed her, sobbing, into the bedroom. Upending his wooden bed in the outer room he blocked up the doorway before collapsing on the veranda. How long he lay there was unclear but by the time he struggled to his feet it was almost dark.

Hearing his sister's laboured breathing, interspersed with sobs, Geoffrey knew the time had come for them to leave, ready or not. Having alerted Archie to the situation, he began making preparations first thing the following morning.

To all outward appearances Marguerite was behaving normally, getting ready to leave the cabin but the crazed look in her dark eyes said differently. Inherently graceful, even in her father's old boots, she wore one of her late mother's underslips but for modesty's sake had pinned an embroidered shawl around her waist. Even more incongruous was the holster attached to a bandolier slung threateningly across her upper body. Unlike the robust figure she had presented when they had first been abandoned at the compound, she was now an elegantly slim and graceful woman.

"We should get off, Maggs. With only damp wood to stoke up the boiler, Archie is finding it a devil of a job to keep it in."

"You want my sympathy for the stoker?"

"You know damned well that is not what I mean. His name is Archie, so I would suggest that you show him the respect he deserves and refer to him as that, or use his title since he outranks mine. After all, he risked his life by coming down this backwater of the Amazon to rescue us, not once but twice and his best friend was crushed to death."

"Ironic is it not that his well-meaning intentions only served to get his friend killed instead of that monster he chose to engage?"

"Well take comfort that you will not be seeing Giorgio Papas again."

"In Hell perhaps but then it will not matter." Marguerite had packed what clothing she had in Lady Claudia's Gladstone bag and also carried the water-stained journal. "Can you put this safe for me inside the satchel?"

"Of course; is there anything else?" Geoffrey asked, unzipping a compartment on the leather satchel.

"Yes, Geoffrey, there is… you seem to have forgotten the musical instrument you made for Edwin," Marguerite said.

"You surely cannot be serious about taking that useless piece of junk back to England?"

"Why ever not? If we are creating a winter garden as a memorial to our loved ones, it could not be more appropriate to hear you playing some of your own compositions. It has a strangely beautiful tone." Her eyes narrowed, daring him to object.

"Rubbish. That lashed-up stick with a gramophone horn stuck on the end sounded more like a catfight than anything resembling music. Besides, there would not be room on board, as well you know. The three of us can barely fit as it is, not with all of your potted plants too." Geoffrey wondered why she had never expressed an interest in his knocked-up parody of a Stroh violin before.

"Then I will leave some of them behind. I will not set foot on that vessel until I see it on board and that is final!"

"Very well then, if you feel that strongly about it."

"Decidedly so and you will also need those articulated fingers that Lorenzo carved for you."

"Like hell I will… I refuse to take those bloody things with me. They would make me look more of a freak than what you have already turned me into."

"Then wear gloves over them Geoffrey, as you cannot play without them. If you will not carry them, then I will keep them safe with the spare ammunition in mother's bag."

Having no option but to do as she asked, Geoffrey reluctantly removed the intricately crafted fingers from a tin box he had kept out of sight. "There, are you satisfied?"

"For the moment."

"And what about that?" Geoffrey asked, indicating the flood-damaged crib on the veranda. Inside was a fresh flower that his sister must have placed there earlier.

"No one will take that." She glanced around at the devastated compound as she brushed past him. "It will still be here when I return."

"What do you mean by that? You cannot intend coming back here?" he asked but there was no response. "We will never come back here for Pete's sake."

"I was not including you, Geoffrey, I referred only to myself," Marguerite said. "When I have been delivered of that rapist's child, then I will be returning here to continue with my search for Edwin but this time alone!"

"Dear God in Heaven, no… you cannot be having that bastard's child… you cannot!" Geoffrey protested but he knew instinctively by the rigid set of her mouth that she was speaking the truth.

THE END
(of Book Two)